DISNEY ✦ SQUARE ENIX

KINGDOM HEARTS
THE NOVEL

Tomoco Kanemaki

Original Concept
Tetsuya Nomura

Illustrations
Shiro Amano

YEN ON

NEW YORK

KINGDOM HEARTS: THE NOVEL
TOMOCO KANEMAKI,
ILLUSTRATIONS: SHIRO AMANO,
ORIGINAL CONCEPT: TETSUYA NOMURA

Translation: Melissa Tanaka

Yen On
Hachette Book Group
1290 Avenue of the Americas,
New York, NY 10104
www.HachetteBookGroup.com
www.YenPress.com

Yen On is an imprint of Hachette Book Group, Inc.
The Yen On name and logo are trademarks of
Hachette Book Group, Inc.

The publisher is not responsible for websites
(or their content) that are not owned by
the publisher.

First Yen On Edition: March 2015

ISBN: 978-0-316-26019-0

10 9 8 7 6 5 4 3 2 1

RRD-C

Printed in the United States of America

CONTENTS

CONTENTS

Goofy

The captain of the knights at Disney Castle. Kind-natured and easygoing, he fights only with a shield rather than a weapon designed to hurt. He's on a journey with Donald Duck to find their king.

Donald Duck

The royal magician of Disney Castle. Along with Goofy, he leaves in search of their king and friend, Mickey Mouse, who suddenly disappeared. He's a good guy, but hotheaded and stubborn.

Chip'n'Dale

The chipmunk brothers in charge of the design and maintenance of the Gummi Ship. The one with the black nose is Chip, and the one with the red nose is Dale.

Jiminy Cricket

A polite little cricket gentleman who goes along with Sora, Donald, and Goofy to watch over them.

Alice

A girl who followed the White Rabbit into Wonderland. She's true to herself and quick to speak her mind. She is accused of stealing the Queen of Hearts's heart and found guilty in a sham trial.

Maleficent

A tremendously powerful evil witch, capable of controlling the Heartless. She interferes with Sora and the others at every step of their journey. She's especially good at exploiting the weaknesses in other people's hearts.

Sora

A fourteen-year-old boy who lives on Destiny Island, a sunny, peaceful little place surrounded by the sea. He can usually be found out playing with his longtime friend, Riku, and a girl their age, Kairi. With a strong sense of right and wrong, he's always poking his head into things that seem unjust to him.

Riku

Sora's best friend on Destiny Island. At fifteen, he's a year older and has a cooler, more mature outlook, but a deep inquisitiveness. He and Sora have done everything together ever since they were little, but Riku is always a step ahead, almost like a big brother to Sora.

Kairi

A cheerful fourteen-year-old girl who's always with Sora and Riku. Several years ago, she came to Destiny Island from somewhere across the ocean. She doesn't remember much before that, so she's curious about the world beyond their island, but she's afraid of it at the same time. It's a little confusing for her.

A boy who lives in Neverland, where he will never grow up. He's full of mischief and a little fickle but brave and willing to take action. He snuck onto the pirate ship, where Captain Hook had kidnapped Wendy, a girl who is precious to him.

Peter Pan

Genie

Beast

He was once a prince, but he was selfish and cruel and judged others only by their appearances. As punishment, he was transformed into a hideous beast. Then he met a warm-hearted young lady, Belle, who opened his eyes to love and kindness, but their world was destroyed. He made his way to Hollow Bastion, where she was taken.

The lively and genial Genie of the Lamp. Whoever possesses the magic lamp becomes his master, and he can grant them three wishes. But in his current master, Aladdin, he has more of a friend.

Ansem

He was once a sage, held in high regard by his people. He became obsessed with researching darkness and the Heartless, and he turned into something else. Sora, Donald, and Goofy are collecting pages of his report on their journey, trying to understand just what he is now and what he's done.

Sora's friend back on Destiny Island. A year older, he has a cooler, more mature outlook but a deep inquisitiveness. He's always been a step ahead, almost like a big brother to Sora. Here and there on the journey he visits Sora then soon leaves after acting mysteriously...

Riku

Kairi

A cheerful fourteen-year-old girl who came from across the sea to Destiny Island. She was always with Sora and Riku, but she went missing when their island was destroyed. A headstrong girl, she has a few mysteries about her.

Goofy

The captain of the knights at Disney Castle. Easygoing but sturdy and kind-natured, he fights only with a shield rather than a weapon designed to hurt. He met Sora on a journey with Donald Duck in search of their king.

Donald Duck

The royal magician of Disney Castle. Along with Goofy, he leaves in search of their king and friend, Mickey Mouse, who suddenly disappeared. In Traverse Town, they met Sora, the Keyblade wielder, and took him along on their adventure.

Sora

A fourteen-year-old boy who lived on Destiny Island, a sunny, peaceful little place surrounded by the sea. He was always playing with his longtime friend, Riku, and a girl their age, Kairi. Then their island was destroyed, and the three friends were separated, and to find them he's embarked on a journey through the Worlds of Disney with Donald Duck and Goofy.

PART 1

PROLOGUE
dive to the heart

ON AND ON—THE DARKNESS WENT ON AND ON.
With a tiny little light to guide him, he walked on.
He heard a soft voice—then he felt a presence.

There you are!

So much to do. So little time.
But take your time. Don't be afraid.
The door is still closed.

Now, step forward. Can you do it?

Power sleeps within you. Give it form...and it will give you strength.

And then the light will shine where you are.

But the closer you get to the light, the greater your shadow becomes.

But don't be afraid. And don't forget.
You hold the mightiest weapon of all.

*   *   *

So don't forget—
You are the one who will open the door.

Now, go.

And—the door to destiny began to open.

CHAPTER 1

DESTINY ISLANDS & DISNEY CASTLE
first impression

AS HIS EYES SLOWLY OPENED, THE SUNLIGHT STREAMED
in dazzlingly bright. The sound of the waves was the same as always, brushing softly against his mind.

Sora got up and stretched.

Before him the blue sky and sea stretched on and on. As far as he knew, that was the entire world.

These were the Destiny Islands—a little cluster of islets floating in the sea.

"Huh… What was it?"

He felt like he'd had a bad dream.

Was it scary…? No, something about it felt nice, too.

That voice—that light. And that dark black shadow—

And—was it really just a dream?

"Sora…"

"Whoa!"

Kairi suddenly appeared in front of his face. Sora jumped to his feet.

"Gimme a break, Kairi."

"Sora, you lazy bum! I knew I'd find you snoozing down here."

Kairi leaned in, peering into Sora's face, and smiled. Her red hair glinted in the brilliant light that poured down from the sky and reflected off the sea and sand.

"No! This huge black thing swallowed me up, I couldn't breathe, I couldn't—ow!"

Whatever he was going to say got lost when Kairi knocked him on the head.

"Are you still dreaming?"

As she stared at him again, Sora began to feel uncertain about what he remembered. How could there be a pitch-dark monster thing like that around here, under such a bright sky?

"It wasn't a dream! …Or was it? I don't know…"

Sora hung his head. Kairi gave him an exasperated look and walked down to the water's edge. Turned away from him, she felt just a little bit distant somehow. He didn't know what to say to her, but as he hesitated, Kairi looked back with a smile.

"We better start working on it. Riku's getting annoyed."

"Huh?" Startled, he turned, and Riku was standing there, holding a log and scowling.

"So, I guess I'm the only one working on the raft."

It was a fairly heavy log. Riku tossed it to Sora with a shake of his silver hair.

"Ack!" Sora fumbled to catch the log.

Riku turned to Kairi. "And you're just as lazy as he is!"

"So, you noticed." Kairi grinned and began ambling toward the inlet. "Okay, we'll finish it together. Race you!"

Laughing, she took off at a run.

"Huh? Seriously?" Sora hurried after her, and then Riku.

"Ready? Go!"

Kairi was already running, but at her words the other two broke into full speed.

The sun was still high. They had plenty of work ahead of them.

"Riku, you get the logs...and some cloth and rope. Sora, you find some drinking water and mushrooms for us to take. I'll wait here."

"Got it!"

Sora and Riku took off running like it was another race, footsteps scrunching over the dry sand. A little ways off, they could hear Tidus and Wakka playing with wooden swords.

"Want to join them, Sora?"

"But won't Kairi be mad?"

Sora threw that out as an excuse. The truth was, he just couldn't win against Riku, which made it hard to be interested.

"Don't worry about that." Riku thumped him on the back and ran toward Tidus and Wakka.

"Aw, geez…"

On this little island, pretty much any game the boys played was something competitive, and the perennial favorite was sword fighting. Wakka, a few years older than everyone else, acted as a teacher. Just recently Sora and Riku had become good enough to beat him once in a while. They were about even with Tidus.

"Here I come!" Tidus closed in on Wakka.

"Go, boys, go!" Selphie was hopping up and down, making the outward curl at the end of her hair bounce in time.

"I'm not done yet!" Wakka's voice rang out over the sound of wood striking wood, and Tidus's sword flew from his hand.

"Aw, nuts."

Tidus dejectedly plopped down on the sand.

Riku picked up the sword that had fallen some distance away and turned to Wakka. "My turn!"

"Hey, hey, gimme a little breather here," said Wakka, scratching his head through his bandanna, and tossed his stick over to Sora. "You take him this time, Sora."

"But Kairi'll be upset…"

"You're wide open!"

As Sora stood there trying to get out of it, Riku leaped in to attack.

"Hey! No fair, Riku!"

"Fights don't have to be fair!"

Sora dodged his strike with a jump and finally grabbed a sword. There wasn't any getting out of it, then.

"All right, come get me!" Riku smirked like he knew he hardly had to try. Sora couldn't stand it.

"Here I come!"

The wooden swords met with a *clack*! Sora threw himself into fighting just like Wakka had taught him, swinging straight down at Riku from over his head. *Clack, clack, clack* over and over. Sora's style mainly involved staying on the offensive.

"Ngh!"

"That's it, Sora! Keep going, push him right into the water!"

Just as Wakka cheered him on, Sora made a huge swing.

"Ouch!"

The sword leaped from Riku's hand and spun up into the air, then landed point down in the sand.

"Wow!" Tidus yelled.

Breathing hard, Sora held out a hand to Riku, who'd fallen on his rear.

"*Tch*. Let my guard down."

"Or I'm just better than you!" Sora grinned and pulled Riku to his feet, then took off toward the hill. "Race you to get all the supplies!"

"All right!" Riku replied, dusting off sand, and ran in the other direction.

"Hey, hey, a race to get what?"

But Wakka's question went unheard as Sora and Riku ran off.

"Those two lately, and Kairi, too… I get the feeling they're up to something…" Selphie screwed up her face and tilted her head in concentration.

Wakka shrugged. "Well, they've got Riku, so I wouldn't worry, yeah?"

"That's not the point!" Selphie said in a huff, kicking the sand.

"It's not fair! I wanna be in on it, too!" Tidus tried to follow them, but Sora had already disappeared into the bushes on the hillside and Riku into the sea.

"Mushrooms… Where do I find more mushrooms?"

Sora wandered around the hill in search of mushrooms. The ones that grew on this island were all edible, and a while ago they'd even roasted some over a campfire. If they were planning to sail across the ocean for however many days, though, he needed to find more than that.

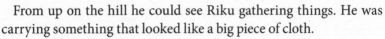

From up on the hill he could see Riku gathering things. He was carrying something that looked like a big piece of cloth.

Must be nice being Riku…

The thought stung in his chest. It felt like nothing more than an accident that he'd managed to win the sword fight. Sora was always the one who lost. School grades, sprinting, it didn't matter what—he couldn't beat Riku. If he could just win at *something…*

Sora slid down the hill and jumped into the thick foliage that grew beside the waterfall. Through there was the entrance to a little cave. It was their secret spot. Sora and Riku had found it and told Kairi.

"…Haven't been here in a while…"

Inside the cave, the constant sound of the waves was hushed to a whisper. Further in, the space was more open, like a great big room. And at the other end of it—that door. It was a big door, but without a doorknob or anything. It just sat there, as if in wait for a visitor from somewhere.

On the cave wall beside the door, there was a little doodle.

"…There it is."

Years ago, Kairi and Sora had drawn each other's faces on the wall, and they were still here. Sora crouched down and softly touched the scribbles.

If he could just be better than Riku…

Sora turned toward a small sound. "Who's there?"

It was a man in a brown robe.

"I've come to see the door," he declared in a deep voice. Sora couldn't see the face beneath the hood. "This world has been connected."

"What are you talking about?"

The man showed no reaction to Sora and kept talking. "A world tied to the darkness…soon to be completely eclipsed…"

At that, a chill crept up Sora's spine. "Well, whoever you are, you're freaking me out! …Where did you come from, anyway?!"

He didn't answer the question but said slowly, "There is much to learn. You know so little."

"You're from another world, aren't you?"

"You do not yet know what lies beyond the door. One who knows nothing can understand nothing."

Sora had been staring at the mysterious man, but now he looked at the door.

That door, he thought. *That big door… Didn't I see a door like that somewhere else, just a little while ago…?*

"Hey, who are you—"

Sora looked back again, but the man was gone.

When he left the cave, the brilliant sunlight made him blink. The island spread out before him with its brilliant sea and sky, and what had just happened in the cave seemed like a dream.

Arms full of the mushrooms he'd gathered in the cave, he began to run down to the inlet where Kairi and Riku would be waiting.

That man—and the door. It did feel like a dream. And no one would believe him if he said anything about it. Here on this little archipelago called the Destiny Islands, there wasn't a single person they didn't know. Not even anyone from across the ocean—no, wait, there was one person.

Kairi.

She came from across the ocean, people said. Kairi came from another world across the ocean, somewhere we've never seen or even heard about. That's why we're going to find…

"Sora! You're late!"

"Sorry! It was hard to find enough mushrooms…"

Winded from running, Sora held up the stockpile of fungi for Kairi to see. As soon as he saw her face, the incident with the strange man was gone from his mind. Kairi and Riku were standing beside a soaringly tall tree trunk.

"Wooow. You really found a lot, huh!"

"Not bad for you!"

They both laughed, relieving him of the armfuls of mushrooms.

"Right, Sora—this looks like a good sail, don't you think?" said Riku.

Sora looked up at the cloth tied to the tree trunk like a flag. "Where'd you find a piece that big?"

"Oh, nowhere." Riku shrugged and smiled and then began to climb up the trunk. "If there's a storm, we have to climb up the mast and lower the sail."

"I know that."

Kairi watched their back-and-forth, giggling.

The three of them were building a raft, a nice big one. A raft that would take them to worlds they'd never seen before. They lashed several logs together with some rope and stood up the trunk for a mast. Then the sail went up, made from the cloth that Riku had found, flapping in the sea breeze.

"She looks seaworthy already!" Kairi exclaimed.

Riku leaped down from the mast. "Yeah. On this, we can go anywhere we want," he said, gazing into the distance beyond the perfectly smooth horizon. The sun was sinking low, the sky shifting from clear blue to deep crimson.

"Hey, Sora," he said, looking at the mast again. "We haven't given our ship a name yet."

"Heh. Right, we should!" Kairi looked up at the mast, too. "A sail like that is sure to catch the wind."

The sail hung quietly over them, the sail that would fill up with wind and take them gliding over the sea.

"What should we call her?"

At Kairi's prompting, Sora mentioned the name he'd been thinking of all day. "How about…the *Highwind*?"

"The *Highwind*…" Riku softly repeated it. "When the winds are high, she'll take us as far as we can go."

"Pretty good, right?" said Sora. Riku gave him a nod.

"The *Highwind* it is, then!" Kairi grinned and clung to the mast, turning her gaze out to the open sea. "…It's getting late, huh?"

Riku and Sora, too, saw that the sky above the horizon was glowing brilliant red and the sun would soon disappear below it.

"If we go to the very end of the sea…I bet we'll find the world where you came from, Kairi."

Sora said it like he wanted confirmation. Kairi turned slowly away, staring into the distance.

"We don't know that for sure."

"If we don't go and see, we'll never find out," Riku replied, arms folded.

"Do you really think we can get that far on a raft?" said Sora.

Riku looked at him, and back out to the sea. "Well… If it doesn't work, we'll think of something else."

The sun sank lower toward the horizon, turning the sea and even the sand red.

They had watched this very scene together countless times, but to Sora, it looked just a little bit different today. Something about that made him uneasy.

After this…what's going to happen to us?

I want to see other worlds, he thought.

There was the sea, always so calm, though storms came once in a while. There were the beautiful sandy beaches. There were birds on the hills and even mushrooms to eat, and…Riku and Kairi, Tidus and Selphie and Wakka. Mom and Dad and the other people in town. All the wonderful friends he had fun with here on the Destiny Islands. But the landscape that Sora saw was always the same. If he could just see a different world…maybe something would change.

So he wanted to try going somewhere else.

"Suppose you get to another world. What would you do there?" Kairi asked Riku a little nervously. "Do you just want to see, like Sora?"

"Well, I haven't really thought about it. It's just… I've always wondered why we're here, on this island. If there are other worlds out there, why did we end up on this one?" Riku paused for a moment, as if listening to the waves, and then went on. "And suppose there are other worlds. Then ours is just a little piece of something much greater…" Then he turned to Sora and Kairi. "So, we could have just as easily ended up somewhere else, right?"

A little piece of something greater. This was pretty complicated. Not quite following, Sora flopped over on the raft. "I dunno."

Riku looked at him with a little sigh and started walking down toward the shore. "That's why we need to go out there and find out. Just sitting here won't change a thing."

Sora turned to the sea, his eyes following Riku.

"It's the same old stuff. And I want to go."

"You've been thinking a lot lately, haven't you?" Kairi said softly.

"Thanks to you. If you hadn't come here, I probably never would have thought of any of this." Riku turned away from the setting sun to look at her. "Thanks, Kairi."

Those words sounded more earnest to Sora·than anything he had ever heard. He felt his heart skip a beat.

"Um, you're welcome…," Kairi said with a shy laugh, turning to the sea again.

"Well… Guess I better get going. You two shouldn't stay out too late, either." Riku took off for the pier at a brisk pace, as if suddenly embarrassed by what he'd said.

Staring after him, Kairi said in a tiny voice, "You know, Riku's changed."

"What do you mean?" said Sora. If there was anything different about Riku, he couldn't tell. It seemed like the usual Riku to him.

"Well… Hmm. You don't think so?"

"Nope, it's just you."

Kairi looked a little sad at that. But then she blurted, "Hey, let's take the raft and go—just the two of us!"

She peered at Sora with a mischievous grin.

"Huh? What's gotten into you? You're the one who's changed, Kairi."

"…Maybe."

She started ambling down to the beach. Something small and bright fell out of her pocket.

"Kairi, you dropped something."

"Oh—" She carefully picked it up and showed it to him. It was a pendant made of seashells, tied together into the shape of a star.

"What is it?"

"I'm making thalassa shell charms. In the old days, sailors always wore them. They're supposed to ensure a safe voyage."

"A sailor's amulet, huh…"

Sora gazed at the charm in the palm of Kairi's hand.

"I'm making them so even if one of us gets lost, we'll make it back here safe and sound. …So the three of us will always be together."

She placed it gently back in her pocket. The sun had already fallen halfway below the horizon.

"You know, I was a little afraid at first…but now I'm ready." Kairi looked at Sora, speaking like she'd made up her mind. "No matter where I go or what I see, I know I can always come back here."

He ran to catch up with her. "Yeah, of course!"

I still want to come back to Destiny Island, too, he thought. *I want to see other worlds, but I'll come back. To the sea and the sky and everyone here. To this place with Kairi and Riku.*

"I'm glad… Sora, don't ever change."

"Huh?"

Kairi smiled at his startled sound. "I just can't wait. Once we set sail, it'll be great."

"Yeah… We'll make it, for sure."

The sun was nearly gone now. The waves went on and on with their calm, soft rush.

A great trumpet fanfare rang out.

The castle stood tall against the clear blue sky. The broom servants swept by on their important task of morning cleaning. Donald strode past them, chest puffed out, tail waddling to and fro. As the royal magician, his first order of business for the day was to greet the king.

"A-hem!"

Putting even more puff into his chest, he cleared his throat and knocked on a grand door ten times his size. A little Donald-size door cut into the big door opened, and he entered the great hall.

Here, in the biggest room in the castle, was the king's throne, and Donald walked up to it on the long red carpet.

"Good morning, Your Majesty! It's nice to see...*quack*?"

The king should have been sitting there. But the throne was empty. Instead the king's dog, Pluto, poked out from behind it.

"Pluto?"

Hearing his name, Pluto trotted up to Donald. He held a white envelope in his mouth.

"...*Quack*?"

Pluto held his head out, waiting for Donald to take the envelope. Frowning, Donald did, and opened it to find a single sheet of notepaper. The moment his eyes took in the writing...

"*Gawawawawawawaaaaaa! QUACK!*"

Donald ran back out of the great hall, shouting all the way.

> *Donald,*
> *Sorry to rush off without sayin' good-bye, but big trouble's brewin', and there's no time to lose. I'd better leave right away.*
> *The stars have been blinkin' out one by one, and that means disaster can't be far behind.*
> *I hate to leave you all, but I've gotta go look into it.*
> *As the king, I'm askin' you and Goofy to do something.*
> *There's someone out there with a "key"—the key to our survival. So I need you two to find him and stick with him. Got it?*

We need that key, or we're doomed.

Go to Traverse Town and find a man called Leon. He'll point you in the right direction.

P.S. Would ya apologize to Minnie for me? Thanks, pal.

That was the note he left behind. A very important letter from their beloved king—and their dear friend. If this was all true, things were serious. That strange problem with the stars vanishing from the night sky and the disaster on the way. Did this mean the king had gotten involved in something really dangerous?

Donald hurtled down the long hallway and out to the gardens. That was where he'd find Goofy, the captain of the royal knights.

"Captain Goofy! This is bad!"

Goofy was sound asleep. Donald tried to wake him up to no avail.

"Goofy!" His shouts echoed in the peaceful courtyard, but Goofy didn't stir. Now totally out of patience, Donald snapped his fingers and yelled, "*Thunder!*"

A little crackling bolt of lightning struck the end of Goofy's black nose.

"*A-hyuck?*" Goofy blinked a few times and finally saw Donald. "Hey there, Donald. G'mornin'. Nice weather, isn't—"

Donald cut off his carefree hello. "We-we've got a big problem!"

"Problem?"

"Now, don't tell *anybody!*"

"Anybody? Tell 'em what?"

"I'm telling you, it's top secret!" Donald said, flapping his arms.

Goofy wasn't quite grasping the urgency of the situation. He got up slowly and stretched, looking at Donald. "…Queen Minnie?"

"Not even the queen!"

"Daisy?"

"Definitely not Daisy!"

"G'mornin', ladies."

Goofy looked past Donald's flailing and nodded.

"...Er...?"

Finally realizing what Goofy meant, Donald turned around to see Queen Minnie and his girlfriend, Daisy.

"What's all the commotion, Donald?"

"Quack...gawawawawa..."

Hearing the queen's voice, Donald began flapping around again. Daisy pointedly cleared her throat.

The castle's bell chimed the hour. Donald, Goofy, Daisy, and Queen Minnie were in the king's room, deep in serious conversation.

"...That's how it is," said Donald after explaining to the others.

"Oh, dear! What could this mean?" Daisy worried.

"It means...we'll just have to trust the king," Minnie replied softly.

"Gawrsh. I sure hope he's all right," said Goofy, unhurried as usual.

Donald kicked him in the shin and spoke with determination. "Your Highness! Don't worry. We'll find the king, and this 'key.'"

"Thank you."

"Daisy," asked Donald, "can you take care of the queen?"

"Of course. You be careful now, both of you." With a scatterbrain like Donald for a boyfriend, Daisy herself was quite steady. She'd be able to protect the castle and the queen in their absence.

"Oh. And Donald, take him with you." The queen gestured toward "him"—but Donald couldn't see anyone there.

"Er...who?"

Then Donald saw him, hopping up and down. "Over here!"

"...Him?"

He was much smaller than Donald or Goofy. He wore a tiny suit and a silk hat, which he politely doffed, and bowed to them.

"Cricket's the name. Jiminy Cricket, at your service."

And Jiminy sprang up onto Donald's hat.

"*Wak!*"

"I'll just stay nice and quiet like this. No worries!" With that, Jiminy jumped into Donald's pocket and made himself at home.

"Jiminy said his world disappeared, too." Queen Minnie lowered her long lashes.

"…Disappeared?" said Goofy.

Jiminy poked his head out from Donald's pocket again, his brows furrowed. "That's right. It all just disappeared. Everyone's scattered—I'm the only one who made it to this castle."

"Maybe you'll be able to find the others from your world, Jiminy," the queen said.

Jiminy leaped out onto the desk, doffing his hat again to Donald and Goofy.

"So, that's how it is. Thanks for taking me along."

"All right, but…" Donald looked at the queen.

"Outside of this castle, you mustn't let anyone know that you've come from another world," the queen told them firmly.

"Oh, to keep the order—right?" said Goofy.

"Right. To maintain the order of each world," Donald replied. It was a closely guarded secret that he and the others could leave Disney Castle and travel to other worlds. If the secret got out, other people might try to go between worlds willy-nilly, and the order would break down.

A heavy silence settled into the room. The queen spoke brightly to dispel it. "Your Gummi Ship should be ready soon. We hope for your safe return. Please help the king."

Donald saluted with his hand at his breast. Goofy returned the salute to see him off…

"You're coming, too!" He grabbed Goofy by the arm and dragged him out.

*   *   *

The Gummi Ship factory was at the end of a long spiral staircase that wound down beneath the castle. Puffs of steam rose from chugging, clanking machinery. In the middle of it all, a little orange rocket ship sat waiting for Donald and Goofy. This was the only kind of vessel capable of flying between worlds—a Gummi Ship.

Great big magic hands were readying the ship for departure, giving it a final inspection.

"Donald Duck to launch crew!" he said into a big pipe, and his voice quacked through the control room. "Is she ready to go?"

The two crewmen smartly saluted in return. The one with the black nose was Chip, the designer, and the one with the red nose was Dale, the mechanic. Chip pulled the big lever in the control room and the whole factory began to groan.

"What's goin' on?" Goofy wondered, and just then a big magic hand picked him up. *"A-hyipe!"*

"Be quiet!" Donald snapped, and another magic hand grabbed him by the tail. Jiminy nearly fell out of his pocket, hanging on to his silk hat and clinging to Donald's hem for dear life.

"Maybe go a little easier…" Just as Goofy said that, they plopped down into the cockpit. Pluto, who must have been following them for some time, jumped in, too.

"Pluto!" Donald exclaimed. Pluto barked in reply.

The cockpit smoothly closed up with the four of them inside, and the door at the front of the factory opened. The Gummi Ship slowly rose into launch position.

"Gawrsh, I'm kinda nervous," said Goofy.

"—Hush, it's gonna be fine."

Just as Donald scolded him, the Gummi Ship reached its mark.

Queen Minnie and Daisy had come to see them off. "Please help the king…and the worlds…"

The soft plea didn't reach the cockpit, but Donald gave a thumbs-up and a wink to the queen and Daisy.

The engine started with a *bomf!* and the little ship shook.

"Blast off!" Donald pointed to the track ahead—but the arrow there pointed down. *"Quack?!"*

A hole in the floor opened up and sucked in the Gummi Ship. It kept falling and finally popped out the other side of Disney Castle upside down, then righted itself and sped into the stars.

Lightning flashed, and in nearly the same moment, rain came pattering down on the roof.

"...Rain?"

Sora sat up and looked out the window. His house was on a bigger island, a little ways off from the small one where he and his friends always went to play. A little house in a little town—that was where he lived. Since he came home, he'd been spacing out, staring up at the ceiling, thinking about what happened today and what was going to happen soon.

The rain started to come down harder. Showers after sunset weren't that rare here. The ocean here was usually calm, but once in a while, there would be downpours or storms.

Still...

Lightning flashed again. Sora could tell...

"It's coming from our island!"

He jumped out of bed.

Sora took his kid-size rowboat and hurried to their island. There was a nice big reef surrounding it, so anything less than a hurricane wouldn't cause much damage. But at the moment, there was a raft to worry about.

If the raft got swept away...

Luckily the waves weren't very high yet. The raft should be okay if he just tied it good and tight to a cocoyum tree.

Rolling thunder enveloped the island. Sora looked up at the starless night sky to see a ball of darkly glowing energy floating in the air. "What's *that?!*"

When he climbed up onto the dock, he saw that there were two other small boats.

"Riku and Kairi are here, too?"

He ran in from the dock to the beach, but some kind of shadow rose up from the ground, blocking his path.

"...What's going on?!"

He swung his wooden sword around, and it felt like he hit something, but the shadow didn't go away. In fact, more and more of them appeared.

"Ugh, they just keep coming..." Sora gave up trying to beat them and ran along the beach, looking for Kairi and Riku. The wind swallowed up his voice as he shouted their names. At the waterfall, he paused and looked around. Then he saw it—in front of the bushes that hid the path to their secret spot, there was a big white door.

"What...?"

Suddenly he remembered the strange man he'd met in the afternoon.

Soon to be completely eclipsed——

No way, Sora thought. *But he was definitely saying something like that... Anyway, I have to find Riku and Kairi.*

Holding the shadowy things at bay with his wooden sword, Sora looked around again.

"Riku!"

He could see Riku standing in the darkness, facing the sea, his silver hair whipping in the howling wind.

Sora ran to him. "Where's Kairi? I thought she was with you!"

Riku slowly turned. "The door has opened..."

"Riku?"

Something wasn't quite right about him. He was different. And what was this about a door? Did he mean that white door? Or…

"The door is open, Sora! Now we can go to the outside world!" Riku said in a rush, a strange excitement in his eyes.

"What are you talking about? We've gotta find Kairi!"

"Kairi's coming with us!" Riku shouted at the top of his voice. "Once we step through, we might not be able to come back. But this might be our only chance. We can't let fear stop us! I'm not afraid of the darkness!"

As he went on, eerie dark energy gathered above his head.

"…Riku?"

"Let's go, Sora!"

Smiling, Riku stretched out his hand, but at his feet the darkness swarmed and grew, twisting itself around his legs—and in the blink of an eye, it had covered him completely.

"Riku!"

Sora tried to run toward him, but when he stepped into that darkness, it began twining up his body, too.

Smiling in the midst of the darkness, Riku called his name. "…Sora…"

But Sora couldn't reach him. Riku was engulfed in darkness, and just as Sora was about to be swallowed up, too, a light shone from inside it and drove it away.

For a moment Sora had to shut his eyes against the brightness. When he opened them again, there was a giant shining key in his hand. A voice echoed in his head—

Keyblade…

As if on cue, the dark, shadowy things came up from the ground again. Sora swung the key—the Keyblade—at them, and this time they disappeared.

"…Riku?" With the Keyblade still firmly in his hand, Sora looked around, but couldn't see Riku anywhere. "Riku! Where are you? Riku!"

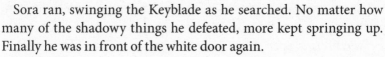

Sora ran, swinging the Keyblade as he searched. No matter how many of the shadowy things he defeated, more kept springing up. Finally he was in front of the white door again.

"…Huh?"

The door was opening, almost as if to invite him inside. This was the only place left on the island where Kairi and Riku could be. Sora ran through the door.

"Riku… Kairi!"

There was the cave—their secret spot, just the same as ever. The only difference was that glowing door at the end. And in front of the door, Kairi stood silently staring at it.

"Kairi!" Sora dashed toward her.

She turned to look at him, slowly and sadly. "Sora…?"

The moment she reached out for him, the door began to open. Ink-black darkness erupted out, blowing her toward him like the blast from an explosion. He tried to catch her in his arms—but her body just faded out. She passed through him and vanished.

It was like she'd been sucked into Sora himself. He called her name, but with a huge rush, Sora and the door and the island were all hurled away in the wind.

"What's happening—?!"

Thrown out onto the sand, Sora pounded the ground with his fist. Inches away, the ground just dropped off, like a cliff. He looked up and saw that dark sphere covering the entire island. And a huge black shadow was standing right in front of him.

This isn't our Destiny Island anymore, he thought.

Riku isn't here. Kairi's gone, too.

So how am I still here?

Sora was still on his hands and knees. The huge shadow swiped at him, knocking him aside.

He groaned, and the Keyblade glowed in his hand.

*　　*　　*

"Power sleeps within you. Give it form…and it will give you strength."

I feel like someone's speaking to me. Power sleeping within me…? I don't have any power. I can only just barely beat Riku. So how…

"No matter where I go or what I see, I know I can always come back here."

But Kairi disappeared. Riku, too. And now even the island's about to disappear. Can we really ever come back here? All three of us?

"Make it so the three of you can always be together."

Sora thought of Kairi's smile. *Kairi and Riku and me. So we'll always be together. So we can come back here.*

The Keyblade shone brightly, like it was reacting to Sora's emotions. *There's no way I'm gonna lose. So I can go see other worlds, so the three of us can run on the beach together…*

He stood up and took a huge leap, and his attack became trails of light that wounded the shadow.

"*Yaaaaah!* I won't lose!"

Two, three blows from the Keyblade he wielded, and wounds made of light kept appearing on the giant shadow.

"You're not gonna beat me!"

Sora felt the Keyblade pierce something, and the shadow let out an enormous roar.

"…I did it…"

Bellowing in fury, the shadow was sucked into the dark sphere up above.

"Kairi…," Sora whispered. Before he could take another breath, the sphere raged and howled, swelling up and dragging what remained of the island into it, along with Sora. With a terrible rumbling, it swallowed up the cocoyum trees, the rowboats, even the sea...

Sora strained to hold on to the wreckage of the wooden bridge, but the huge force pulled him off. In a swirl of debris, he fell into the dark sphere and disappeared.

TRAVERSE TOWN

encounter

THE TOWN ALWAYS GREETED EVERYONE WARMLY.

This was Traverse Town. It was full of people who had nowhere else to go, who had lost their homes to those strange events. Donald, Goofy, Jiminy, and Pluto had just arrived in the Gummi Ship. The man the king had mentioned in his letter, the one who knew about the "key," was supposed to be here somewhere.

Donald took the lead, his webbed feet smacking on the cobblestones.

"Y'know, maybe we better find Leon…," said Goofy, following behind. Pluto brought up the rear. "D'you think this is a big city?"

"How should I know?"

Goofy made a tiny sigh and looked up at the night sky. It looked pretty much the same here as it did from Disney Castle, which made him feel just a little bit better. What with the stars going out, and the king disappearing, and this "key"… Well, there sure was a lot Goofy didn't know and a lot that made him uneasy.

There was one star sparkling more brightly than the others. What kind of star could it be…?

Just as Goofy thought that, it happened.

"Donald…!"

Donald looked up to where Goofy was pointing.

"Look, a star's goin' out!"

The star's light sputtered and vanished.

"They really are goin' out…"

Goofy had heard of it in the castle, but this was the first time he'd seen it happen. It was the kind of thing you couldn't really believe until you saw it yourself. He thought of what the king had said in the letter. *"Big trouble's brewin'."*

And it was really true—the stars were going out. That couldn't mean anything good.

Donald and Goofy exchanged glances and started walking faster through town.

"C'mon, Pluto!" Goofy called.

But Pluto was busy sniffing around. He followed a scent into a back alley. There was hardly any light, but Pluto kept tracking farther in.

In that dim alley, lit only by faint moonlight, there was a boy sprawled on the ground. Pluto trotted up to the boy, tail wagging, and licked him on the nose.

Sora groaned and opened his eyes. What came into focus wasn't the sea or the sky of Destiny Island, but a place he'd never seen before—and a dog.

"What a dream…"

Right. This place has to be a dream. I've never seen anything that isn't our bright sunny island.

He began drifting off again, and Pluto jumped on his stomach.

"Oof! …This isn't a dream!"

Sora stood up, rubbing his eyes, and looked around. He was still in the same totally unfamiliar scene. The night sky spread out above like it did over Destiny Island, but it looked a little hazier than the one he remembered.

"Oh, boy…" Sora helplessly turned to the dog. "Hey, do you know where we are?"

The dog wagged his tail and scampered away.

"Hey, wait!"

Sora began to chase the dog, but he must have run down another alley, and Sora couldn't see him anymore. He came to a wide-open spot like a town square and looked around again.

There were lots of people here, after all, going to and fro through the square.

"This is weird… Am I in another world?"

It felt like he'd gotten lost in a fairy tale. There was nothing like this in the Destiny Islands—a town square laid with cobblestones and lit by lanterns.

So after he was sucked into that sphere, somehow he'd made it to another world?

But what about the island? And Riku and Kairi?

Where the heck am I...? he thought.

Just then the Keyblade gleamed in his hand.

He couldn't do anything to those shadowy things with a wooden sword, but he could beat them with the Keyblade. He told himself that. Maybe he'd be okay.

"Well, I dunno. Maybe someone— Wait, what's that?"

Sora tried talking to the funny-looking creature in the middle of the square. "Um, where am I?"

"Kupo?"

The funny-looking creature with a red pom-pom sprouting from its head looked up at him.

"I'm Sora. I just woke up here..."

"I'm Kupo the Moogle, kupo."

So Kupo was its name, and Moogle was its species...if Sora was making that out correctly.

"Shadows destroyed my home. I've got nowhere to go, kupo..."

"There were shadows after you, too?"

"Sure were, kupo." The pom-pom swayed as Kupo hung his head.

"Wow..." So it wasn't just the Destiny Islands.

Kupo didn't seem to want to talk anymore, so Sora walked away.

"New around here?" an older woman said to him.

"Where am I?" Sora asked again.

"This is a place where people end up when they have nowhere else to call home... Traverse Town."

"I'm from Destiny Island. What about you?"

The woman just smiled sadly. "You shouldn't ask people that here. We all have painful memories."

"Then the shadows got your—"

"Don't ask such rude questions...," she said with sorrow in her eyes. "Now, maybe the owner of the accessories store can tell you what you want to know." She pointed to a store up some steps from the square.

"Okay. Thanks!" Sora ran across the square and leaped up the steps.

In the sky up above, another star went out.

"Hey there, how can I… Aw, it's only a kid."

The man who came up to the counter had goggles on his head, a cigarette hanging from his lip, and a bellyband over his T-shirt—a middle-aged man, hardly the sort of person Sora would have expected to find running the Accessory Shop.

"I'm not a kid! And the name's Sora!" he shot back, posing with the Keyblade.

"Okay, okay, simmer down. So what's up, Sora? Need a present for a girlfriend?"

"That's not it!" Sora pouted at the teasing.

"You lost, then?"

"No! Well, maybe. I mean, I just woke up here…"

The man folded his arms and rumbled, "Okay, why don't you start at the beginning, Sora."

"Umm, well, I came from a place called Destiny Island…"

Sora told him everything—about the island, the shadows, Kairi and Riku. Now that someone was really listening to him, he felt a little better.

"Uh-huh, I see…"

When Sora finished, the man fell quiet, looking pensive.

"So, gramps, is this really another world?"

"Don't call me gramps! The name's Cid!"

"Okay…Cid. So this is another world, isn't it?" Sora said, staring at him closely.

"Not sure what you're talkin' about, but this sure ain't your island."

He hadn't left the island the way they'd planned. But there was no doubt now. He was in another world. So where could Kairi and Riku have ended up?

And everyone else on the islands?

"Yeah… Hey, Cid. Do you think Kairi and Riku are here, too?"

"Hmm. Couldn't tell ya." Cid frowned.

"I'd better start looking for them."

With that Sora sounded more determined, and Cid gave him a brash grin in return. "Well, good luck with whatever it is you're doing. If you ever run into trouble, you come to me. I'll look out for you."

"Thanks!"

Holding tight to the Keyblade, Sora nodded and rushed out of the shop. Cid rested his elbows on the counter and stretched over to make sure that Sora shut the door behind him.

"…The Keyblade… So that's the 'key' thing, huh…," he mumbled to himself. "Maybe I better tell Leon…"

"It sure would be nice if they were here somewhere…"

Sora ran through the town. From what the people who lived here told him, it was a pretty big place. The part where he woke up was the First District. Beyond that was the Second District, and then the Third District. And if there were lots of other worlds that had been swallowed up like the Destiny Islands, there must have been more worlds like Traverse Town that were still safe from the shadows. So that meant Kairi and Riku might be in other different worlds, Sora thought with a sigh.

He ran up streets and down alleys and emerged in front of a big door.

"Hey, you look like you're new," said a boy who came through the door. "It's kinda dangerous through there. Be careful."

"Dangerous?" said Sora. Had the other boy come from a world that got swallowed up by the shadows, too? From what he'd seen of the First District, this town definitely didn't seem all that dangerous.

"Go see for yourself. There sure have been a lot of newcomers today, though... Did the shadows take over another world?"

Sora missed the question. "Newcomers... You mean, there are people besides me who showed up here today?"

"Yeah, looks like. I saw a couple in the Second District through this door. Kind of a weird-looking pair..."

"Thanks!"

"Hey, be careful!"

Maybe it was Kairi and Riku... Hope swelling up in his chest, Sora opened the door to the Second District. On the other side was a narrow street.

"Kairi! Riku!" he shouted. No one answered. He kept walking, a little let down. Right in front of him a man turned a corner and fell over.

"Whoa! Are you okay?!" Sora went to help him, but the man's chest began to glow with red light. A glittering heart-shaped thing floated up and was sucked into a small shadowy orb that appeared in the air.

Was that...the same sort of shadowy orb he'd seen on the island?!

Without thinking, Sora held the Keyblade out ready to fight. The orb took on a humanoid shape for an instant, then disappeared. And then a little black monster came up out of the ground.

"These things were on the island...!" It was the same as the little shadowy things he'd fought off before. "They're here, too?!"

They appeared one after another, and they were all coming for Sora.

He brought the glowing Keyblade down on them, and after one or two blows, they disappeared.

"There's no end to 'em!" More and more little shadowy creatures came, and Sora ran through the Second District square, striking them down as he went.

Donald and Goofy were in the Second District hotel.

"Doesn't look like there's anybody here," said Goofy, opening the front door. It certainly did seem lonesome.

"Leee-on!" Donald called as he left the hotel.

"Wonder where he could be?" Goofy looked this way and that, then squinted, looking out at the Second District square. "Huh."

"What now, Goofy?"

"I thought I just saw someone go by."

"*Quack?*" Donald stared out toward the square, but didn't see anyone. "Are you seeing ghosts?"

"Gawrsh, maybe…"

Sora hurtled down another street to avoid more shadows and caught his breath. Nobody would be able to handle that many. He stretched his arms and took a deep breath. To win, you have to start with a clear head. Then you can outwit your opponent. That's what Wakka always said.

I'm okay. I won't lose.

And Sora opened the door to the Third District.

Donald and Goofy glanced every which way as they walked through the alleys of the Second District.

"Guess there's nobody here after all," Goofy said, sounding spooked.

"Aw, don't be such a fraidycat. And you call yourself captain of the royal knights! …*Wak?!*"

Something poked Donald in the back. He jumped high in the air and came down clinging to Goofy.

"Excuse me. Are you friends of the king…?"

Standing behind them was a smiling young lady in a pink dress.

"Gawrsh, you know the king?!"

"Oh yes," she replied brightly.

"Careful, Goofy. It could be a trick!" Donald brandished his magic wand.

"But she looks way too nice to be trouble," said Goofy.

"How do you know?" Donald was still inching back.

Confused, Goofy looked from him to the girl. Her long brown braid swayed, and she looked a little worried, then she smiled again.

"You must be looking for Leon, right?"

"…Leon?!"

Hearing that name, Donald and Goofy both sprang up.

"The king already contacted him. Let's go—it's not very safe out here."

"Gawrsh, er… What should we do, Donald?"

"What's the matter with you? She looks way too nice to be trouble!"

The girl looked back and laughed. "So you two are Donald and Goofy. I'm Aerith. It's nice to meet you."

"I guess they're not here…"

After running around the Third District, Sora came back to the Second District and stood in front of the fountain, looking up at the night sky.

That pair of newcomers the other boy had mentioned probably weren't Kairi and Riku after all…

Somehow, he got the feeling that he'd meet someone here in this town. But after all this searching, he still hadn't found Riku or Kairi.

"What do I do now…?"

Then Sora remembered what Cid at the Accessory Shop had told him. He could go there if he was ever in trouble. But just as he was thinking about it, more black shadows came up out of the ground.

"These things just won't go away…!" Sora ran at them with the Keyblade ready. It felt like he was getting better at using it.

"I just know I'll find them."

He took down the shadows and hurried back to the First District.

*   *   *

"Hey there, how… Oh, it's just Sora."

"What d'you mean, *just* me?" It wasn't unlike their exchange when Sora had first walked into the Accessory Shop, but this time instead of dashing up to the counter, he plodded.

"Still can't find your buddies, huh?"

"No…" Cid sure did seem to read him easily, Sora thought. "…But I keep feeling like I'll find somebody here!"

"Hmm…" Cid stroked the stubble on his chin. "Well then, you don't wanna give up now. Why don't ya take another look around town?"

"I guess you're right…"

Cid gave him a grin and a thumbs-up. "'Course I am."

"Okay. I'll look some more!"

"There ya go. Good thing you got plenty of energy, kid."

"I'm not a kid!"

Feeling more encouraged, Sora ran out of the shop again.

Then he heard another man's voice. "They'll come at you out of nowhere."

"Who's there?!" Sora jumped down the steps in front of the shop and turned with the Keyblade ready to face the man behind him.

"And they'll keep coming at you…as long as you continue to wield the Keyblade." The man had a strange kind of sword across his back, a huge gun with a blade at the end of it. His long hair fluttered in the night breeze, and a smirk tugged at the corner of his mouth.

Then he let out a sigh, his shoulders drooping. The breeze moved his hair aside, revealing a big scar on his face. "But why would it choose a kid like you?"

"Hey, what's that supposed to mean?"

"Never mind. Now, let me see that Keyblade."

The man came closer. Sora shifted, ready to fight. "What? There's no way you're getting this!"

He smiled coldly. "...All right, then, we'll have to do this the hard way."

He took out the strange sword—the Gunblade—and lunged straight for Sora. A chain attached to the barrel jingled. At the end of it was a silver charm in the shape of a lion's head, gleaming in the moonlight.

"I knew it! You're with *them*!" Sora yelled.

"I wouldn't be so sure about that." The man closed in and attacked Sora with a ferocious blow.

Sora barely managed to block with the Keyblade, but it almost seemed like the force might break it. He was stronger than anyone Sora had fought before. Stronger than Wakka or Tidus or Riku.

"You're not bad," the man remarked, smiling and leaping back. From just that one attack, Sora was out of breath.

Maybe he was no match for someone like this...

"So, how about this?" The Gunblade came at him from the side. Sora dodged by a hair's breadth, nearly defeated by the man's speed. His invincible smirk made Sora feel like he was being toyed with.

"I'm not done yet!"

This time the Gunblade rained down blows from above. *Clang! Clang!* Sora could feel the impact right through the Keyblade, all the way in his bones.

Groaning, he jumped back, dodging again, and then rushed in to attack. "Hyaaaah!"

He attacked upward, from below, and he definitely made contact. But...

"You really aren't done, huh?"

A blow came down hard onto Sora's head, knocking him back, and then he wasn't sure what happened. But it felt like he was thrown into the air for a long time, and he could see the night sky drifting peacefully above.

He fell flat on his back and his head met the cobblestones with a thump. Everything went dark.

"Whew…" The man shouldered his Gunblade. From behind him, he heard someone applauding.

"We lucked out finding it here, huh, Leon?"

He turned and a black-haired girl was standing there. She shrugged and grinned. With the giant shuriken strapped to her back, she looked like a fighter, too.

"Cid told me," he said.

"Hmm."

She ran up to Sora and knelt down to gently touch his head. For someone who'd lost a fight, the kid looked pretty comfortable, his eyes closed as if he was just napping. "Looks like he's not hurt too badly."

"Of course he isn't. I did go easy on him." Leon put the Gunblade away and picked up Sora to carry him on one shoulder.

His head was spinning. And it hurt a little, too. *Huh, what was just happening…?*

"Come on, you lazy bum. Wake up."

It was Kairi's voice. Sora regained consciousness, and Kairi was staring into his face, looking worried.

Finally…!

"You okay?"

"I guess…" He sat up slowly, hazily trying to focus on Kairi. Was he dreaming?

"Those creatures that attacked you are after the Keyblade. But it's your heart they really want, because you wield the Keyblade."

"I'm so glad you're okay, Kairi…" Sora sighed in relief. Now they just had to find Riku…

"Kairi? Who's that? I'm the great ninja Yuffie!"

"Huh?"

Sora looked closer at the girl in front of him. Her hair did look like Kairi's, except that it wasn't the same color, and her face was different, too.

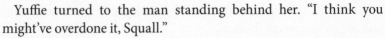

Yuffie turned to the man standing behind her. "I think you might've overdone it, Squall."

"That's *Leon*."

It was the man Sora had fought in the square. He stiffened. "You're…"

"We're not bad guys. Take a look around," Leon said reassuringly.

"Where…"

It looked like they were in a room in the hotel he'd seen in the Second District. The bed Sora had just woken up in was nice and soft, and next to him there was a cool, damp towel they must have been using to ice his head. The Keyblade rested against the wall.

"We had to get the Keyblade away from you to shake off those creatures," said Yuffie. "It turns out that's how they were tracking you."

"It was the only way to conceal your heart from them," Leon went on.

Conceal his heart…? Sora looked up at him.

"Once you lost consciousness, they lost track of your heart. But it won't work for long. Still hard to believe…that you of all people are the chosen one." Leon picked up the Keyblade and swung it through the air. It sparkled and vanished from Leon's hand, then reappeared in Sora's. "Well, I suppose beggars can't be choosers."

"None of this is making any sense!" Sora complained. "What's going on here?"

Leon and Yuffie looked at each another.

Back in another room at the hotel, Donald and Goofy listened to Aerith, patient and serious. When they'd come looking for Leon before, there hadn't been anyone here, but now they could hear people in the next room, too.

"Okay, you know there are many other worlds besides this town and your castle, right?"

"Yup!" Goofy nodded. "But they're s'posed to be a secret."

"That's right—they've been secret because they've never been connected. Until now." Aerith looked down sadly. "When the Heartless came…everything changed."

"The Heartless?" said Donald.

"Maybe you haven't seen any yet. Dark, shadowy creatures… Those are the Heartless." She stood restlessly.

"Do they look like ghosts?!"

"Yes. They're like ghosts that live in the darkness." Pacing slowly, she paused in front of the window and looked out at the city lights. "The darkness in people's hearts—that's what attracts them. And there's darkness within every heart…"

"Well, not ours!" said Donald, hopping to his feet.

Aerith shook her head. "Even a little fear is enough to turn a heart to darkness. Sometimes." She looked as if she'd remembered something painful—then she smiled, as if to shake off her own darkness. "Have you heard of a man called Ansem?"

"Ansem…?" Goofy cocked his head and exchanged glances with Donald. Neither of them had heard a name like that.

"He was studying the Heartless. He recorded all of his findings in a very detailed report."

"Gawrsh, er, can we see it?" Goofy held out his hand, but Aerith shook her head.

"The pages are scattered everywhere."

"Scattered?" said Donald.

"Across many worlds." Aerith sat down on the bed again.

"So these Heartless things came… Then the worlds were connected… And the stars started going out… And there's a report about the Heartless… And the king left…," Donald thought aloud. "So…?"

Goofy pounded a fist into his other palm. "Oh, then maybe the king went…!"

"To find the report. Yes, that's what I was thinking, too," said Aerith.

"We've gotta find him, quick!" Goofy tapped Donald on the back as if they had to hurry right away.

Donald stood fast with his arms folded. "But don't we need that key first?" he asked Aerith.

"That's right. The Keyblade." Aerith looked toward the neighboring room.

"So...this is the key?" Sora held up the Keyblade, staring at it.

"Exactly!" Yuffie nodded.

"The Heartless have great fear of the Keyblade," said Leon. "That's why they'll keep coming after you no matter what."

"Well, I didn't ask for this," Sora protested.

"The Keyblade chooses its master. And it chose you!" Yuffie poked the Keyblade.

Leon gave them a cynical smile. "So, tough luck."

"Tough luck? C'mon... I mean, how did all this happen? I remember being in my room..." Then Sora gasped and leaped to his feet, looking at them frantically. "Wait a minute! What happened to my home? My island? Riku! Kairi!"

Leon only shook his head.

"But...!"

"Calm down. There's still more to explain." Leon quieted him with a look.

Somehow feeling like he had to listen to Leon, Sora sat down again. But his heart was still racing.

Kairi, Riku... Our island...

What could have happened to them?

"Did you see a large door open?" Leon asked.

"...Yeah, I did."

That big white door, and then... But there must have been a door before that.

"Each world has a Keyhole. And each Keyhole is connected to the heart of that world."

"The heart of a world...?"

"No one knows what the heart of a world looks like yet. But the Heartless come in search of the Keyholes." Leon pushed his hair back and glanced toward the neighboring room.

"The Heartless enter through the Keyhole and do something to the world's core," said Yuffie, peering closely at Sora and poking at the Keyblade.

"And then what happens?" Sora asked.

"Darkness comes out from the Keyhole. And then the world disappears."

"What?!" Sora jumped up again, staring at the other two. That great big door. And the darkness that poured forth from it. The collapsing island… "Like our world did?"

"That's right," Leon said gravely. "That's why you have to lock the Keyholes."

Sora weakly shook his head. "But I have to find Kairi and Riku…"

"The worlds that are destroyed get scattered across other worlds," Yuffie told him gently. "So, while you're visiting other worlds, maybe you'll find your friends."

At that Sora looked up.

"Maybe. There's still a lot we don't know," said Leon.

"Okay… So I have to lock these worlds, right? But how do I get to…"

Sora trailed off. They felt a strange presence.

"Leon!" Yuffie pointed at the corner. A shadow had appeared there—a Heartless.

"Yuffie, go!" Leon shouted. She took the shuriken from her back and dashed out to the neighboring room. Sora sat there bewildered. "Let's go, Sora!"

"But—!"

"The Heartless have sniffed you out. The darkness in your heart… in the heart of the Keyblade wielder!"

"Darkness—?"

"Sora, stay with me!"

One after another, Leon destroyed the Heartless that came for Sora. But Sora wasn't moving—he couldn't.

The Keyblade was shining in his hand.

Worlds were disappearing. Worlds had already disappeared—like Destiny Island.

And his friends were gone. Kairi and Riku.

I have to do this, he thought.

"SORA!"

"Right!" Finally he stood up, holding tight to the Keyblade.

"Take *this*!" Leon swung his Gunblade and sent the Heartless flying. The window shattered, and Leon simply leaped through it to the outside. Sora followed and landed after him. The alleyway behind the hotel was swarming with Heartless. No matter how many they defeated, more appeared.

"Don't bother with the small fry," said Leon. "We have to find the leader! Let's go!" He ran with Sora close on his heels.

"So, that's how it is…"

"Sounds like we really need that key," said Donald, and just then there was a commotion from the next room.

The door flew open and a black-haired girl came running in. "Aerith!"

"…Yuffie?!" Aerith stood up from the bed.

"The Heartless are here! It's not safe in here anymore!" Yuffie shouted, attacking the Heartless that were coming in from the other room.

"Gawrsh, are these the Heartless guys?" said Goofy, hunkering behind his shield.

"That's right!" Yuffie replied.

"Let's go get 'em, Goofy!" Donald readied his wand, and then—

"Look out!"

Heartless flew into the room and slammed themselves into Donald and Goofy.

"*Wak?!*" Knocked back, they crashed through the window and out into empty air.

"*Gawawawawawawaaaaaaak!*"

"*A-hyoooooooooohooohooohooooo!!*"

Their howls echoed through the city.

Hearing some odd shrieks from overhead, Sora looked up, but just a moment too late.

"*Waaak!*"

"*Ahweee!*"

"Oof…"

Donald landed tailfirst on top of Sora, and Goofy crashed headfirst on top of them.

"What just happened…," Sora mumbled, still holding on to the Keyblade even while being smooshed.

Two voices chorused from on top of him, "The key!"

And then something strange came over the Second District.

"Wh-what's going on?!"

The three got up nearly all at once and readied their weapons—Sora with his Keyblade, Donald with his wand, and Goofy with his shield. With a roaring rumble, stone walls rose up out of the ground, trapping them in the Second District square.

And then Heartless after Heartless sprang up and headed straight for them.

"Here they come!" Sora shouted.

They had no choice but to fight.

"Lemme at 'em! *Fire!*"

"Here goes!"

Flames burst from Donald's wand and Goofy rushed the Heartless.

Not to be outdone, Sora leaped into a swarm of Heartless. There were more than a few, but he was pretty sure that three could handle it.

"Hey, not bad!" he called.

"Well, I am the royal magician, y'know!" Donald shot back.

"Here come some more!" Goofy told them.

Sora knocked a Heartless back and Donald finished it off with magic. Goofy attacked another one and threw it into the Keyblade's path. They fought perfectly together, almost as if they'd been comrades all along.

When the Heartless were all defeated, the trio finally got to look at one another for the first time, and they smiled.

But in the very next moment, a huge bundle of metal fell clanking out of the sky.

"*Waaaak?!*" Donald skittered back and forth, trying to avoid being flattened.

The metal pieces bounced up off the ground and amassed together in the center of the square into the shape of an enormous suit of armor.

"Gawrsh, is that a Heartless, too?!" Goofy said, huddling behind his shield.

Sora nodded. "I bet this one's the leader!"

A helmet landed atop the suit of armor. Sora, Donald, and Goofy were confronted with a giant Heartless—the Guard Armor.

"D…d'you think we can beat it…?"

"…If we all fight together, we'll be okay." Sora rested the Keyblade on his shoulder to look at Donald and Goofy.

"But we've never fought together before…," said Goofy.

"We'll be fine! I'm Sora!" He gave them a lopsided grin.

"Donald Duck here."

"Uh, I'm Goofy!"

They introduced themselves just in time before the Guard Armor came rushing at them.

"Here we go!"

The three of them ran under it. First, Sora jumped up and attacked the main bulk of it, but the Guard Armor didn't seem to take the hit at all.

"*Quack!*" The parts started moving on their own and a foot stomped down on Donald.

"Gawrsh, are you okay?" Goofy ran over to help him up. In the meantime, Sora was dodging the other foot that came for him.

"Ow, ow, ow, ow! Why, you! *Fire!*" Donald hit the right hand with his magic wand, but that didn't do much damage, either. The torso and the two feet, stomping around with minds of their own, came after them.

"It's not doin' any good!" With the left foot pursuing him, Goofy held up his shield and ran off to a corner of the square.

"Take that! And that!" Donald kept shooting magic at the right foot, and it finally seemed to weaken. Sora ran up and attacked it, striking with a huge clang.

"I got it! If we're gonna beat this thing, we have to gang up on one part at a time!" he shouted, whaling away at the right foot.

Goofy came dashing out of his corner. "Wahoooo!"

"*Fire!*"

Goofy's shield dealt a heavy blow, and a hit from Donald's magic exploded on its target.

"There we go!" As Sora pumped his fist in the air, the right foot burst apart. "Now the left foot!"

They concentrated their attacks again as he said, and this time easily disabled the left foot.

"Wowee! That was pretty good!" Goofy yelled, and this time he rushed the Guard Armor's right hand. It was spinning around, which made it hard to hit, but the three of them together took it out, and then the left hand, too.

"Now it's just the torso!"

Donald attacked the torso with a barrage of magic, and Goofy leaped up to hit it with his shield. At this point, all they could do was wear down the Guard Armor's strength.

"Take this!"

Sora took a flying leap and struck the torso, and the Guard Armor fell like a marionette with its strings cut.

"Is…that it…?"

"*Quack, quack, quack!*" Donald kept on attacking the immobile Guard Armor.

And then… A big heart floated up out of the torso.

"Huh…"

As the three of them watched, the Guard Armor dissolved into little sparks of light and disappeared.

"All right! We won!" Sora jumped at Donald and hugged him.

"*Wak?!*"

"We did it!" cried Goofy and did the same thing.

Smooshed between them, Donald let out an odd noise. "*Waaaak!*"

"Not too shabby, Sora."

Sora looked up to see Leon standing atop the wall.

"Well, I didn't beat it myself, you know." Sora smiled, speaking over Donald's head.

"That's right! He had the royal magician Donald Duck to—"

Goofy hushed him from butting in.

"So you've already met?" said Leon.

"Met…? Well, we know each other's names…," Sora replied.

"I see." Leon jumped down from the wall. "They've been looking for you."

"…For me?"

"For the Keyblade wielder."

Sora turned uneasily back to Donald and Goofy.

"Hey, why don't you come with us?" Goofy said, taking a step toward Sora. "We can go to other worlds on our vessel."

"Other worlds…"

"We're lookin' for the king," Goofy explained.

"I wonder if I could find Riku and Kairi..."

"Of course!" said Donald.

Sora looked at Leon, hoping for some kind of advice.

"Sora, go with them. Especially if you want to find your friends."

"Yeah...I guess..."

Could he really find Kairi and Riku?

And he had just been fighting alongside these two so well, but could he keep doing that?

Anyway, it was really just about the Keyblade...

Wait, no. Sora remembered. He'd already made the decision that this was something he had to do.

But...can I really do anything?

"Sora..." Donald gave him a serious look. "You can't come along looking like that."

"Huh? Why not?!"

It was Goofy who protested first. Sora kept staring at Donald unhappily.

"No frowning, no sad face. Okay?" Donald made a sad face and a frown, scrunching his brows on purpose.

"Oh yeah, that's right. Only smiles can come aboard the Gummi Ship." Goofy brought his face closer to Sora's and screwed up his face in a dorky smile. "Ya gotta look funny, like us!"

"Our ship runs on happy faces!" Donald said with a beaming grin.

Still hanging his head, Sora thought about it a little, and...

"Ngeeeee!" He made his eyes pop and smiled as wide as he could.

Donald and Goofy burst out into laughter. "Yeah, like that, Sora!"

"But that face...is too funny..." Goofy was rolling on the ground laughing.

"Seriously..." Even Leon cracked a wry smile.

"Okay. I'll go with you guys," Sora said with a real smile. "I'm going to find them."

"So, let's do this right. Donald Duck!" He held out his hand.

"The name's Goofy!" He placed his hand on top of Donald's.

"And I'm Sora!" Finally Sora did the same, adding his hand atop theirs.

"All for one, and one for all!" Goofy's voice rang out.

With no Heartless for the moment, Traverse Town felt a little quieter but friendlier.

"So, if there's any trouble, just come back here," Leon told Sora and the others once they had prepared to leave.

"Got it!" Sora replied, smiling.

"And we might hear from the king!" said Donald.

Aerith nodded. "Besides, we still haven't found the door in Traverse Town. As long as the door stays unlocked, the Heartless will probably keep coming."

"Even if they do, there's nothing to worry about with Yuffie on the job!" Yuffie grinned.

"We'll make sure to find the door before you come back," said Leon.

Sora nodded.

Aerith took a step closer, looking a little worried. "Be careful, Sora."

"I'll be okay. I've got Donald and Goofy with me now!"

"Yeah! Leave it to us!" Donald pounded on his chest, making Aerith smile.

"Good thing you've made some friends."

"Yeah!"

"Let's go, Sora!" said Goofy, and Sora started toward the gate.

"Don't let your guard down," Leon said after him. "Hold on to your heart."

Sora waved the Keyblade over his head in reply.

A mysterious space opened up outside the gate, and a strange little ship was there to meet them, not quite an airplane and not quite a submarine.

"This is our Gummi Ship. C'mon, let's get going!" Donald

apparently preferred to hurry, but at that moment, Jiminy came out of his pocket.

"Aren't you forgetting someone?"

"Ack!" Startled by Jiminy, Sora fell back on his behind.

"The name's Jiminy Cricket. I'll be going with you, too."

"Gee, you surprised me! I'm Sora. Nice to meet you." Sora got up and held out his hand, and Jiminy took a hold of his fingertip to shake.

"Likewise, I'm sure! I'll stay on the ship to watch over things. So, is everyone ready?"

"Ready! We got plenty of items and snacks and accessories, too." Goofy thumped his chest.

"Well then, let's be off! There must be some pretty big adventures coming your way. I'll be here to help you on your journey."

"Thanks, Jiminy."

Jiminy politely doffed his hat and bowed and jumped into Sora's pocket this time.

"Okay, here we go. Let's hurry up and find the king..." Donald headed toward the ship.

"And I'm gonna find Kairi and Riku!" said Sora, following him.

Goofy came after them. "And we gotta lock the Keyholes, too!"

So together they took off into the Other Sky, to unknown worlds.

WONDERLAND
first princess

THE GUMMI SHIP HURTLED THROUGH THE OTHER SKY.

"So, how does this thing move?" asked Sora.

"Well, it—*wak*! Can't really talk much right now!" Donald replied, gripping the control stick, and the ship banked a full forty-five degrees.

When Sora looked past him to the expanse of the Other Sky, he could see big rocks like meteoroids and strange shapes floating around. It did look like piloting would take some concentration.

"Let me fly the ship!"

"No way!"

"Hmph." Sora moved away from the cockpit and plunked himself down in a corner of the little ship. Donald could let him try it a *little*.

Goofy saw him sulking and went to sit next to him. "Hey, Sora…"

"C'mon, don't you think I could do it for a little bit? Donald's so mean!"

"Well, y'know, I've tried it before, and it's not that easy, flyin' the Gummi Ship."

"Really?" Just as Sora said that, the Gummi Ship made a huge turn, and he nearly fell over. "I bet I'd be better at it…"

With all his attention on the control stick in his hands, Donald didn't seem to hear them.

"Maybe he'll let me try it soon?"

Jiminy hopped out of Sora's pocket. "They say this Gummi Ship runs on some mysterious power."

"That's right," said Goofy. "That's why it can go between different worlds."

"Hmm…" Sora looked around the cabin. There was plenty of space for them to move around, but it had the feeling of any other vehicle.

"The stuff used to make this ship is pretty special," said Jiminy.

"Special? What is it?"

"It's made of a particular material called Gummi blocks. And this material—"

"*Quack!*"

Jiminy, explaining with his memo in one hand, found himself interrupted by Donald's shout.

"There's something up ahead!"

Sora and Goofy went running into the cockpit.

"Is that what a world looks like from outside?" said Sora, fascinated. He'd never seen anything like it before. The world floating there in the Other Sky was covered in a heart pattern, and there were green arches and a castle. Somewhere he'd never been before—never even dreamed of. He wanted nothing more than to land there.

"Yep," said Donald. "The worlds are all like this, floating here and there in the Other Sky."

"Wooow." Sora's eyes shone with wonder.

Goofy and Donald exchanged glances, and the Gummi Ship swooped down to land.

The Gummi Ship touched down in the middle of some strangely colorful fog. They couldn't see far ahead of them.

"Okay, we're off!"

Sora, Donald, and Goofy waved to Jiminy, who stayed to watch the ship, and looked around them, then finally stepped off the ship.

And—

"Whoa!"

There was no ground. The three of them drifted softly down and down into a deep hole.

"It kind of feels like we're flying…" A strong wind coming up from below buffeted Sora in the face.

"Hey, watch this!" Goofy waved his arms as if he were swimming, then he rested his head on his elbows in a napping pose.

Then Sora and Donald landed lightly on their feet, and Goofy crashed spectacularly into the ground.

"Owww…" Goofy staggered to his feet, rubbing his side. Even the Gummi Ship had floated down next to them.

"Whoa!"

"Gee, that sure was a surprise." Jiminy poked his head out. And then, right in front of them, a white rabbit went scurrying by.

"Oh, my fur and whiskers! I'm late, I'm late, I'm late! Oh, dear, oh, dear, oh, dear—I'm here, I should be there. I'm late, I'm late, I'm late! The queen—she'll have my head for sure!"

The white rabbit disappeared down a hallway and around a corner with his glasses and his giant watch.

"Why's he in such a hurry?" Sora wondered, staring after him.

"Well, let's find out!" said Donald. "The ship's all yours, Jiminy!"

The trio ran after the rabbit and finally came to a stop.

"A door!"

It looked like they should be able to get through it.

"Well, there's no keyhole," said Goofy. "But looks like that white rabbit went through here."

He opened the door, and beyond it, they could see another door through which the white rabbit was just running.

"Let's go!"

They went through that door and then another… And then they came into a big room.

It had a fireplace and a clock, like someone's living room but a little bit off—there was a giant faucet.

"Hey, there he goes!"

Goofy pointed at the white rabbit, which shrank to a fraction of his size, then opened a tiny door and ran through it.

"He shrank?!" Sora ran to the door and crouched down. The door was definitely too small for him to fit through. "How did he get so small?"

As he peered closely at the little door, the doorknob moved drowsily and spoke. "No, you're simply too big."

"It talks!" Donald shouted.

The doorknob looked annoyed and made a huge yawn. "Must you be so loud? You woke me up."

Goofy moved closer and said cheerfully, "Good morning!"

"Say, have you seen a girl and a boy about as old as me?"

"Or the king!"

"Or a Keyhole maybe…"

The three of them had burst out with questions, but the doorknob only yawned again.

"Well, don't ask me all at once. I have seen a girl. The queen must know more."

"It has to be Kairi!" Sora exclaimed.

The doorknob's eyelids drooped. "Good night! I need a bit more sleep."

"Hold on! Where do we find that girl and the queen?"

"Why, don't ask me."

The doorknob had nearly dozed off already. Sora leaned in closer. "Wait—what do we have to do to get small?"

"Why don't you try the bottle…over there?"

The three of them turned to look, and indeed, there on the table were two little bottles, one with a red label and one with a blue label.

"We should drink these?" Sora asked, but the doorknob was fast asleep.

"He said something about a queen, right?"

"But, Sora, we're looking for the king." Donald and Goofy both looked at Sora, a little anxiously.

"But…he said there was a girl…"

"Gawrsh, I guess he did, but…" Goofy folded his arms, thinking.

"Besides, isn't it suspicious how that white rabbit was in such a hurry?"

"Gee, it was a little odd."

"And we do have to look for the Keyhole," said Donald, picking up the bottle with the red label. "Hey, it says something."

Goofy looked closer at the label. There was a picture of a small tree growing into a bigger tree. And on the blue label, there was a big tree shrinking into a smaller tree.

"So, if we drink the red one, we'll get bigger, and if we drink the blue one, we'll get smaller?" said Sora.

"It's okay to drink, right?" Goofy stared uneasily at the bottles.

"The doorknob said to. So it must be fine." Sora picked up the blue one and put it to his lips.

"Whoa— Sora!" Goofy yelped, and right before his eyes, Sora shrank down.

"All right. Our turn!" Donald drank it, too, and likewise shrank. Still looking a bit worried, Goofy finally followed suit.

"Well, it looks like everything's in order."

"Except that we're tiny…"

They looked at one another, making sure everything was in one piece. The table was the size of a house now and the chair next to it like a very odd tree. Only that door with the talking doorknob on it was the right size for them now.

"Let's go!"

Just as Sora began to run toward the door, they heard a strange noise—and Heartless appeared.

"Wha-hoooey!" Goofy jumped back. These were different from the Heartless they'd fought in Traverse Town—some looked like dragons floating in the air, some were squat and round. But what they had in common was that they had no face. Just two shiny little eyes.

"They're over here, too!" Donald shot magic at them and the battle began. And just like in Traverse Town, as many as they defeated, more kept appearing.

"We'd better get moving!" Donald yelled, fending them off. "There's no end to 'em!"

"I wonder if there's a big Heartless around here, too…," said Goofy.

"Let's just go!" Sora pushed him along and went up to the door-knob again. "Hey, let us through!"

He knocked and even tried kicking, but the doorknob wouldn't wake up.

"What do we do…?"

"Sora! There's a tunnel over here!" Donald had found the way out—a hole in the wall. They headed into it.

Through the tunnel, there was a garden full of greenery. The shrubs were neatly trimmed into leafy arches shaped like hearts.

"Gawrsh… It kinda looks like the gardens at our castle!"

"*Wak!* Disney Castle's gardens are definitely more impressive!"

Bickering, Donald and Goofy walked under an arch. Sora hardly heard them as he turned to and fro, gazing around him. He had never seen anything like this before.

This was Wonderland—a mysterious place ruled by the Queen of Hearts. And they were in the queen's enormous courtyard.

"Hey, look!" Goofy pointed to a dais, atop which a rotund woman sat with an air of puffed-up authority—the queen.

Some playing-card soldiers holding spears shaped like spades were blocking the way through the next arch. "Aw, let us through," said Donald, but they didn't even look at him.

The white rabbit ran up to a platform beside the queen and sounded a bugle.

"What's going on?" Donald wondered, watching the scene unfold.

"Court is now in session!" cried the white rabbit.

"I'm on trial? But why?" said a girl with blonde hair, who stood atop some stairs in front of the dais. She wore a light blue dress with a white apron over it, and her shoulders were bunched up in anger.

"A trial?" said Goofy.

"What's a trial?" asked Sora. He'd never even heard the word on Destiny Islands.

"Well, it's kind of like a meeting to decide whether to punish someone for a crime."

"So that girl did something wrong?"

"Maybe we'll find out…"

Sora decided he'd have to see.

"Her Majesty, the Queen of Hearts, presiding!" the white rabbit announced.

The queen loudly cleared her throat. "This girl is the culprit. There's no doubt about it. And the reason is—because I say so, that's why!"

"That is utterly unfair!" the girl cried.

"Well, Alice, have you anything to say in your defense?" the white rabbit asked.

"Of course! I've done absolutely nothing wrong!" Alice glared back up at the dais. "You may be the queen, but that doesn't give you the right to be so *mean!*"

Hearing her forthright speech, the white rabbit ducked his head fearfully, anticipating a fit from the queen.

"*Silence!* You dare defy me?!" The queen snapped the fan she held and jumped to her feet. "The court finds the defendant *guilty as charged!*"

It sounded as though this was an awful sort of trial, in which a single word from the queen decided the verdict and everything else.

"Hey, we should help her out," Sora said, gripping the Keyblade.

"Yeah, but, uh… That'd be muddling," said Goofy.

"Meddling!" Donald corrected him with a jump.

"Oh yeah! 'Cos we're not supposed to get involved with stuff on other worlds…"

The queen's booming voice cut off their hushed conversation. "For the crimes of assault and attempted theft of my heart…!"

"Theft of her heart?" said Sora.

"That must mean Heartless!" said Donald. The three of them nodded. If there were Heartless involved, they couldn't stay out of it.

"Off with her head!" the queen bellowed.

"No, no! Oh, please!"

At the queen's command, the playing-card soldiers began to close in on Alice—but Sora, Donald, and Goofy got there first. "Hold it right there!"

The queen scowled at the three running up into the clearing. "Who are *you*? How dare you interfere with my court!"

"Excuse me," Sora loudly addressed the queen. "But we know who the real culprit is!"

"That's nonsense. Have you any proof?"

"Umm…"

They might have known that Alice was innocent, but they didn't have any proof at all. There was just the fact that only the Heartless would try to steal hearts.

"If you don't have any proof, the verdict is *guilty*!"

"Then we'll find some!" said Sora.

"*A-hyuk!* Yeah!" Goofy agreed.

"Bring me evidence of Alice's innocence! Fail, and it's off with all your heads!" the queen declared. "Court is now adjourned!"

The playing-card soldiers returned to their posts—after Alice was placed in a prison cell, which looked more like a giant birdcage.

Goofy spoke to her first. "Are you okay? We'll find the evidence for sure!"

"My name is Alice. Who are you?"

"I'm Sora."

"I'm Goofy. And this is Donald."

She smiled a little. "Pleased to meet you." Then she looked down, speaking quickly. "I do wish we hadn't met at a time like this… I'm sorry to get you all caught up in this strange trial."

"Why are you on trial?" Sora asked.

"Well, that's what I'd like to know! The moment she saw my face, the Queen of Hearts decided I'd done something wrong. But I've never seen her before!" Alice sighed.

"That's terrible!" Donald stamped his feet. "We'll bring charges against *her*!"

"How did you get here?" asked Sora.

She had to concentrate a little and then spoke hesitantly, as if choosing her words. "Hmm… Well, I don't really remember. I was sitting in a meadow, with the older girls reading to me, and then I found a mysterious hole in the ground."

"A hole?"

"It must be the same hole we fell into!" Goofy said, exchanging glances with Donald.

"When I tried to look inside, I just tumbled in…and then I woke up here."

Goofy cocked his head and murmured, "Gawrsh, it almost sounds like she came from another world…"

"That's funny," Donald whispered. "People usually can't travel between worlds."

"Well, why not?"

They wouldn't have been able to come here themselves without the Gummi Ship. How Alice could have made it here from a different world, they had no idea. Maybe she had some kind of secret power, like Sora had the Keyblade.

"What do you mean by another world?" asked Alice.

"Err… That's private."

"The defendant will remain silent!" shouted one of the playing-card soldiers standing guard. The trio moved up closer to the cage to whisper to Alice.

"Don't worry. We'll find the evidence!"

"Thank you. I hope so." Alice shrugged, then finally smiled.

"No loitering! You're all an eyesore! You want to be thrown in prison, too?!" The playing-card soldiers chased them off. The three ran into the shelter of a heart-shaped arch to hold a strategy meeting.

"Evidence… Does that mean we'll have to bring a Heartless into court?"

"Even if we showed up with a Heartless, that wouldn't necessarily prove anything…"

As Donald and Goofy discussed, Sora folded his arms and thought. "Well, what about their smell...or claw marks... Wouldn't that be more like evidence?"

"Have you seen anything like that around, Sora?" Goofy asked.

"Well, not around *here*, but..." Sora pulled at his own sleeve and showed them.

"Oh...it's torn!"

"One of them got me when we were fighting just before. So, if we look around, I bet we can find some more traces like this here in this world."

Goofy sniffed at Sora's sleeve. "They do have a weird smell..."

"Maybe that'll work for evidence!"

The three looked at each other and ducked back into the hole beside the arch. They emerged into a forest thick with giant water lilies.

"Sure would be nice if there was something around here...," Donald said, looking around, and then— *Waaaak!* he shouted and jumped behind Sora.

"What, Donald?"

"Th-th-th-*there*!" Donald's trembling hand pointed at a disembodied cat's head floating in the air.

Goofy yelped and ducked behind his shield and Sora.

"Who are you?!" cried Sora.

The cat's head drifted to and fro and settled at last on the ground. "Who, indeed?" The cat's plump, striped body appeared, balancing on the head and rolling it around, as if it were a ball in a circus trick. "Poor Alice. Soon to lose her head, and she's not guilty of a thing!"

The cat's head floated up again and stuck properly onto his body. He grinned down at the trio from up atop a lily pad.

"Hey, if you know who the culprit is, tell us!" said Sora.

"The Cheshire Cat has all the answers...but doesn't always tell."

"Meanie!" Donald yelled.

The Cheshire Cat only grinned. "The answer, the culprit, the cat all lie in darkness..."

And then the cat vanished.

"Wait!" Sora called. If they couldn't find any evidence, they wouldn't be able to help Alice.

The cat's disembodied voice echoed in the lotus forest. "They've already left the forest. I won't tell you which way. But even I don't know whether there might be anyone else who knows…"

"Should we trust him…?" Donald said uneasily, and then the Cheshire Cat appeared again right in front of him.

"To trust or not to trust? I trust you'll decide!" Grinning, the cat vanished once again.

"I guess we should go through this forest," said Sora.

"Do you believe the cat, Sora?" asked Goofy.

"I think we've got to!"

Donald nodded at Sora's determination, then looked around again. "So…which way is through the forest?"

"Hmm… let's try that way."

They started deeper into the forest, but Heartless popped out to waylay them.

"Whoa!"

"Gawrsh, these things are following us everywhere…" Goofy took a breath and readied his shield. He still didn't like fighting the Heartless, but now that he was getting used to fighting alongside two others, they didn't scare him so much anymore.

"Of course they are! Aerith said they'd follow the Keyblade wielder, and that's Sora!" said Donald, attacking with his magic.

"Guys…I'm sorry," Sora told them sadly, even as he finished off a Heartless.

"Aw, don't feel bad, Sora," said Goofy. "We serve the king, and he sent us to find the key, so we're stickin' with you. There's nothing for you to be sorry for!"

Sora's face fell. "But…"

So if the king hadn't sent them, these two wouldn't be going any-where with me at all… It was a terribly lonely thought. They'd only been together for a little while, but they were fun to be around—hot-tempered Donald and easygoing Goofy.

Of course, they didn't compare to Kairi and Riku...

"Augh!" While he got lost in thought, a Heartless swept him with its claws, and Sora fell backward.

"Hang on, Sora!" Goofy ran to him and gave him a healing potion.

"Thanks, Goofy."

"It's not a good idea to be spacin' out like that!" And Goofy dashed off to help Donald fight. Sora got up, too, and rushed at the Heartless.

Having finally defeated all the Heartless, the three collapsed on the spot.

"Whew... A little tired now." Goofy sighed, looking up at a big lotus blossom above his head.

"*Quack...*" Donald flopped back as if he'd overspent his magic.

And then they heard a tiny voice. "Thank you."

"Huh?" Sora sat up, glancing around.

"Over here..."

"Who is it?" Donald asked rather nicely, and the lotus blossom above them gently swayed. "The flower?!"

"That's right. I'm a lotus blossom!" The blossom slowly opened.

"Wooow..."

A sweet fragrance filled the air. Pollen fell on their heads, and somehow, it made them feel more awake.

"We couldn't open with those things around," the blossom said.

"Those things—you mean the Heartl—" Goofy started, then covered his mouth with both hands. They couldn't even tell anyone about the Heartless. That would be meddling.

"Those dark things!" the blossom explained.

"Hey, have you seen a great big shadow?" Sora asked.

"A big shadow...?" The blossom seemed to think for a moment. "Well, perhaps... That way..."

The blossom pointed with its biggest petal to a lily pad not far away.

"Up there?"

"This should make it easier to climb." As the blossom said this, a lotus stalk rose up out of the ground and spread out a lily pad at the right height for Sora and the others to jump to.

"Thanks!"

"Our pleasure," the blossom replied and closed again.

The trio leaped onto the lily pad and from there to a higher one. And there was another lily pad above that, which looked like they could just barely reach it.

"Wow, that's high up!"

"We can make it!"

There were more lily pads up at the top, surrounded here and there by bushes. They looked around for where to go...

"There!" Donald pointed to a hole in the greenery that looked like it could lead somewhere else.

"Gawrsh, d'you think it's safe to go in...?" Goofy looked a little apprehensive again.

"That flower didn't seem like it would lie to us," said Donald.

"But the Cheshire Cat could've been..."

"Well, let's go see!" Sora urged them, and they all headed into the hole.

"Whoa!"

Through the hole there was no floor. They fell through the air and landed in another odd place.

"Are we...on top of the faucet in that funny room?"

Just as Donald said, somehow they'd come back out into that first room where the bottles were. "Wow, we sure are!"

"Shucks, we got turned around..." Goofy's shoulders drooped.

"Hold on!" Sora stared at the cupboard, which it looked like they might just be able to reach with a jump. "Isn't there something over there?"

"Footprints!" cried Donald and leaped to the cupboard. "Look at this! Great big footprints! Definitely from a Heartless!"

Sora and Goofy jumped over to join him.

"If we take off this piece and bring it back, we'll have some evidence, huh?" said Goofy, rummaging around.

"Why, look what you've found," a voice said out of nowhere. "Nice going."

When the three turned to look, the Cheshire Cat was sitting on the faucet, grinning away.

"Now we can save Alice!" said Sora.

The cat only grinned and stood up on his hind legs. "Don't be so sure! She may be innocent, but what about you?"

And the Cheshire Cat somersaulted in the air.

"What's that mean?" asked Goofy.

"I won't tell," the cat replied, floating playfully around, and then he disappeared again.

"What was that about…?" Sora tilted his head as Goofy went back to pulling off the piece of the cupboard. "Well, there's no reason to trust anything he says! This'll let us help Alice!"

Goofy finally pried it off. "We've been lookin' around here and there, but we haven't seen any Keyholes yet, have we…?"

"We've found some evidence, but we still haven't beaten the Heartless that's trying to steal hearts… *Oof.*" Sora jumped down to the floor.

Donald followed. "Leon said there'd be Heartless around the Keyholes, right?"

"So that means…maybe we'll have to fight another big Heartless…" Goofy leaped down, carrying the piece of wood over his shoulder.

"I don't know…," said Sora. "But let's go help Alice!"

They headed back to the queen's court.

"We'll help you, I promise!" Sora told Alice, who was still shut in the birdcage prison. The Queen of Hearts glared at them.

"Thank you…"

A curtain fell over the bars, and the cage was lifted up high, out of reach.

"Court is now in session," the white rabbit cried. "Counsel, step forward!"

Holding the plank with the footprints on it, Sora stepped up to the defense podium. Donald and Goofy took seats in the jury. The Queen of Hearts was leaning forward from the bench, already in a foul temper.

"Now, show the evidence you've found!"

Sora offered the plank.

"Hmph… Is that all? Compared to what I've gathered, it's as good as junk. Cards! Bring forth *my* evidence!"

At the queen's command, the playing-card soldiers brought out a big box. Then they put the plank from the cupboard in another box and spun them around out of Sora's sight. He couldn't tell which box was which now.

"Hey, what are you doing?!" Sora shouted.

The stubborn Queen of Hearts was deaf to any protests. "Why don't you choose which one has the correct evidence! I'll decide who's guilty based on that!"

"After we went through all that trouble of bringing it?!"

"Didn't I just say I'm allowing *you* to choose? Do you dare object to the rules of my court?!"

"All right…" Helplessly, Sora stood in front of the boxes and craned his neck, staring at them. He had no idea which one it might be.

"The one on the right, Sora!"

"No way, the left! Definitely the left!"

"I'm pretty sure it's the right!"

Goofy and Donald argued from the jury. Sora stood the Keyblade up in front of him, closed his eyes, and took his hands from it.

The Keyblade spun around for a moment as if it was confused and then fell over to the right.

"It's this one!"

"Are you certain?" snapped the Queen of Hearts. "No second chances!"

"Yeah, I'm sure!" Sora picked up the Keyblade and looked straight at her.

"Now we shall see who the real culprit is."

A playing-card soldier opened the box Sora had picked. A Heartless jumped out and disappeared.

Even the queen couldn't hide her shock. "What in the world was that?!"

"There's your evidence. Alice is innocent!"

"Yeah! That's right!" Goofy and Donald cheered from the jury.

"*Rrrrgh...* Silence! I'm the law here!" the queen bellowed. "Article Twenty-Nine! Anyone who defies the queen is *guilty*!"

Donald jumped up and down. "That's crazy!"

"Seize them at once!" The queen raised her heart-shaped fan, and playing-card soldiers rushed at Sora.

"You guys help Alice!" Sora shouted to Donald and Goofy and launched out of the defendant's stand.

"Got it!" Donald and Goofy ran to the tower that held Alice's cage.

"Cards! If they touch that tower, you'll lose your heads!" yelled the Queen of Hearts.

Donald jumped at the handle on the side of the tower. "It won't turn!"

"Let's break it!"

Goofy and Donald worked on breaking the handle while Sora kept the playing-card soldiers away from them.

"There, it's broken!" With the handle broken, the winch chain went slack and Alice's cage lowered again.

"Alice!" Sora ran toward the cage and threw off the curtain...but Alice wasn't there. "She's gone! Alice?!"

"Did she run away while we were fighting...?" Goofy wondered.

"Or maybe—she was kidnapped by the Heartless!" cried Sora.

The Queen of Hearts yelled over him, "You fools! Find the one who's behind this—I don't care how!"

The card soldiers all stopped fighting and scattered. Sora, Donald, and Goofy were right behind them, heading back into the lotus forest.

"Gawrsh...I can't believe she disappeared..."

"Well, c'mon, let's find her." Sora walked ahead.

"But how do you know it was the Heartless?"

"Who else could've kidnapped Alice?"

They had been right there when the cage went up the tower with Alice in it and when it had come back down empty. That could only mean that whoever had gotten to her must have done so while she was up in the air.

And only the Heartless could pull off something sneaky like that, Sora thought.

"Let's go and ask the flower that told us about the shadow," he said.

When they came upon the lotus blossom that had spoken to them before, it opened with a *poof*. But what appeared was the Cheshire Cat.

"I don't really like him much...," Goofy grumbled.

But Sora took a step closer. "Have you seen Alice?"

"Alice, no," said the grinning cat. "Shadows, yes!"

"Where'd they go?" Donald demanded.

The cat stood up and swayed to and fro.

"This way? That way? Whichever I say, I can only tell you lies."

"What's that supposed to mean?" Sora shot back a little angrily.

"Up, down, left, right—all mixed up thanks to the shadows. Step deeper into the forest, to the deserted garden... And you might find shadows in the upside-down room." Twitching his tail, the Cheshire Cat vanished again.

"...The deserted garden?"

"He said deeper into the forest. Let's go!"

They started to go farther but ran into trouble.

"Aw, more Heartless…" Goofy sounded reluctant but dashed into the fray, only to bounce off a Heartless with a big round belly. "Huh? Do they seem stronger to you this time…?"

"Ack! These ones shoot fire!"

It seemed they wouldn't get deeper into the forest that easily.

Goofy rammed himself into a Heartless and asked Sora, "Farther in is…this way?"

"Looks like it…! Let's hurry up!" Sora ran, swinging the Keyblade.

"Fire—I'm on fire! *Gwaaaaak!*" A Heartless had caught Donald on the tail with a burst of flame. He put it out with magic. "*Blizzard!*"

"This way, Donald!" Sora jumped up onto a lily pad and stretched out his arm for Donald.

"*Wa-ahoooey!*" Goofy climbed up frantically, pursued by magic-wielding Heartless.

"Bah…what a disaster…" Donald's shoulders fell.

Sora was already climbing onto the next lily pad. "But we still have to find Alice."

"Right. *A-hyuck!* There's a damsel in distress!" Goofy jumped up after Sora.

"*Quack!* I know that!" Donald waddled over and jumped, too. "Over there… There's another hole."

"There's gonna be a floor this time, right?" Goofy worried.

"Let's go!" Sora ran in.

Sight rushed back all at once after the darkness of the tunnel, making them blink. A big table set with plates and teacups sat out in a garden.

"Gawrsh, is somebody having a party?" Goofy wandered around the table.

Sora stared at it, too. But no one was here. "Maybe this is the deserted garden."

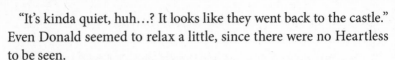

"It's kinda quiet, huh…? It looks like they went back to the castle." Even Donald seemed to relax a little, since there were no Heartless to be seen.

Sora followed the other two in walking around the table. A plate in the center was heaped high with cookies.

"They can't be bad to eat, right?"

"Nah, it's fine!"

With that brief exchange, Goofy and Donald were already popping cookies into their mouths.

"Hey, no fair! Me, too!" Sora ate one himself. "…It's sweet!"

The sweetness was somehow familiar and very elegant, and without thinking on it, he reached out to take another one.

"They're pretty tasty."

"Yeah! Hey, this kind's got fruit in it."

"This one has chocolate!"

Hungry from all the running around, the trio had finished off the whole plate in no time at all.

"Wow. It's been a while since we've had a treat like that!" Goofy crunched down on the last cookie—and the table tipped over. "Whoa!"

Heartless jumped out from under it.

"Aw, no way!" Still munching, Donald took out his wand.

"Over here, Donald!" Sora took his hand and pulled him into the little house beside the garden. Yelping, Goofy practically fell in before the Heartless could attack.

"Wait, huh…?"

There was something strange about the room. The floor had a door in it, and the fire in the hearth was burning *sideways*. And the back of the chair was resting on the floor.

"Whoa… It's makin' me dizzy!" Goofy wobbled, trying to look around.

Sora tilted his head. "Things that go on the wall are on the floor, and things that go on the ceiling are on the wall…?"

Donald did the same. "But it feels like we've seen it before somewhere…"

Goofy struck his open palm with his fist. "Isn't this…the same room we were in before?"

That made Sora think of what the Cheshire Cat had said. "Up and down, left and right, they're all mixed up… Gah!"

Right in front of his face, the cat's mouth appeared—and nothing more. Sora jumped back. "Hey, don't scare people like that!"

"The shadows are hiding somewhere. And the momeraths outgrabe. Why don't you try turning on the light?" Swaying, the cat's grin floated toward the lamp in the middle of the room.

"All right, leave this to me! *Fire!*" A ball of fire shot from Donald's wand and lit the lamp.

"Still too dim." Now the Cheshire Cat's face appeared in front of Donald. "You'll have to make it brighter."

"There's another lamp over there, Donald!" Sora pointed.

"Okay, here goes! *Fire!*" Another fireball set the other lamp alight, and brightness filled the room.

"You'll see the shadows soon. They'll arise in this room…but somewhere else. And they might go after that sleepy doorknob, too…"

With that the cat disappeared again.

"This room, but somewhere else… What's that mean?" Goofy cocked his head.

"Where the doorknob is!" Sora and Donald said at once and jumped back out of the room.

"H-hey, wait up!" Goofy scrambled to follow them.

"Gee, all this runnin' around…is pretty exhausting," Goofy panted as they ran through the lotus forest.

"And this world is just one weird thing after another!" Donald said to Sora.

"It's like a land of wonders," Sora replied.

"Yeah! It's crazy! I hope we can find the king and go back to our castle soon…" Donald trailed off with a sigh.

Once Donald and Goofy find the king, will I ever see them again? Sora wondered sadly.

"Our castle's the most fun anywhere," said Goofy, "and the fanciest and the most exciting!"

Sora broke into a smile. "Well, our island has an amazing beach, where you can swim all year round!"

Even though he didn't know if it was still there.

But he'd promised Kairi they would go back.

"Gawrsh, that sounds nice. We don't have a beach…" Goofy sounded especially envious.

"When I find Kairi and Riku, you should come visit!"

"You can come to our castle, too!" said Donald, glancing at Sora. "And meet the queen and Daisy!"

"Yeah!" Sora agreed loudly.

Even if they found the king and Kairi and Riku, and he went back to Destiny Island, he wouldn't forget this. He'd keep this memory of running through the lotus forest with Donald and Goofy. When Sora realized that, it lifted his spirits.

They would lock the Keyholes to keep the Heartless from coming, and then they'd find everyone, and his connection with Donald and Goofy wouldn't disappear.

"Promise, Sora!" said Goofy.

They grinned at one another and ran back through the court of the Queen of Hearts to the room with the talking doorknob.

"Whew… Doesn't look like there are any shadows here." Donald looked around and let out a breath. "But we gotta keep on our toes!"

Goofy ducked behind his shield and inched into the room.

"You'll have a better view from higher up."

Sora looked up at the voice to see the Cheshire Cat lazily stretched out on the table.

"Should we really listen to the cat, Sora?" said Goofy, as if he really would rather not.

"You're the fraidycat, Goofy!" Donald teased and looked at Sora. "Well?"

"Yeah, let's go!"

Sora jumped up onto the table. Donald followed him, and then Goofy gingerly climbed up.

The Cheshire Cat stood and pointed at the ceiling. "The shadows should be here, so…are you prepared for the worst?"

"We're ready!" Sora replied, even though Goofy was still cowering behind his shield.

Seeing him, the Cheshire Cat grinned mischievously. "Well, if not—too bad!"

Then the cat disappeared and down from the ceiling came a huge Heartless. The Trickmaster. Its long arms stretched out like springs, and it held clubs in its hands. Moving like a dance, it stepped closer to the trio.

"This must be the one that kidnapped Alice!" Sora leaped down from the table and headed straight for the Trickmaster. It whirled its long arms, bringing the clubs down at him, but Sora dodged and closed the distance.

"*Quack!* Wait up, Sora!" Donald rushed in after him.

"Gawrsh, it's huge… I don't like this…"

"C'mon, Goofy, you too!"

Goofy groaned and finally jumped off the table, but the Trickmaster's arm batted him away. "Yeeeow!"

"Goofy!" Sora ran over to him.

"Ouch…" A lump was rising on Goofy's head.

"Hey! This is for Goofy! *Fire!*" Fireballs shot from Donald's wand at the Trickmaster—but all that did was to light the clubs it held aflame. "*Wak?!*"

Then the flaming clubs flew at Donald's head.

"*Gwaaaak!*" He ran away with his hat on fire.

"You can't use fire magic on it, Donald!"

"*Waaaak!*"

"Water! Where's some water?!" cried Sora.

Donald ran under the faucet and turned the handle. Water gushed down on him and doused out the fire on his hat.

"Looks like it's another really strong one, huh…" Goofy sighed and stood up.

"Are you okay?" Sora stared with concern into Goofy's face.

"Well, not really… But if we don't beat it, we won't find Alice or the king or your friends, either! And if we don't lock up the Key-holes, the Heartless will keep on coming. So here goes!" Raising his voice, Goofy jumped at the Trickmaster and landed a hit.

Goofy's fighting for Alice and to find my friends, Sora thought. *And I have to fight so Donald and Goofy can find the king, too.*

We're not just fighting only for ourselves…

Sora went after Goofy, and one after another they struck the Trickmaster.

"*Wak!* Leave some fighting for me!" Donald joined in and this time attacked with ice magic. "*Blizzard!*"

They jumped out of the way of the Trickmaster's long arms and wore it down bit by bit.

"Now, Sora!"

At Donald's words, Sora climbed back up on the table and took a flying leap to swing the Keyblade into the Trickmaster's face. He felt it clang all the way up his arms.

"Hah! We did it!" Donald jumped up in joy as the Trickmaster fell to the floor with a huge thud. And a heart floated up out of its body, the same as the Guard Armor.

"I wonder if that's a heart it stole from someone…"

The trio watched the heart float up and up. It was sparkling beautifully—one could hardly imagine that it came out of something as terrible as a Heartless.

As the heart seemed to vanish into the ceiling, the Trickmaster's body turned into motes of light and disappeared. All that remained was silence.

"Oh yeah—Alice! Where could Alice be?" Donald ran around the room, searching.

"I thought we'd find her once we defeated the Heartless…" Dejected, Sora hung his head. Just then they heard a yawn.

"What a racket… How's a doorknob to get any sleep?"

The doorknob yawned hugely again, and inside its mouth—

"A Keyhole!" Donald shouted.

The Keyblade pointed toward the doorknob and a beam of light shot from its tip. "Whoa!"

The light shone into the Keyhole, and with a *click* it disappeared.

"Did that just lock the Keyhole?" Sora stepped closer and tried to look inside the doorknob's mouth.

"Now go on and let me sleep!" the doorknob complained and refused to open its mouth again.

Sora gave up and shrugged to Donald and Goofy. "Well, it looks like we locked the Keyhole, but Alice isn't here…"

"We haven't seen the king, either."

"Or Sora's friends."

A little discouraged, they looked at one another, and then the Cheshire Cat appeared between them.

"Splendid. You're quite the heroes."

"*Wak!* You again!" Donald lunged to catch the cat, to no avail.

"Oh, dear. Defeating me wouldn't do anything for you. …Or maybe it would."

"You're just talking nonsense again…" But Goofy didn't seem to mind the Cheshire Cat much anymore.

"By the way…" Now only the Cheshire Cat's head was floating there, looking down at the three. "If you're looking for Alice, you won't find her here."

"What do you mean?!" Sora tried to grab the cat's head, but it just floated away out of their reach.

"Alice isn't in this world at all."

"But normal people can't leave their world—"

"I wouldn't be so sure." The rest of his body materialized, still floating. "Alice is off with the shadows, in the darkness…"

And that was their only hint before the cat disappeared.

"What…did he mean by that?" Sora folded his arms. They'd been trying to help Alice all this time, but now they couldn't even find her.

"…Maybe there's something we don't know about Alice," said Donald, putting a hand on Sora's shoulder.

Goofy tried to cheer him up, too. "Well, it might feel like giving up, but let's go back to the Gummi Ship. Maybe we'll find her on another world. …Once we get back to our normal size!" He jumped up on the table and picked up the bottle with the red label.

"I guess so…" Sora stared at the bottle.

"Not with a gloomy face like that, though," said Donald. "If that's the face you're making…"

"I know, I can't get on the Gummi Ship." Sora looked up with a tiny smile.

"Right, only smiles!"

Sora stuck out his tongue at Goofy, took the bottle, and drank from it. Before their eyes, he grew bigger and bigger, back to normal.

"Us, too!" Donald and Goofy drank it in turn and grew.

"Okay, let's go!" They ran back out of the strange room.

DEEP JUNGLE
friends

THE GUMMI SHIP GAINED SPEED AND ROCKETED through the Other Sky. Sora and Goofy were talking behind the cockpit.

"We're not finding much, are we…?"

"About the king?" said Sora.

"Not just the king. Your friends, too. And then Alice disappeared, too." Goofy sighed.

"Hey, you can't tell Sora to keep smiling and then go around sighing yourself!" Donald yelled from the cockpit.

"But gawrsh… While we're looking for someone, another someone disappears! Don't you think it's pretty fishy? And on top of that, there's one of those big, mean Heartless in every world."

"…What's it all mean?" Sora asked in a tiny voice.

"That's what I'd like to know!" Jiminy Cricket hopped out of Sora's pocket.

"And there's the Keyblade… It happened in my world, too—but the Heartless in Wonderland were way stronger than the ones in Traverse Town." Sora clutched the Keyblade tightly in his fist.

The shining Keyblade didn't give him any answers, but he could feel that bit by bit, he was getting stronger. At the same time, though, it seemed like the Heartless were getting stronger, too. He'd never be able to beat them without Donald and Goofy.

"And I bet they'll keep getting stronger…" Goofy sighed again.

"But I think at the same time, we'll be getting that much closer to the truth," said Jiminy.

"Maybe…"

Sora didn't have much confidence in what Jiminy was saying, either. As the atmosphere grew heavier, the ship suddenly banked.

"Whoa! C'mon, can't you fly any better, Donald?" Goofy complained.

"If you think it's so easy, why don't you try!"

"I can pilot!" Sora eagerly interrupted and grabbed the controls for himself.

"*Waaak!* Bad idea!" Donald wrested the controls back from Sora. In the same moment a world covered in green emerged from the midst of the Other Sky. They could see an enormous tree twined with hanging vines, and a hut, and a great big waterfall.

"What is it...?"

Deep Jungle. The world was all but untouched tropical forest, a wild paradise.

"Why would the king be in a backwater place like this? It'd be a waste of time looking here," Donald argued.

"But Riku and Kairi might be down there," said Sora. "C'mon, Donald, let's just check it out!"

Just because the king wouldn't be here didn't mean that they could just ignore this world. Besides, weren't Donald and Goofy helping him look for Riku and Kairi, the same way he was helping them look for the king?

"No way. We're on an important mission!" Donald accelerated the Gummi Ship.

"Just land!" Sora tried to take the controls again.

Donald was too stubborn to be swayed at this point. "No!"

"Aw, guys, cut it out...," said Goofy.

"That's right! No quarreling!" Jiminy tried to get between them, but Sora and Donald went on wrestling over the controls. Neither one was prepared to give in.

"C'mon!"

"Forget it!"

"We're landing, so there!" Sora shoved Donald aside, grabbed the stick, and pushed it all the way back.

"Hey, don't touch that! *Wak-wa-waaaaak!*" Donald tried to pull the Gummi Ship back up out of its sudden descent, but it was too late for that. The ship was out of control, falling headfirst straight into the green world.

"*Quack!*" Now there was nothing to do but try to save the landing. Donald mashed buttons here and there. "This is all your fault,

Sora!" he shouted, and hit a red button. The cockpit opened up and the three of them went flying out of the Gummi Ship, screaming all the way.

"Whooooa!"

"Gwa-waaak!"

"Aaaah-hoohoooey!"

Jiminy was hanging on to the control stick for dear life. "Good luck, everyone…!" he called after them.

With a crash and a rustle and a thump, Sora tumbled down through the trees and then through the roof of the little house. Finally he hit the ground in one piece…more or less.

"Ow, ow, ow…" He stood up, rubbing a bump on his head. "Donald…? Goofy?"

The other two were nowhere to be seen. He was in what looked like a wooden hut. Outside the window, the green jungle went on and on. They must have gotten separated in the fall.

"What do I do now…?" Sora heaved a big sigh, and just then, he felt a rush of wind beside him. "Huh?!"

It blew him backward, and as he fought to regain his balance, he swung the Keyblade. And there in front of him was a growling leopard. It clearly wasn't friendly. Sora inched back and the leopard pounced at him.

Slammed back into the wall, Sora couldn't speak, but he stayed on his feet and barely avoided being knocked over. The leopard snarled and crouched down, ready to spring again. Sora felt sweat go down his back. Unlike the Heartless, the leopard's hostility was so focused and ferocious it felt searing hot.

It growled again deep in its throat and stopped only to launch another attack. Teeth closed on the Keyblade with a clang. With all his strength, Sora was just able to throw off the leopard, but before he could take another breath, it lunged for him once more. This time the Keyblade met its claws, and they were both thrown back from the force.

They clashed again and again until finally both Sora and the leopard began to tire. The next move would have to end it…

Sora put the last of his strength into his arm holding the Keyblade—but his hand was sweaty, and his grip failed for a moment—and that was when the leopard sprang.

I'm done for!

Just as he shut his eyes, a man with a spear leaped in through the window. The leopard found the handle of the spear in its jaws instead, and the man flung it back.

"Sabor…" the man murmured and rebounded at the leopard. It fled out the window. Sora felt all the remaining strength go out of him.

That was close…

He kept himself from falling to the floor in exhaustion. The man came closer. He wore a scrap of animal skin like a loincloth, his long hair looked like it hadn't been so much as trimmed in years, and he was staring closely at Sora. "Sabor, danger."

"Is Sabor the leopard?" Sora asked, but the man only shook his head as if he didn't understand at all. "Um… Thank you."

When Sora nodded, the man did, too. "Thank you."

"Huh?" How had Sora done anything that deserved thanks? "Er… What is this place?"

"This place, this place."

Apparently the man was only repeating back what Sora said.

"Okaaay… Where did the others go?" Sora scratched his head. "I mean, I got separated from my friends. Have you seen them?"

The wild man only looked confused.

"*Friends,*" Sora said slowly.

"Friends!" the man echoed happily. Did he understand at all…?

"Right, my friends! There's two of 'em. The loud one is Dona— No. Never mind!"

The man cocked his head at Sora, who had practically started talking to himself.

It's not that Donald and Goofy aren't my friends… But Donald only seems to care about finding the king. So I should put finding Kairi and Riku first, Sora told himself.

"I'm looking for my friends, Riku and Kairi," he went on.

"Look for Riku, friends?" said the man. "Kairi…friends?"

"Umm…yeah…" Kairi's smile flashed in his head.

"Friends here."

"Really?!" Sora perked up with a jump.

The man smiled back and said something Sora couldn't understand.

"Huh?"

He repeated the same sound in a strange voice, like no words Sora had ever heard before. "…Friends here." The man was gesturing intensely.

"Not sure I understand…but show me!" Sora didn't know if Riku and Kairi could really be here… But he couldn't just ignore what this person was telling him. "Take me to Riku and Kairi!"

The man tilted his head a bit and tapped his chest. "Tarzan. Tarzan go."

Sora pointed to himself, too. "And I'm Sora. Tarzan go, Sora go, go!"

Tarzan nodded, and Sora followed him out of the hut.

Outside, lush green spread out as far as the eye could see. They leaped down into the jungle.

Meanwhile…

Donald woke up atop a boulder in the middle of a bamboo thicket. He'd never seen a place like this before. He stood and looked around, bewildered, and finally noticed Goofy out cold beside him. But he didn't see Sora anywhere.

"Goofy!"

"Hmm…?" Goofy yawned and stretched, easygoing as ever. "What a good night's sleep. Mornin', Donald!"

"Don't gimme that! He's gone! S-so-so…"

"Huh? Sora's not here. Gawrsh, I sure hope he's okay…"

"…Aw, who needs him! We can find the king without him." Donald stamped his foot and reached out for his wand, which should have been beside him. But instead his hand felt something fuzzy. *"Quack… Waaaak?!"*

He looked at what he was touching, and a small gorilla stared back.

Then something in the thicket behind them moved.

"Who's there?!" As Donald and Goofy turned, the little gorilla dropped something shiny and ran away.

"Hey, is this…"

"A Gummi block?"

The two looked at each other and nodded.

If there were Gummi blocks here, that might mean someone else had been here…

"Who goes there?!" a voice boomed suddenly.

Donald and Goofy jumped. When they turned, slowly and timidly, a man holding a shotgun was standing there.

Sora and Tarzan landed in the midst of the thick jungle. Tarzan moved by swinging on vines from tree to tree, and Sora did all he could to keep up.

"Hey—Tarzan, slow down!"

Tarzan looked back at him and cocked his head.

"Umm, could we have a break? I guess you don't understand…"

"Go, go!"

"Okay, okay… Go…," Sora replied, out of breath, but just then, a Heartless appeared from the foliage behind Tarzan. "Look out!"

Tarzan turned as the Heartless attacked, but his long spear threw it off.

Sora had seen it before when Tarzan saved him from the leopard, but—he was *strong*.

"Let me at 'em, too!" Sora fought beside him, and they dispatched the Heartless that came out one after another.

After they'd defeated all of the Heartless, Sora rested the Keyblade on his shoulder. "...Well, that wasn't so bad!"

"That wasn't so bad," Tarzan repeated, smiling brightly. They took off again through the trees.

They made it through the jungle to a clearing where a small tent stood. It looked like people were living there, which made Sora feel a little better.

But still... Are Donald and Goofy okay...?

The thought crossed his mind and he shook his head. Even without them, he could still fight the Heartless... And if he could find Kairi and Riku here, they'd be able to manage, for sure.

"Jane!" Tarzan called and went into the tent. Sora followed him.

Inside, a pretty young lady was fiddling with some kind of machine. "Tarzan!" she exclaimed, looking up, and then saw Sora. "And who is this?"

"Uh, hi there. I'm—"

"Oh, you understand!" She looked rather surprised. "So then, obviously you're not related to Tarzan..."

"I'm Sora."

"And my name is Jane. Are you here to study the gorillas?"

Just as he was about to answer, a man with a shotgun strode into the tent. "Highly doubtful."

Behind the tall man, Sora could see Donald and Goofy.

"Sora?!" They both ran for him happily.

"Gee, we didn't know if we'd see you again!" Goofy cried.

Sora ran to them, too, but then he remembered the fight on the Gummi Ship and refused to look at Donald. "I was worried about you, Goofy!"

"We were pretty worried, too! Weren't we, Donald?" said Goofy, but Donald stubbornly faced the other way.

"Well, at least we're all together now!" Jiminy Cricket hopped out from behind Jane.

"Jiminy!" The trio ran up to him.

"I wasn't sure how this would turn out when we all fell out of the Gummi Ship, but here we are."

"Where's the Gummi Ship?" Donald asked.

Jiminy grinned. "Why, it's hidden behind the tent."

"That's good to hear!" Relieved, Donald took a deep breath.

"So, you're all friends!" Jane smiled.

The man folded his arms. "A circus of clowns. Not much use for hunting gorillas."

"We're studying them, Mr. Clayton, not hunting them," said Jane. "This is research!"

Without any sign of having heard her, Clayton turned and left the tent.

"Er... I'm Jane. We've come to the jungle to study the gorillas. And that was Clayton. He's a hunter, but he's acting as our guide in the jungle. And you are...?"

"Donald Duck. This is Goofy, and that's Jiminy Cricket. We're looking for our king."

"Your king? Goodness, is the king your friend, too, Sora?"

Donald and Sora exchanged glances, and both turned away again, sulking.

"Well, the more the merrier," said Jane, trying to soften the atmosphere between them. "Do make yourselves at home."

"Well, there's nothing for you to do here, is there, Donald?" Sora pouted.

"Actually, I'm staying!"

"…Huh?"

Goofy showed Sora a small bright block. "Look, it's a Gummi block. We found it here."

"Which means the king might just be around here somewhere," said Donald. "So we've gotta work together to look for him. *For now.*"

"Fine," Sora shot back. "I'll let you tag along. *For now!*"

Jane stooped down to peer at him. "Are you looking for something, too, Sora?"

"I'm looking for my friends. Tarzan said that they…that Kairi and Riku would be here… I wish I could actually talk to him, though." Sora hung his head.

If he understood what Tarzan was saying, maybe he could get some more clues about Kairi and Riku.

"Tarzan was raised in this jungle by the gorillas," said Jane. "He doesn't understand very much of our language yet, so I don't know much more than that… Well, Tarzan?"

Beside her, Tarzan cocked his head.

"Where are Kairi and Riku?" asked Sora.

"And the king!" Donald chimed in.

Tarzan only shook his head.

"Our friends are here, right?"

"Friends…here."

"Then…tell us where!" Sora looked up at Tarzan, almost pleading.

But someone replied from behind him, "There's only one place they could be."

"Clayton!" Sora turned. He'd practically snuck back into the tent.

"Young man, we've been in this jungle for some time now," Clayton said. "We were in the jungle before you arrived. But we have yet to encounter these friends of yours. I'd wager they're with the gorillas. But Tarzan refuses to take us to them."

"Really, Mr. Clayton," Jane began, "Tarzan wouldn't *hide*—"

He cut her off to browbeat Tarzan. "Then take us there! Take us to the gorillas. *Go-ril-las.*"

Tarzan stared at Sora instead.

Sora looked back. "Tarzan…"

He smiled and then nodded to Clayton.

"Tarzan, are you sure?" Jane worried.

"Tarzan go see Kerchak," he told her.

"Kerchak?"

"He must be the leader," said Clayton. "Perfect. I'll go along as an escort. The jungle is a dangerous place, after all." He smirked.

"Gawrsh, I've got kind of a bad feeling about this fella," Goofy whispered to Sora.

"Well, I'll get back to watch the Gummi Ship as usual!" said Jiminy. "See you all later!"

The trio nodded to him and he left the tent.

"Is it really okay, Tarzan?" Sora asked as they ran through the jungle.

"Go see friends!" he answered with a smile and ran ahead of them.

"Did he understand what I said…?"

"*Quack!*"

Donald jumped back. As Sora worried, a Heartless had appeared right in front of him.

"You guys don't have to do anything," Sora said, ready to fight with the Keyblade. "Tarzan and I can take care of them!"

If they started fighting, Tarzan should sense the commotion and come back, and they'd be able to catch the Heartless between them.

"*Wak!* Are you tryin' to tell me you don't need my magic?!"

"I guess that's what I'm saying…" Sora swung the Keyblade.

"*Quack!*" Donald shouted, waving his wand. "Then we aren't one for all *or* all for one anymore!"

"Aw, cut it out, guys…," said Goofy, but Sora and Donald went on fighting the Heartless without looking at each other. Finally, after defeating them all, they caught their breath—and more Heartless flew out of the brush to attack Donald.

"Look out, Donald!" cried Sora.

Shouting something they couldn't understand, Tarzan jumped to the rescue just barely in time.

"*Qua-waaaak...!*" Startled, Donald had fallen back onto his tail.

Sora breathed a sigh of relief, but when he spoke, it came out mean. "I *said* leave it to us!"

"*Quack!*" Donald jumped to his feet and stamped them. "Don't underestimate the royal magician!"

"I don't care how royal you are! I can get rid of the Heartless without your dumb magic!"

Donald harrumphed and turned away.

"Aw, no..." Goofy fretted, holding his head.

Tarzan looked at them with concern. "Sora, Donald, friends? Not friends?"

"...Gawrsh...I dunno." Goofy stared anxiously at Donald and Sora, who still wouldn't look at each other.

Weaving between the huge trees, they finally reached a rocky wall, a little break in the lush jungle. In a particularly enormous tree, there sat two gorillas. The bigger one had to be Kerchak.

Tarzan started talking to Kerchak in the gorillas' language. The one beside Kerchak gazed at him fearfully.

"Uh...did you get that?" Goofy murmured.

Donald tilted his head. "Nope."

"Kerchak," Tarzan called up to him again. But Kerchak suddenly got up and began ambling away. "Kerchak?!"

There was no reply. Kerchak climbed higher and left. The other gorilla gave Tarzan a look of deep concern and followed Kerchak. Tarzan's shoulders fell.

Sora moved closer to him. "Hey, don't worry about us. Actually…"

Something was bothering him about the direction the gorillas went.

"I've got a bad feeling. Let's go…"

They headed back for the house in the treetops.

"They just don't understand what the gorillas are really worth," Clayton grumbled, crouched in the brush with his shotgun at the ready. Inside the tree house, a small gorilla was spinning a globe. "A young gorilla is worth more than an adult…"

He took aim at the small gorilla. And then—Donald Duck came into his sights.

"Gwa-waaaaak!" shouted Donald, noticing the gun barrel.

Clicking his tongue in frustration, Clayton pulled the trigger. But his aim was just the slightest bit off, and instead he hit Donald's hat. The little gorilla fled.

"Hey, what's the big idea?!" Donald yelled at Clayton.

Then Kerchak emerged. Tarzan called to him, but he disappeared again. Dejected, Tarzan hung his head.

Sora, Donald, and Goofy jumped down from the tree to glare at Clayton.

"You don't understand. I was only trying to— Ah, a snake slithered by, you see. I saved that poor gorilla's life."

At Clayton's attempt to justify himself, Tarzan only closed his eyes and quietly shook his head.

They returned to camp for the moment, and Jane gave Clayton an earful.

"How could you do such a thing, Mr. Clayton!"

"Now, Miss Porter, I told you— I was not aiming at that gorilla."

"You are not to go near the gorillas again!"

"All because of one mishap? Come, now...," Clayton tried to protest, but everyone else was there staring him down.

"All right, then, all right...," he amended grudgingly and left the tent.

"Honestly...I just don't know what to do with him," said Jane. "I'm sorry about this."

"You don't have to apologize," Sora replied.

Jane looked downcast. "But...I'm the one who asked him to come with us as our guide, after all..."

A gunshot rang out.

"Oh no...!"

Sora and Tarzan and the others jumped up and dashed out of the tent. "Heartless!"

There was a gorilla surrounded by them.

"Then where did that gunshot come from...?"

"Let's help the gorilla first!"

Sora and Tarzan exchanged glances and ran in.

"Tarzan, you stay in the tent and protect Jane! Goofy, you help the gorilla! And Donald..." Sora was shouting back behind him, but he had no idea what to say to Donald, and he faltered.

"*Wak!* Well, we're not friends!"

"C'mon, this isn't the time for that!" Goofy shouted, running toward the gorilla. Tarzan was already cutting down the Heartless with his spear.

"Anyway—let's just get rid of these Heartless!" Sora barged into the fray. Donald looked a bit confused, but he waved his wand and attacked with magic.

"The Heartless are after another gorilla over there!" Goofy cried, trying to let the first one escape into the jungle.

"You guys take care of this!" Leaving the rest of that cluster to Tarzan and Donald, Sora ran to help Goofy.

"Maybe that gunshot we heard just now really was Clayton trying to help the gorillas," said Goofy.

"Well, I'd like to believe that…" Sora just wasn't as optimistic as Goofy. Anyway, there was no sign that the Heartless had been attacking that gorilla before. So why…

"Whoa!" While he was thinking, a Heartless hit Sora with all its might, knocking him flat on his back. And it was coming for him again.

This wasn't good—

"*Thunder!*"

From across the clearing, he heard the voice casting the spell. Donald's voice.

"You owe me for that! *Quack!*" Donald yelled with a sullen glare.

"Well, I don't want to owe you anything!"

"*Waaaak!*" While Donald launched into the air to stamp his feet harder, a figure ran up to him. "Oh, it's you…?"

It was the small gorilla. It clung to Donald nervously.

"Aw, it's okay… But I can't fight with you like this…"

Goofy rushed over, too. "Hey, maybe the gorilla can hide in the tent?"

"Yeah!" Donald picked up the little gorilla and ran into the tent. In the pause, Tarzan saw the other gorilla under attack by the Heartless.

He cried something in the gorillas' language and ran over. Sora and Goofy went on fighting, and then Donald after leaving the little gorilla with Jane.

The four ran around the jungle helping the gorillas who were being attacked by Heartless. But even while they fought a common enemy, Sora and Donald were not on friendly terms.

"Aw, guys, can't you make up already…?" Goofy mumbled help-lessly, but he couldn't get through to that stubborn pair. After an entire circuit through the jungle, they arrived back in front of the tent. Seeing that there weren't any more Heartless for the moment, they could breathe easier. But Tarzan was still looking around nervously.

"Are Jane and that little gorilla okay…?" Donald lifted the flap of the tent. "Jane!"

There was no reply. They all frantically ran into the tent. "They're not here."

They looked all around, but there was no sign of Jane or the little gorilla. Tarzan was staring hard at the ceiling.

"What is it, Tarzan?" said Sora.

"Strange smell… Jane, danger. Jane near…near tree house!"

"Let's go!"

They left the tent and headed for the tree house.

Standing in front of the enormous tree that held the house, they heard Jane's voice. "Tarzan!"

The door to the house was boarded up. Jane and the little gorilla peeked out.

"Jane!" cried Tarzan.

"What's going on?!" Sora yelled to her.

"Mr. Clayton came to the tent, and…that's the last thing I remember…"

Then there was a gunshot from behind them.

"Clayton!"

Sora and the others turned, and Clayton appeared with his gun at the ready.

"Not Clayton!" Tarzan shouted and then said something in the gorillas' language. "Not Clayton!"

And as if on cue, Clayton let out a horrible roar that didn't even sound human.

"That's…not Clayton?!"

That was when it happened—*something* came out of the greenery from behind Clayton. Its huge footsteps shook the jungle floor. And it was coming closer.

Clayton had disappeared while Sora watched. "Where'd he go?!"

"There he is!" Goofy pointed up in the air. Clayton was sitting up there as if possessed by something.

"He's *flying*?!"

"No, he's just on something that we can't see…"

They stared bewildered up at the Heartless, the Stealth Sneak, with no idea how to fight it. Something invisible knocked Tarzan flat.

"Tarzan!"

Sora, Donald, and Goofy tried to go to him, but a dark brown shadow stood in their way, almost as if to protect the wounded Tarzan.

"Kerchak!" cried Sora. The big gorilla growled in reply and swung his powerful fists in the air. The part that he hit turned a vague yellow green.

"There it is!" Sora ran to it and slashed out with the Keyblade at the place where Kerchak had struck. Wherever he did any damage, slimy reptilian skin became visible. Behind him, Kerchak picked up Tarzan and leaped to the tree house. He knocked the boards from the door so Jane and the little one could get out.

"…Tarzan!" Seeing him hurt, Jane threw her arms around him.

"Now we can fight it all we want!" Donald waved his wand.

"Well, I can take care of it myself!" Sora yelled, swinging the Keyblade.

Donald stomped his feet again. *"Gwa-waaaaaak!"*

Goofy tried to intervene, but the Stealth Sneak rammed itself into them as if it had been waiting for the chance.

"Whoa—!"

All three of them were thrown back.

Shouting, Sora got up and started slashing away at the Stealth Sneak's feet, but it just kicked him aside again.

"C'mon, Donald," said Goofy.

"…No!"

"Well, fine then!" Goofy left Donald to sulk and ran over to Sora.

Thanks to Sora's all but reckless attacks, the Stealth Sneak was gradually revealing its form, which looked like a giant chameleon.

"Ack!" Sora got thrown aside again.

"Hey, are you okay?" Goofy ran over and gave him a potion, and Sora was soon on his feet again.

Donald glanced over in time to see Sora hurt. "Take care of it yourself, my tail feathers…"

Sora jumped up angrily and attacked again, but this time he was tossed aside by a swipe of the Stealth Sneak's tail.

"Just can't do it without me, huh? *Fire!*" A fireball shot from Donald's wand, even bigger than usual. It knocked the Stealth Sneak off-balance.

"Donald!"

"You're not much use without me, are you?!"

Sora frowned at Donald's smug expression, but there was no time for them to argue.

"Here it comes!"

The Stealth Sneak was heading straight for them with its mouth open wide. Sora went for its feet and dealt a blow, stopping it in its tracks, and Donald shot magic into its gaping mouth. The impact sent Clayton sliding from its head.

"Now!" Sora leaped up and brought the Keyblade down on the creature's head.

"We did it!"

He hugged Donald and Goofy—then remembered that he didn't want to be hugging Donald and backed off to turn away and pout.

He saw the Stealth Sneak turn to light and disappear and Clayton tumbling to the ground.

Clayton groaned and picked up his shotgun, but as if the effort was too much, he fell backward and collapsed on the spot.

"Sora…," Tarzan called, leaning on Jane. And then the hoots of gorillas cheering them rang out from the treetops.

"Heh…" Grinning, Sora rubbed under his nose. Suddenly something lifted him up. "Whoa— C'mon, Kerchak, put me down!"

Even though he was kicking in protest, Kerchak lightly tossed him up high into the air—and then Donald and Goofy, too.

"Whoaaaaaa!" Sora yelled, and the gorillas kept cheering.

With Kerchak's help, Sora went flying through the air and finally landed atop a cliff. Then Donald landed on top of him tailfirst and Goofy headfirst—just like the first time they'd met.

"…Could you get off?"

"Wak!" shouted Donald, and he and Goofy climbed off from Sora.

"Seriously…" Sora brushed dust from his knees and stood up.

There was an almost-deafening sound of rushing water, and when he looked up, he saw the enormous waterfall.

"Wow… Look at that…," Goofy said in wonder.

"Just so we're clear… This doesn't mean we're friends!" said Sora.

"You took the words right outta my mouth!" Donald snapped.

Then Tarzan appeared, still leaning on Jane.

"Tarzan! Are you okay?!"

"Okay. Tarzan home." With his uninjured arm, he pointed to the waterfall.

"Your home…?"

Tarzan jumped up into a cave atop the rocky wall. Sora and the others scrambled to follow.

"Wow… This sure is somethin'!" Goofy marveled loudly, peering into the cave.

"This must be behind the waterfall," Donald whispered to him. Water trickled inside the cave, and boulders lined up almost like steps. Holding Jane with one arm, Tarzan climbed up.

"Tarzan, wait!"

Sora, Donald, and Goofy rushed to keep up.

They climbed up a huge tree trunk that the three of them holding hands wouldn't be able to encircle.

"Wow…"

They looked quietly up at the tree, which seemed to spread into the heavens.

Tarzan said something in the gorillas' language. Sora recognized it as the word he'd said when they first met.

"…Here…?"

Tarzan hushed Sora and held a hand to one ear and silently closed his eyes.

They could hear the roaring of the waterfall in the distance. It was echoing up through the cave, bringing with it a mysterious melody.

Jane gazed at Tarzan and repeated the word he'd said. "It means 'heart,' doesn't it?"

"Understand?"

"I think I do… Friends, inside our hearts…"

"Heart," Tarzan repeated, smiling.

"Oh, so they're not actually here…," Sora said glumly.

"Friends, same heart. Clayton, lose heart. No heart, can't see friends. No heart…no friends." Tarzan was trying with all his might to tell them something important about friendship.

"Sora…"

"Donald…"

They both said the other's name at almost the same time.

"You go first, Donald!"

"No! You first!"

"Aw, you guys…," Goofy scolded them with a smile.

Sora rubbed the back of his head. "Sorry for what I said."

"I'm sorry, too." Donald looked a tiny bit embarrassed.

"Yeah! We're friends, right! All for one and one for all!"

Goofy hugged Donald and Sora around the shoulders.

Then a blue light shone down on them.

"What's that light…?"

They looked up, and in the middle of the tree trunk, blue butterflies clustered, their wings glittering in a sunbeam.

Gazing closely at the butterflies, Donald pointed to the trunk. They were surrounding something, almost as if to protect it—a Keyhole.

Sora quietly raised the Keyblade and a thin, bright beam of light shot from it into the Keyhole. It locked with a click, and something tumbled down.

"A Gummi block!" Goofy picked it up. The little block sparkled in his hand.

"But it's sure not the king's…," Donald said sadly. The little gorilla nuzzled up to him.

"Why, I think someone has a new admirer," Jane remarked.

Donald frantically waved his hands in refusal. "No, no, no! Daisy would kill me!" He tried to run away and the gorilla chased him.

Sora nearly fell over laughing. But then Tarzan called his name. "Sora, Tarzan friend," he said, smiling.

"Tarzan, Sora friend!"

Light shone around them, sunlight through the leaves or glittering butterflies, or both.

Friends.

Hearts.

Tarzan.

Donald and Goofy.

Kairi and Riku.

They were all dear friends… And there was nothing as important as friends.

"Donald, Goofy… Let's go!" Sora said to his friends. They went back to the tent where Jiminy Cricket was waiting.

And they left Deep Jungle behind them.

SHORT CHAPTER

FRAGMENT
secret conversation

THE BLACK SHADOWS GATHERED AROUND A STONE pedestal. In the center of it was a ring of light, showing a vision of Sora, Donald, and Goofy.

"That little squirt took down another Heartless! Who'd a thunk! What's that now, three?"

"And the brat's friends are the king's lackeys. Swoggle me eyes, they're all bilge rats by the look of them…"

"You're no prize yourself."

"Shut up!"

The man in a black cape, with a staff shaped like a snake, and the man in a great red hat with a feather in it and a piece of sharp curved metal in place of his left hand—Jafar and Hook—had begun to argue. A third chilly voice cut them off. "Enough."

This was Maleficent in a cloak as black as the shadows.

"That is the power of the Keyblade. The boy's strength is not his own." She walked toward the ring of light on the pedestal and raised her staff to it.

"Why not turn him into a Heartless? That'll settle this quick enough!" said Hook with a cruel grin.

With a sweep of her cloak, Maleficent smiled. "The Keyblade has chosen him. Will it be he who conquers the darkness? Or will the darkness swallow him? Either way, he could be quite useful."

The shadowy figures all peered closely at the image of Sora.

"At any rate—what could have drawn the Heartless into a jungle like that?" Hook wondered.

Maleficent answered without looking away from the ring of light. "The hunter lured them there. His own lust for power became the bait."

"A weakhearted fool like him stood no chance against the Heartless," said Jafar, raising his snake-headed staff and moving toward Maleficent. "But the boy is a problem. He has been finding the Keyholes."

"It will take him ages to find the rest," Maleficent replied, her gaze still locked on Sora, Donald, and Goofy in the ring of light. "Besides, he remains blissfully unaware of our other plan."

"The princesses…," Hook said, folding his arms.

"Yes. They are falling into our hands one by one. And speaking of which…" Maleficent gestured with her staff to the prisoner, who had gone missing in Wonderland—Alice.

TRAVERSE TOWN
meeting again

SORA WATCHED DEEP JUNGLE VANISH INTO THE DIS-
tance behind them. It felt like such a long time since he'd left
Destiny Island.

He'd met so many people and said farewell to some of them again.
But he still hadn't found Kairi and Riku.

They have to be out there somewhere, Sora thought, staring out at
the Other Sky.

The sparkling stars were so beautiful. He wanted Kairi and Riku
to see this too. No... He wanted to see it *with* them.

"Say...this Gummi block looks kinda strange..." Holding the
block that they'd found at the Keyhole in Deep Jungle, Goofy cocked
his head.

Sora moved away from the cockpit window and looked at the
thing in Goofy's hand. "What's strange about it?"

"I dunno, it just doesn't look like a normal Gummi block." Goofy
held it up to the starlight.

"I've never seen one like that, either," said Jiminy Cricket, hopping
onto Goofy's hand.

"How's it different?" asked Sora.

"Hmm... I can see somethin' inside it."

"Where...?" Sora looked closer, and the light came through it,
revealing something else in the middle that glittered like a tiny star.

What *was* it...?

"Maybe Leon'll know," Donald said from the cockpit.

"Yeah... Maybe. Should we go back to Traverse Town?" said
Goofy.

"I wanna be pilot!" Sora tried to edge Donald out of the pilot's
chair.

"Hey, stop it!"

The battle for the pilot's chair began once again.

"Oh, c'mon! I'm the Keyblade master!"

"I don't care who you are! No!"

Watching the two argue, Goofy and Jiminy smiled and shrugged.

*   *   *

On their second visit to Traverse Town, the nighttime city was calm and friendly.

"Looks like there aren't any Heartless in the First District…" Donald looked around. "There's Yuffie!"

She was standing by the post office in the First District square. They ran over to her.

"Hey, Sora!" Yuffie greeted them with a grin. "Welcome back!"

"It's good to see you!" Donald and Goofy replied, but Sora couldn't say anything.

Yuffie didn't seem bothered by his reserve. She kept talking. "How have your travels been?"

Bit by bit, interrupting one another, the trio told her about Alice and what had happened in Deep Jungle.

"Gee, I wish I could've been there, too… That sounds hard, Sora." Yuffie gave him an affectionate gaze, almost as if she were his big sister.

"It's all right! I'll do whatever it takes to find Riku and Kairi!"

"And the king!" Goofy added.

"Actually," said Sora, "we came back to Traverse Town to ask Leon something."

"He's probably training in the underground cavern," said Yuffie.

"Underground cavern?"

Sora had walked around the city quite a bit, but he didn't remember seeing anything like that. Come to think of it, they still hadn't found the Keyhole in Traverse Town, so maybe there were lots of things they didn't know about this city.

"You know the channel in the alley?" Yuffie explained. "That's connected to the cavern."

"The alley behind the hotel?" said Donald.

"Right! You can go underground from there. You didn't know?"

The trio exchanged glances. They would just have to go and find out. "Okay, see you!"

"Watch out for the Heartless in the Second District!"

"Thanks!" They headed to the Second District.

The moment they stepped through the door between the districts, Heartless came up from the ground.

"*Quack?!*" Donald jumped away from a Heartless attack.

"Gawrsh, it's so quiet in the First District, I couldn't believe there'd be any…" Goofy rushed at the Heartless that had gone after Donald.

"And it feels like they're stronger than before!" Sora slashed at a big Heartless from behind. They were definitely stronger. There were Heartless that attacked spinning around like a tornado and Heartless that used more powerful magic. "I wonder if that means the darkness is getting stronger…"

They ducked into the hotel.

"Whew… Bet they won't come in here," Goofy said, catching his breath.

"They were swarming all over last time we were in the hotel!" Donald went into a guest room. It was the one with green wallpaper, where Sora and Leon and Yuffie had discussed things before.

"I haven't been in the other rooms…" Sora opened the door to the neighboring room.

"You've been in this green one?" said Goofy, peeking into both of them.

"I was talking to Leon here, right before I met you guys."

"And Aerith was telling us everything in that room. Then Yuffie came, and the Heartless attacked…"

They looked at one another.

"…So that means we were all here at the same time, but in different rooms?" said Sora.

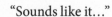

"Sounds like it…"

They laughed.

"When you guys fell on me all of a sudden, I thought you must be more Heartless!"

"We had no idea you'd be down there! Right, Donald?"

"The biggest surprise was when the one who broke our fall turned out to have the key!"

They found themselves talking about the time they met as if it happened a long time ago and not just the other day.

"And now here we are on a journey together!" Goofy folded his arms and nodded.

"Well, we don't have time to stand around jabbering about it," said Donald. "Let's go!"

They went out on the balcony and jumped down into the alley.

In the dim alley, no matter how many Heartless they defeated, more kept rising out of the ground as always.

"They just won't quit!" cried Donald, shooting off magic.

"Goofy, did you find the channel passageway?" Sora called. He was fighting them alongside Donald, while Goofy looked for the passageway that led underground.

"Nope… But the only place I can't look is behind this grate…"

In the corner, the channel ran through a grate. Goofy tried shaking it, but it stayed firmly in place. At a pause in the fight, Sora and Donald ran over to join him.

"So it's here?"

"Probably…"

Sora peered into the grate, but it was pitch-dark inside.

"*Wak!* Here they are!" A swarm of Heartless were coming up behind Donald.

"Maybe if we all run into it at once, we can break it?" said Goofy.

They looked at one another…

"On three. One, two…*three!*"

With a running start, they crashed into the grate, and it came off almost too easily. They tumbled into the water.

"Whoa!" A huge splash echoed in the underground passage. It looked like the Heartless weren't following.

"Gee, it sure is dark in here." Goofy helped Donald up, and they went farther down the waterway.

"But it does go somewhere…"

They swam gingerly on, and suddenly a space opened up that they could see.

"Wow…"

It was a big cavern, and on the little bit of dry land in the middle, Leon stood silently swinging his Gunblade.

"Leooon!" Donald went splashing through the shallow water. Leon must have noticed them, but he went on practicing. Aerith was there beside him. "Aerith!"

"Sora, Donald, Goofy! Welcome back," she said, smiling, when they had all reached the island.

"Say, Aerith…"

"Yes?"

"Yuffie said, 'Welcome back' to us, too… Isn't it kind of weird?" Sora had felt like something was off when Yuffie said it, but now he brought it up.

"How?"

"Well… I mean, this isn't where I'm from…" Sora looked down.

Aerith looked a little sad.

"Traverse Town is a city where people come when they have nowhere else to call home," said Leon, still swinging his sword. "So the people here greet you like you've come home. Even if you're really from someplace else."

"Oh… Okay, I get it. Well, thanks! It's good to see you guys again!"

"Welcome back, Sora," Aerith said again with more affection in her voice.

Leon finally paused in his training. "So, have you found anything?"

"Well, I don't know if it counts…"

They related to Leon and Aerith the same story they'd told Yuffie about Alice and Deep Jungle.

"So you locked the Keyholes…" Deep in thought, Leon folded his arms.

Aerith spoke as if she'd made up her mind about something. "You're the only one who can save the worlds, Sora." She clasped her hands together almost as if to pray.

Worry clouded over Sora's face. "But…can I really do that?"

"Well, if you want to look for your friends," said Leon, "I doubt seeing other worlds would be a waste of your time."

Even if that's true…can I really do something this crazy? Sora thought.

"C'mon, Sora, we can do it!"

"We gotta find your friends! And King Mickey!"

Donald and Goofy were staring at him.

I've already done a lot of things I couldn't have imagined, Sora thought. *I didn't think I could, but I did them. And…I'm the only one who can, because the Keyblade chose me.*

"Sora," Aerith said softly.

"I guess you're right… Okay!"

"There, that's what the Keyblade wielder is made of," said Leon, as if Sora still needed persuading.

"Oh yeah, Leon. We've got this Gummi block…" Goofy took out the sparkling block and showed it to him. "It looks different from the other ones. Do you know what it's for?"

Leon stared at the Gummi block, but didn't have an answer.

"Ask Cid," Aerith told them. "He knows a lot about Gummi blocks."

"Okay! We're off, then!" Sora started back toward the waterway. "Thanks for everything!"

He waved the Keyblade. Leon and Aerith quietly watched him go, with Donald and Goofy close behind.

"But…," Leon began when the trio were out of sight.

"I know." Aerith seemed to read his mind. "You're worried about the Keyhole in this world, aren't you?"

"If we could seal off the Keyhole, the Heartless shouldn't be able to get here."

"But just sealing it isn't enough…" Aerith's brows knit.

"So all we can do is gather information and watch over Sora."

"It's kind of frustrating, isn't it?"

Leon went back to swinging the Gunblade.

And Aerith went on praying.

Please don't let the worlds disappear.

Please let him be safe.

She prayed for the worlds…and for Sora…and for him.

The trio returned to the First District and ran into the Accessory Shop. Cid was there as usual, resting his elbows on the counter. "Hey there," he greeted them.

"Cid!" They dashed up to the counter and handed him the Gummi block.

"Well, if it ain't a Gummi block."

"Yup." Donald nodded.

The Gummi block's sparkling reflected in Cid's eyes as he stared at it.

"So, what's this one for?" Goofy asked.

"You're kiddin' me, right?!" Cid exploded dramatically. "You're flyin' a Gummi Ship and you don't even know the different kinds of Gummi blocks?! You pinheads! The Other Sky ain't no playground!"

"There's a lot we don't know. So what!" Feeling like a kid getting scolded, Sora pouted. "We have to use the Gummi Ship to go to other worlds. We don't have a choice."

"Oh— Well, I guess ya do," Cid said quietly, looking at the Keyblade in Sora's hand. "All right, I'm here to lend a hand."

"Thanks."

Cid took a deep breath and explained, "So this Gummi is pretty dang handy—if we install it in your ship, it'll open up new routes. You know what that means?"

"New routes…" Goofy cocked his head.

Donald picked up the hint. "That means we'll be able to go to new worlds!"

"Bingo. So, you want to install it?"

"Yeah!"

If they saw more worlds, they might find Kairi and Riku…and King Mickey.

"Naturally, I'll take care of that, no worries," said Cid. "But I'm gonna need something from you in the meantime."

"What? We gotta pay?!" Donald complained, jumping up and down.

"Now hold on! I just want you to deliver something. And while you're doin' that I'll install this Gummi. It'll take a while. Plenty of time for you to make a little delivery, okay?"

"I guess so…," said Sora, still not convinced.

"And anyway… Eh, well…" Cid scratched his head. It looked like he had something important to say but couldn't get it out. "Well, you'll see when you get there!"

Sora, Donald, and Goofy looked at one another. "Okay. So what do we need to deliver?"

"Just this…" He held out a beat-up book. "It's pretty old, and it looked like it was gonna fall apart, so I fixed it."

There was a little keyhole on the book, but it didn't seem to be locked or anything. They opened it to an illustration of a forest, torn here and there. It looked like a children's picture book.

"Are there some animals in here, too…?" said Goofy, peeking at the book over Sora's shoulder. Just as he said, there were some drawings of creatures that looked like stuffed toys.

"Careful there. This is a precious book. And it seems like it's got a special power. So I want you to take it to the old house in the Third District. Look for the fire sign. Say, can you pip-squeaks use fire magic?"

"Whaddaya think?! You're speaking to a royal magician!" Donald snapped, waving his wand.

"That'll do, then. Well, I'm leavin' it to you."

"Got it!" Sora put the book in his pocket.

And just then, the air trembled with the ringing of a giant bell from somewhere.

"Wow, what's that?!" Sora looked around.

Cid didn't seem startled at all. "Sounds like the Gizmo Shop bell is ringing..."

"The Gizmo Shop?"

"It's a weird shop in the Second District. They say if you ring it three times, something'll happen, but nobody's ever heard it ring three times in a row. Maybe you can check it out after you deliver that book." Cid grinned at them over his folded arms.

"Okay. Donald, Goofy, let's go!" They left the shop and headed to the Third District.

"Man, it's been a while," Cid said to himself. "Good to have some real work."

He stretched his arms and disappeared into the back of the shop.

The trio went through the Second District again.

"No matter how many we take out, the Heartless just keep on coming!" Goofy grumbled as he defeated more of them. "D'ya think we could hide the Keyblade somehow?"

"If we did, we wouldn't be able to lock the Keyholes, and besides, the king told us to stay with the key," Donald shouted back. "We'd be disobeying orders!"

It was true that there was just no end to the Heartless, but... Just then the bell rang again, shaking the ground.

"Whoa!" Sora stumbled and fell.

Goofy helped him up. "You okay, Sora?"

"Sheesh… I wonder if we can do anything about that bell ringing…"

"It's that bell up there, right?" Goofy pointed to a tower. "Maybe we can stop it…"

"*Quack!* No slacking off!" Donald scolded them. They'd paused in fighting the Heartless.

"Okay, okay…" Sora picked up the Keyblade. They reached the Third District. "Finally, we made it…"

Fighting off the Heartless, they ran through the Third District square to the hidden house. After all that, they weren't in the best shape.

In front of the big door, they caught their breath and helped heal one another. The door was marked with a flame insignia.

Goofy pushed, then pushed with all his might. It didn't budge. "It won't open…"

"Didn't Cid say we have to use magic?" said Sora, looking at Donald's wand.

"Well, that'd be…*fire!*" Donald shot a flame at the insignia on the door. And then—it slowly opened.

"Let's go!"

They stepped inside and found themselves in a big cavern.

"Gee, I didn't know there was a place like this in Traverse Town…" Sora gazed around. There was a wide pond in the cavern, and in the middle of that, a little island with a single house perched on it. "Is that it?"

Donald moved first, jumping onto the stepping-stones. "C'mon, hurry up! *Quack!*"

Looking back at the other two as he leaped, Donald fell into the water with a spectacular splash.

"Gawrsh, are you okay?" Goofy jumped onto the stepping-stone and helped Donald out.

"*Wak!*" In a huff, Donald jumped to the next one. "You too, Sora!"

"I'm coming!" Sora started across, too. They made it up to the odd little house that looked like a pot with a red hat on top.

"It won't open!" Donald kicked at the door. Apparently falling into the water had been the last straw for him.

"Maybe there's another way in...?" Goofy walked around the house.

"I've about had it! Falling in ponds, houses with no way in! This is the pits!"

"Aw, don't get so mad about it, Donald." Sora tried to calm him down, looking up at the house. The red roof was kind of dilapidated—it didn't really look like anyone could live there.

"Sora! Donald!" Goofy called. "I found a way in!"

They went to join Goofy on the other side, and there was a big hole in the wall.

"Are we really supposed to go in this way...?"

"Why not?"

So they ducked into the house through the hole. It definitely looked abandoned. Sora glanced from side to side, and...

"There's something about this musty old place."

Sora turned. That voice—it was definitely Kairi's voice he'd just heard!

"Doesn't it remind you of our secret spot?"

Kairi was standing there. Her red hair shook as she turned her smile to Sora. It *was* Kairi. That smile was just the same as he remembered, the same as when they'd last parted on Destiny Island.

"With the cave where we used to scribble on the walls. Remember?"

"Kairi..." Sora reached for her hand.

"Sora?"

It was Goofy's voice from behind him. Sora turned, and then when he looked back again to where Kairi had just been standing—no one was there.

"I-I just saw..."

Sora tried to explain, but then another voice addressed them.

"Whew... Well, well. You've arrived sooner than I expected."

Next to the wall stood an old man with a long beard, in a tall pointy hat and glasses.

"You knew we were coming?" said Sora, walking toward him.

"Of course."

"Are you a Heartless?!" Donald had his wand at the ready.

"Oh-ho-ho! My name is Merlin. As you can see, I am a sorcerer. I spend much of my time traveling—it's good to be home. Your king has requested my help."

"King Mickey?" said Goofy. It was the first news they'd heard of the king since their journey began.

"Yes, indeed. Donald, Goofy... And who might you be?" Merlin peered at Sora.

"I'm Sora."

"...Ah. So you have found the key." Merlin nodded and stared at him closer.

Running out of patience, Donald demanded, "What did the king ask you to do?"

"Now, just a moment..." Merlin went to a stone platform in the middle of the room, climbed on it, and waved his wand. "Presto!"

His bag opened itself, and all sorts of furniture and housewares flew out of it, each thing taking its proper place.

"Wow!" Right before the trio's wide-open eyes, the ramshackle house transformed into Merlin's home.

"There, that should do it. Now then..." Merlin waved his wand at a little model of a pumpkin-shaped carriage in the corner. "Bibbidy-bobbidy-boo!"

With that mysterious incantation, an old lady in a deep blue hooded robe appeared. "Why, hello. I'm the Fairy Godmother."

She waved her own wand and a cloud of sparkling motes fell.

"Your king asked us both to help," said Merlin.

"So where is the king?!"

At Donald's question, Merlin and the Fairy Godmother exchanged glances.

"There's not much time left—

"I can't go back—

"But the light is there above the darkness—

"And the darkness is beside the light—"

Merlin and the Fairy Godmother told them as if reciting a poem.

"That doesn't make any sense!" Donald stamped his feet.

"Darkness is lying in wait for you."

"But...that there is darkness means there is also light."

"Darkness and light...," Sora mumbled.

"I don't get it!" Donald complained.

Merlin pointed to the Keyblade. "Stay with the key, and the path will become clear."

"With the key?" Goofy said anxiously.

"That was the hint the king left."

"What am I supposed to do?" asked Sora.

The sorcerer and the godmother looked at one another again. "Go where the light leads you."

"What about Kairi and Riku?!"

The Fairy Godmother shook her head. "I don't know... But...I do feel them. Very close by..."

"Simply go," said Merlin. "Go where the key points..."

"Okay. I will." Determination came into Sora's voice. "Let's go— Oh, wait..."

Merlin already knew. "The book that Cid asked you to deliver, is it?"

Sora turned back and handed him the worn book.

"Ah, look at that. He's repaired it quite nicely..."

Curious, Goofy leaned in. "What kinda book is it?"

"Well...I'm not even sure myself. If you want to find out, you ought to read it."

"We will, next time!" said Sora, and they left the house.

*   *   *

They ran back through the Third District, fighting through the Heartless. "They really just won't stop...," Goofy grumbled as he opened the door to the Second District. The moment they stepped through, the bell rang again with a resounding clang.

The tremble went through the ground. "*Gwa-waaak!*" Donald yelled.

"Isn't there a way to stop it from ringing?" Goofy wondered.

"Never mind that," Donald scolded. "We gotta get back to Cid's shop and go see some more worlds!"

"But there're so many Heartless, I think the Keyhole must be somewhere around here," said Sora, looking up at the bell tower.

"Are you saying the bell's got something to do with the Keyhole?"

"Well, I dunno, but—" In the middle of Sora's sentence, the Keyblade began to shine brightly. "Whoa!"

"It's shining!"

The three looked at one another and then headed for the Gizmo Shop.

"Wooow..."

They wandered to and fro in the Gizmo Shop with all the huge gears turning and turning.

"Hey, how about that way?" said Goofy, and they ducked between some gears. "Aw, it's a dead end..."

They really had no idea which way to go.

"What are we gonna do when we find the bell?" Donald asked Sora as they dodged more gears.

"Well, Cid said if we ring it three times something will happen, right?"

"Huh? Won't it just make that humongous noise again?" said Donald.

"But look at all the mechanisms here!" Sora exclaimed. "They've just got to be hiding some kind of secret."

"I think Sora's right," said Goofy, leaping over some kind of swinging pendulum.

"I guess so…," Donald grumbled.

Goofy found an opening up above some gears. "Hey, we can go through here!"

"*Wa-waaak…*" Fighting for his balance, Donald stepped up atop the gears and jumped across. If his timing was less than perfect, he'd be crushed in the gears.

"Whoa… Here goes…" Sora rushed to jump across. There was a little door.

"Through here?" Donald opened the door, and then they were out on the roof of the Gizmo Shop. At the other end was the tower where the bell hung.

"Gawrsh. It doesn't look like we can get in…" Goofy peered between the wooden slats. The bell was boarded up.

"Well, it can't be as sturdy as the grate in the waterway, right?" said Sora. "C'mon—on three!"

The trio took a running start and crashed into it, and the boards broke too easily.

"So, this is the bell that rings like that…" Sora looked up at the huge bell. "Goofy, can you keep watch?"

"Sure thing!"

Goofy looked down at the Second District.

Donald jumped up and hung on to the rope that would ring the bell. "Three times, Cid said, right?"

"Right!"

Taking Sora's reply as a cue, Donald pulled.

Once…

Twice…

Three times…

But all that happened was the sonorous sound of its ringing.

"Aw… Nothing's happening…" Sora sighed.

But then Goofy called out, "A Keyhole!"

"Huh?"

"There's a Keyhole!"

Sora ran over to Goofy and looked where he was looking. A Keyhole had appeared at the fountain in the square.

"All right!"

They leaped down from the roof and ran to it. "Now there won't be any more Heartless in Traverse Town!" said Goofy.

But an enormous roar shook the ground.

"What's that?!"

A giant Heartless fell from the sky—one they thought they'd already defeated. It was the Guard Armor.

"I guess they're not gonna let us close the Keyhole without a fight…," Goofy complained and held up his shield.

"But we beat this one before!" Sora readied the Keyblade.

Donald raised his wand—but the Guard Armor's huge foot was already coming straight for him.

"*Wak-gwaaak!*" Donald tried to dodge but tripped on the cobblestones.

"Donald!" Sora ran over to cover him. "Hey— Look out!"

Goofy had covered his eyes, and then, with a clang, the Guard Armor's foot went flying back.

"There you are. What's going on?"

It was a voice Sora knew. Silver hair gleamed in the dark night.

Sora looked up, and it was— "Riku?!"

With a cocky smile, Riku helped up Sora and Donald.

"How'd you get here?!"

"I'll explain later— Here it comes!" As Riku spoke the Guard Armor came at them with a furious punch, as if to avenge itself for having a foot knocked away. Riku and Sora jumped out of the way, and then Donald, just in time before its fist crashed into the ground.

"You big, stupid, ugly jerk! *Fire! Thunder! Blizzard!*" Donald pelted the Guard Armor with magic, and Goofy rushed back and forth. Sora and Riku attacked its main body, turn by turn, like comrades who had been fighting side by side for a long time.

"Looks like you've learned a few tricks, Sora!"

"So have you, Riku!"

It was him. That look, that voice—it was definitely Riku. Not an illusion, like he'd seen of Kairi a little while ago. This was the real Riku!

"Here I go!" With a flying leap, Riku landed a fierce blow on the Guard Armor's head.

"My turn!" Sora attacked the torso—and then the Guard Armor fell apart with a clatter. The parts didn't move.

"We did it!" Without thinking, Sora hugged Riku.

"Okay, okay, quit it," said Riku, but he was smiling.

"Is this Riku?" asked Goofy.

"Yeah! The one I've been looking for!" Sora grinned, finally letting go of Riku. "Oh, right— What about Kairi?"

"Isn't she with you?" said Riku, a bit alarmed.

It looked like while Sora thought that Kairi must be with Riku, Riku assumed that she had to be with Sora, too.

"Oh… She's not with you, either."

Riku patted Sora's slumped shoulders and smiled. "Hey, don't worry. I'm sure she made it off the island, too. We made it to another world. So we can go wherever we want." Sora didn't seem to cheer up, so he went on. "We'll all be together again soon. Right, Sora? Just leave everything to me. With me around, you've got nothing to worry about."

"But I've been looking for you and Kairi, too. With their help!" Sora rested the Keyblade on his shoulder and turned his smile to Donald and Goofy. Riku stared as if the pair were somehow suspicious.

"Uh, we're…" At a loss, Donald looked at Sora.

"We've visited so many worlds together," Sora added, "looking for you."

"Really? Well, what do you know? I never would've guessed."

At Riku's reply, Donald and Goofy exchanged glances and each put an arm around Sora.

"And guess what, Sora's the Keyblade master!" said Goofy.

"Who woulda thought it?" Donald remarked, in their usual pattern.

"So, this is called a Keyblade?" Riku held it in his hand.

"Huh? Hey, when did— Give it back!" Sora lunged at Riku, but he dodged and Sora nearly fell over.

"You just never change, Sora." Riku laughed a little and tossed the Keyblade back to him. "Catch!"

"Whoa—" Sora fumbled to catch it and then stared at Riku. "Hey, you should come with us, too, Riku! We've got this awesome rocket. Wait till you see it!"

"Hey! You're not the boss here!" Donald scolded him.

"Aw, c'mon!"

"No!" Donald jumped up and down in a huff.

"Why not?! He's my friend! And we finally found each other!"

"Not gonna happen!"

While the two argued again, Goofy saw the Guard Armor's hand twitch beside them. "Sora! Donald!"

The moment they looked up, the Guard Armor reassembled itself and stood.

Now it had feet in place of its hands and hands in place of its feet, and it had changed color—the Opposite Armor. And it roared and came at them.

"This isn't over, Donald!" Sora shouted.

"*Wak!*"

With the Keyblade at the ready, Sora rushed the Opposite Armor, but it turned aside as if it was ready for him and shot balls of light at him.

"Wh-whoooa!" The attack hit Sora straight on.

"Oh no, Sora, are you okay?" Goofy ran over and healed him.

"*Quaaack!* Why you! This is for Sora! *Thunder!*" After seeing that Sora was mostly all right, Donald hurled out a spell, and a much bigger than usual thunderbolt struck the Opposite Armor right on its head.

"Wow! Nice one!" Once he was back on his feet, Sora ran to Donald without thinking.

"When I get serious, I really— *Wak!*" As Donald puffed out his chest, a giant armored foot kicked him back onto his tail.

"Well, I can get serious, too!" As if Donald's attitude was contagious, Goofy leaped at the Opposite Armor and attacked from up in the air. His shield clanged against its torso and made a dent.

"Wow! I didn't know you could do that, Goofy!" Sora called out, and Goofy replied with a thumbs-up.

"Umm… Wonder what I could try… Here goes!" Then Sora jumped up at the Opposite Armor, too, swinging the Keyblade in a huge arc. "Hiyaaaaaaa!"

The Keyblade drew a wide crescent of light in the air that hit the Opposite Armor with a shock wave.

"Gawrsh, that was amazing, Sora!" cried Goofy.

Shouting with effort, Sora kept attacking. The Keyblade clanged, and the Opposite Armor began to tremble with a clatter, then stopped moving. And at last a glowing heart floated up from its body, which turned to light and disappeared.

"We did it!"

Sora, Donald, and Goofy celebrated another victory they'd achieved together. But—

"Wait… Where's Riku?" Sora realized too late. "Riku…?"

He ran around the square, shouting Riku's name, but there was no Riku to be seen.

"Oh no… Just when I finally found him!" Sora hung his head and kicked at the ground.

I was looking for him all this time. I was so scared for him. But he's just like he was on Destiny Island. He hasn't changed a bit. So that's good...

"Sora?" Goofy looked anxiously into his face.

"He just disappeared again. It's not fair," Sora mumbled, gripping the Keyblade tightly. Then he looked up with a smile. "Oh well. At least he's okay!"

"Huh? Are you okay?"

"Yeah... We'll meet up again. I just know it. Anyway, since we found Riku, I bet we'll run into Kairi soon, too!"

With a smile still on his face, Sora raised the Keyblade to point at the Keyhole and the beam of light shot out at it. The Keyhole seemed to drink up the beam of light and closed with a click.

"Hey, welcome— Oh, you're back."

Cid wasn't alone in the Accessory Shop. Leon, Aerith, and Yuffie were all there, too.

"So, you delivered the book? I'm all done installing the navigation Gummi."

"Thanks! Actually, though—" Sora began.

"We closed the Keyhole!" shouted Donald.

"Really?" said Yuffie.

"Yup, really!" Goofy replied. "We rang the bell, and then the Keyhole appeared by the fountain."

"So you were the ones who rang the bell three times?" said Leon.

"Yeah. The Keyblade told us what to do!" Sora held it up.

Yuffie walked closer to him and stared at the Keyblade. "Wow. That thing sure is amazing."

"But another giant Heartless appeared," said Donald, "and then—"

This time Sora interrupted him. "We found Riku!"

"The friend you're looking for?" asked Aerith.

"Uh-huh. And Riku was helping us, but the giant Heartless woke up, and when we beat it again, he was gone…" Sora trailed off sadly. "But maybe we'll find him again, I hope."

"You will," Aerith said gently.

Yuffie was more curious about other things. "Gee, I wanted to see the Keyhole, too."

"So there was one in Traverse Town," Leon said, completely serious in contrast, his arms folded. "You've got to hurry, Sora. Even while we're standing here talking about it, the Heartless are taking over other worlds."

Sora nodded briskly.

"Yeah, by the way— You guys ever hear of Maleficent?" Cid asked them, his voice hushed.

"Who's that?"

"A witch, man, she's a witch!" Cid folded his arms, too.

Leon went on explaining, "She's the reason this town is full of Heartless. Don't take her lightly."

"She's been using the Heartless for years," said Aerith, looking down.

"We lost our world, thanks to her." Leon looked at Cid until he picked up the thread.

"One day a swarm of Heartless took over our world!" Cid said finally. "…That was nine years ago. I got out of that mess and came here with these guys."

"That's awful…," Donald murmured, looking sincerely troubled and folding his arms.

"Our ruler was a wise man named Ansem," said Leon. "He dedicated his life to studying the Heartless. He was probably searching for some way to defeat them for good."

Remembering the name, Goofy struck his open palm with his fist. "That's the Ansem you were talking about, right, Aerith?"

"That's right," she replied softly. "And his report should tell us how to get rid of the Heartless."

"King Mickey must be looking for that report," said Donald.

Aerith shook her head. "But we don't know where its pages might be."

"I'd bet Maleficent's got most of the pages…," Cid said grimly.

"Well, they've got to be somewhere!" exclaimed Sora.

"Probably."

"Then we'll find them!"

Aerith smiled at him. "Thank you, Sora."

"That's not terribly reassuring." Cid smirked.

Sora turned to him. "Hey! What's that supposed to mean?!"

"Well, you just don't look much like a Keyblade master," Donald joined in.

"What, you too, Donald?!" Sora glared at him with the Keyblade out.

"But you've gotten way stronger than when you started!" Goofy said, grinning.

"Than when I started… Aw, quit it…" Sora weakly sat down on the spot.

"Want to give it another go?" Leon brandished the Gunblade at Sora.

"Huh?"

"Then maybe you want to try a round against the great ninja Yuffie!" She held up her shuriken.

"C'mon, guys, I'm already beat!" Sora groaned.

Then Aerith laughed, and everyone else followed.

"Hey, why're you all laughing at me?" Sora complained, but he was laughing, too.

Outside the window, two shadowy figures stood watching the scene.

One was Riku. And the other…

"You see? It's just as I told you."

Riku made no reply to Maleficent, but kept staring into the window.

"While you toiled away trying to find your dear friend, he quite simply replaced you with some new companions. Evidently he values them far more than he does you," Maleficent murmured to him, terribly gently. "You're better off without that wretched boy. Now, think no more of him, and come with me. I'll help you find what you're searching for…"

But Riku only went on silently gazing at Sora through the window.

To be continued.

PART 2

6 CHAPTER

AGRABAH
promise

THE GUMMI SHIP SAILED THROUGH THE VASTNESS OF the Other Sky.

"It's gotten more comfortable in here, huh?" said Goofy.

Sora was standing on the little dais, gazing out at the Other Sky. Hearing Goofy, he jumped down. "Yeah. There's way more space."

Before the upgrade, it had been rather cramped aboard the Gummi Ship. But with Cid's improvements, there was plenty of room.

"It's not just the interior that's better," said Donald Duck. "Even the operation's powered up!"

With a little tremble, missiles launched from the Gummi Ship and blasted through the boulder that floated ahead.

"Wow! C'mon, Donald, let me fly it…" Standing behind the pilot seat, Sora stared closely at Donald's hands on the controls.

"No, no, no! I'm in charge of the flying!" Donald shook him off and gripped the control stick harder. The field of vision from the cockpit was much wider, too, and it looked easy to navigate.

"Cid's pretty good at what he does, I'd say," Jiminy Cricket remarked.

"He might be even better than Chip and Dale," Goofy agreed, naming the engineer and the mechanic at Disney Castle. "Where are we headed to next, Donald?"

"*Quack?* We decided to go past Wonderland!"

"Past Wonderland…?"

I wonder what happened to Alice, Sora thought. *Is she somewhere out there in the Other Sky? Or…*

"Look, there it is!" Donald pointed at the new world that came into view ahead.

It was a world covered in tawny sand—Agrabah.

"Whoa… That beach goes on forever…," Sora murmured, staring down as the Gummi Ship hovered in the new world's sky.

"Oh, that's no beach—that's a desert," Jiminy corrected him. "You won't find any ocean lapping at those sands."

"There's sand, but no ocean?!"

"That's right."

Taken aback, Sora looked down at the land again.

"I can see a city that way," said Donald.

Sora leaned over to see. Across the desert sands there was a rampart of stone.

"C'mon, Donald, Goofy! Let's go!" Sora couldn't wait to touch down on the desert world.

"Hey, wait!" Goofy rushed to get ready, but Sora was already running out to the open sand.

A city made of stone stood in the middle of the desert, surrounded by huge stone walls nearly the same color as the sand. The city was its own sizable kingdom, where people traveling through the desert would come and go, bringing business for the various shops lining the bazaar. It should have been a lively place. But the city was eerily silent.

A man and a woman, both dressed in black cloaks, walked through the streets.

"Where is the Keyhole?"

"The Heartless are searching for it now. I'm certain we'll find it soon enough."

The one who asked the question was the dark witch, Maleficent.

The one who answered her was the royal vizier of this world, Jafar.

"And what about the other matter?"

"Yes, about that—" Interrupting him, a brightly colored parrot landed on Jafar's shoulder. "Iago! Did you find the princess Jasmine?"

"I looked everywhere for her. She's disappeared like magic!"

Maleficent frowned at the parrot. It was apparent that Maleficent and Jafar were both looking for this princess named Jasmine.

"You said you had this place under control."

"Agrabah is full of holes for rats to hide in."

It sounded as if everyone in the city was imprisoned by some scheme of Jafar's.

"But...with or without the princess, surely this world will be ours once we find the Keyhole," he said. "What do we need Jasmine for?"

This time Maleficent frowned at Jafar's question. "We must have all seven princesses to open the final door. Any fewer is useless."

"Ah, the door, is it. If the princess is that important, we'll find her. —You there, find Jasmine and bring her to me at once!"

Heartless armed with curved swords appeared behind Jafar. They wore turbans on their heads, like desert warriors, but like all known Heartless, they had no faces.

"Now let's get going!" Iago flew farther into town, leading the Heartless away with him.

"Don't steep yourself in darkness too long," Maleficent warned. "The Heartless consume the careless."

Jafar laughed with half a cruel smile. "Your concern is touching but hardly necessary."

A single fat orange tumbled from its pile on a fruit stand, but neither Maleficent nor Jafar noticed.

There, behind the stand, was the beautiful black-haired princess—Jasmine.

The trio stood in front of the huge gate.

"I wonder if this place is full of Heartless, too...," Goofy said, frowning as if he didn't want to go inside.

Donald jumped and brandished his wand. "We'll be all right! Won't we, Sora!"

"Yeah. Leave it to us!"

"Gawrsh, I hope so..."

They went through the gate, and Heartless sprang up out of the ground as if they'd been waiting to ambush the trio.

"Wh-whoa! I knew it!"

"Donald, Goofy, c'mon!" Sora ran straight into the swarm of Heartless.

"They've got funny-looking swords!" Goofy shouted, blocking an attack from a Heartless with a big curved blade.

"These guys have wings!" It was all Sora could do to avoid the low-flying attacks of the winged Heartless.

"All right, my magic will— *Quaaack!*" Just as Donald was about to use his wand, a floating Heartless in a red robe shot magical fire at him. "They got stronger again!" he yelled, batting at his hat to put out the flames.

"Let's just get out of here, Sora!" Goofy ran a step ahead into an alley.

Sora was still intent on fighting. "But we can get more of them!"

"Come on, Sora!" Donald grabbed his arm and dragged him away after Goofy.

"Aww…" Sora kicked a pebble by his foot in the alleyway.

"Those Heartless were pretty strong," said Goofy.

"We could have beaten them all!" Sora retorted, twisting his mouth in a pout.

"Those ones with the swords were really tough…" Goofy let out a huge sigh.

Beside them, Donald was looking around. "Well, anyway… Where are all the people in this city?"

The vendors' stands were all lined up in the market, giving the impression of a very prosperous city—but there was no one to be seen.

"Are these things for sale?" Sora picked up an orange from one of the stands. It was delicious-looking, but…

"Who's there? Hello?"

"Ack!" Sora jumped back from the sudden voice.

"Is someone there?" Goofy peered into the stand from behind its counter.

A beautiful young lady with delicate features and raven hair appeared. A sweet fragrance seemed to waft from her every movement, and her clothes were the color of fresh water, like an oasis in the hot desert city.

"I'm Jasmine," she said. "My father is the sultan of Agrabah."

"Uh, so…that makes you a princess," Goofy replied.

Jasmine shook her head. "…My father was deposed by Jafar, who now controls the city," she told them softly, but it seemed painful for her to say.

"Jafar?" said Donald.

"You haven't heard of him?" Jasmine asked in reply.

"No… We only just came here."

"So you're travelers… Well, Jafar has imprisoned everyone in Agrabah. There's no one here…" Jasmine looked down sadly. She must have thought that Sora and the others were citizens who had escaped Jafar's clutches.

"Jasmine, I'm Sora. Can you tell us anything else about what happened here?"

"Jafar is the royal vizier. He gained evil powers and seized Agrabah. He caught me trying to escape…but someone helped me…"

"Who helped you?" Sora asked, and she looked up at him.

"His name is Aladdin. We were hiding nearby, but he left a while ago to take care of something… Oh, I hope he's all right…" Her gaze strayed down again.

Sora, Donald, and Goofy looked at one another uncertainly.

"Is there anything else you've heard? I think we can help," said Sora.

Jasmine thought for a moment and replied, "Jafar seems to be looking for something."

"What's he looking for?" Donald exchanged a glance with Goofy.

"I think…he called it a 'keyhole.'"

"The Keyhole!" Donald jumped up. "That's what we're looking for, too!"

They leaned closer, hoping Jasmine would tell them more. Could the Keyhole have something to do with the strange events in this city…?

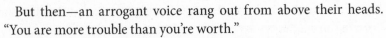

But then—an arrogant voice rang out from above their heads. "You are more trouble than you're worth."

"Jafar!" Jasmine cried.

A man with a snake-headed staff was looking down at them.

"Princess Jasmine, allow me to find you more suitable company," he said, stroking his bearded chin. "These little rats won't do…"

"Jasmine, run!" shouted Sora, who stood ready with the Keyblade.

"Ah, the boy who holds the key." Jafar looked over him and watched Jasmine run away with a nasty smile that said she wouldn't get far. "I suppose we'll get to see what you can do."

Then Jafar waved his staff, and Heartless appeared, rushing at the trio.

"*Wak!*" Donald jumped and dodged an attack.

Looking down on the scene, Jafar turned with a sweep of his cape.

"You're running away?!" yelled Sora. Jafar smirked and left unhurriedly.

"Stop right there!"

"Sora, look out!" Goofy slammed into a Heartless that rushed at Sora as he tried to follow Jafar.

"Whoa!" Trying to jump away, Sora fell flat on his behind.

"Sora, we gotta beat these Heartless before we can go after Jafar," said Goofy.

"And we gotta help Jasmine!" Donald added.

Sora got up, swinging the Keyblade. "Okay! Let's each take on one!"

"Got it!" Goofy winked.

Donald waved his wand. "This one's mine!"

All at once, the three jumped at the Heartless floating in the air like big balloons.

Catching their breath after defeating the Heartless, they sat down on the spot.

"They really are stronger…," Sora said, not quite unscathed.

Donald gave him a potion. "Well, we've got to keep fighting!"

"Yeah." Sora gingerly stood up and looked around. "We have to find Jasmine."

The trio headed toward the direction where Jasmine had escaped.

"Didn't she say she was hiding in a house over this way?" Donald paused in front of a small stone house. "Maybe this is it…"

They opened the wooden door and went into the little house, looking around for Jasmine.

"There's nobody here…"

Donald peeked into a large pot. "Hmm… I wonder where she could've gone. It doesn't look like that Aladdin guy is here, either."

Sora folded his arms, thinking, and they heard a *clunk!* from the corner.

"Huh?" When he turned, somehow a carpet was flapping around by itself.

"Th…that carpet is moving!" Donald exclaimed.

"Gawrsh, it doesn't look like a Heartless…," said Goofy, but he was lifting his shield anyway.

The carpet rattled the cabinet that was on top of it.

"It looks like it's stuck," said Sora.

"Watch out, Sora!" Donald had his wand out, but Sora went closer to the waving carpet and pushed the cabinet off.

"There, now you can move, right?"

The carpet stood on its end and folded itself in half.

"Did it…just bow to thank us?" said Goofy.

Then the carpet went back down and nudged at their feet.

"Are you telling us to get on?" Sora jumped atop the carpet, and it seemed to bounce happily. "Donald, Goofy, get on!"

Donald and Goofy looked at each other and nervously stepped onto the carpet.

And then the carpet flew out the window and on past the edge of the city.

"Whoa!"

Outside the city, the carpet suddenly sped up, and they were zooming over the desert.

"Wow... A flying carpet!" Sora looked down over the dunes.

It wasn't at all like the Gummi Ship—they could feel the wind on their faces. The desert air was hot and dry, but it still felt wonderful. Sora had never experienced anything like it.

"I wonder where we're heading...?" Goofy murmured, his long ears flapping.

"There!"

Where Donald was pointing, they could see a single small figure struggling not to be swallowed up by the sand.

Fighting for his life, Aladdin couldn't hear anything but the soft rush of the falling sand. He was buried up to the knees of his white pants, and with every movement, he only sank deeper. Under his vest, his brown body was fit and tough, but there was nothing he could do against the quicksand.

"...Guess I better use it."

As Aladdin stared hard at the lamp he held, he heard another voice.

"Hey, are you Aladdin?!" Sora called out to the man in the sand and jumped down from the carpet.

"That's right! Who are you?"

"I'm Sora. Let's get you out of there!" He got down in the sand and stretched his hand out to Aladdin. But then—

"*Wak!* Heartless!" shouted Donald, jumping up and down. A huge number of Heartless appeared, surrounding them.

"We have to beat them first, or we won't be able to do much to help!" said Goofy.

"Just hold on—we'll help you, promise!" Sora told Aladdin, who was buried up to his waist now, and got to his feet with the Keyblade ready. "Yaaargh!"

He jumped up and launched himself at the flying Heartless that was coming for him. But it was harder to move on the sand, and he only managed to hit its leg, not doing much damage.

"*Fire!*" Donald covered for him with magic.

"Thanks, Donald!"

"No problem!"

Fighting together, the trio took down the Heartless one by one, but as many as they defeated, more kept rising out of the sand.

"Gawrsh, not again!" cried Goofy.

"But we have to beat them to help Aladdin!" Sora yelled back.

Sinking in the sand, Aladdin held the lamp up high. "Genie, get rid of these guys!"

With that, a big blue cloud spilled from the lamp's nozzle—it was the Genie of the lamp, flying out and roaring.

"Wish number one, coming right up!"

"Whoa!" Sora fell backward in surprise.

The Genie snapped his fingers and all the Heartless disappeared without a trace.

"Wow…"

"Easy peasy, piece of cake!" The Genie winked and folded his arms. His big broad body had no feet, and he floated in the air like a ghost.

"Sora, we gotta help Aladdin!" said Goofy. Sora stretched out his hand to Aladdin, still stuck in the quicksand. As their hands clasped, Donald and Goofy held on to Sora's feet, and they all managed to pull out Aladdin.

"Whew…" Aladdin brushed off the sand that was stuck all over him and smiled brightly at them. "Thanks, Sora! And…"

"Donald Duck!"

"And I'm Goofy!"

Donald and Goofy each shook Aladdin's hand in turn.

"Aladdin, what're you doing out here in the desert?" asked Sora.

"Oh, you know, just hunting legendary treasure. Just paid a visit to the Cave of Wonders." As Aladdin said that, the carpet came down to land.

"Legendary treasure?"

"I found that flying carpet you came here on…and this magic lamp." In Aladdin's hand was the small metal oil lamp.

"How is it magic?" said Sora, staring at it closely, and the Genie put his face level with Sora's to stare back. "Whoa!"

"Leave the explanations to a professional!" The Genie puffed himself up in front of Sora, taking a heroic pose. "The one, the only, the Genie of the lamp! Rub-a-dub-dub the lamp and out comes the Genie to grant your dearest wishes! And today's winner is…Aladdin! Congratulations!"

Dancing around, the Genie snapped his fingers and a fanfare sounded. Confetti sprinkled down on Aladdin.

"*Any* wishes?" asked Donald.

The Genie waved his index finger in front of Donald's face. "Patience, my fine feathered friend! You get…" He flew up in the air and tripled himself—there were three Genies. Each one held up three fingers. "Any *three* wishes! A one wish, a two wish…" The duplicate Genies disappeared. "A three wish—then I make like a banana and split!"

Then he flew behind Aladdin. "Our lucky winner made his first wish—that means he has two left! So, master, what'll you have for wish number two?"

The Genie held his hand out and a spotlight illuminated Aladdin.

"Hmm," Aladdin said quietly. "How about making me a fabulously wealthy prince…?"

"Oooh! Money! Royalty! Fame!" The Genie applauded. "Why didn't I think of that?!"

"Gawrsh, really…?" Goofy murmured, tilting his head.

"Okay, you asked for it. A hundred servants, a hundred camels laden with gold! Just say the word, delivery in thirty minutes or less or your meal is free! I'll even throw in a free cappuccino!" Rubbing his hands together, the Genie sidled up to Aladdin.

But Aladdin shook his head. "No, thanks."

"Okay…"

"I think I'll put it on hold until we reach Agrabah," Aladdin said, looking regretful.

"Uh, why do you want to be a prince?" Goofy asked with his arms folded.

"You see, there's this girl in Agrabah named Jasmine. But, well…" Aladdin looked down sadly. "She's a princess, and I'm… Aw, she'd never fall for a guy like me."

"…Jasmine?" Donald cocked his head. There was something about that name…

"Oh—that's right! She's in trouble, Aladdin!" Sora ran up to him urgently, and the color drained from Aladdin's face.

The carpet flew through the air carrying Sora, Aladdin, Donald, and Goofy.

"Ahh, fresh air! The great outdoors!" Flying behind them, the Genie took a deep breath and stretched.

"I guess you don't get out much, huh?" said Sora.

At that the Genie looked a little glum. "Comes with the job. Phenomenal cosmic powers, itty-bitty living space. It's always three wishes and then back to my little portable prison. So I'm lucky to see the light of day every century or two…"

The Genie hung his head miserably.

If I were shut up in that tiny lamp… Sora tried to imagine it and shivered. That had to be just awful. Destiny Island was full of sunlight and friends, and even there, Sora had wanted to go to other worlds.

Aladdin thought for a bit, too. "Say, Genie, what if I use my last wish to free you from the lamp? What do you think?"

The Genie's eyes shone. "You'd do that?"

"Genie, it's a promise. After we help Jasmine!"

The Genie somersaulted in the air. "Yahoo!" And he kept flying in loops around them.

"So, what is Jafar up to anyway?" Aladdin asked the trio, still watching the exultant Genie.

"We don't really get it, either," said Sora. "But Jasmine said Jafar was looking for the Keyhole."

"That's what we're looking for, too!" Goofy added.

Genie paused to fold his arms and think. "A 'Keyhole,' eh? I could swear I've heard about that somewhere before…"

Donald jumped up. "Really? Where?"

"Now, where was it? It's been a few centuries…"

"C'mon, remember!"

"Hmmm… Can't say." The Genie tilted his head at Donald, who was stomping his feet on the carpet.

"Anyway, we've gotta stop Jafar before it's too late," said Sora. "I've got a bad feeling…"

Aladdin nodded. "Let's go!"

The carpet sped faster over the desert.

The main streets of Agrabah were completely barricaded, but that was no problem with a magic carpet. When flying Heartless came up to waylay them, Donald's magic came in handy.

"*Quack!*" Donald shot off a spell. Sora threw the Keyblade, which whirled through the air and finished off the Heartless, then returned to his hand.

"*A-hyuck!* Wow, Sora, that was a neat trick!" Goofy exclaimed.

Sora gave him a thumbs-up and a grin. He was learning how to use the Keyblade better and better.

They could see two figures down at the great palace gates. "Jasmine!"

"Jafar's there, too!"

Aladdin jumped down from the carpet, and the others followed.

"So, the street rat comes out of his hole at last," said Jafar, sniffing with contempt.

"Let Jasmine go!"

"Setting your sights a little high, aren't you, boy? I will not allow you to trouble the princess any more."

"Aladdin!" Jasmine tried to run toward him, but Jafar held her back.

"Genie... Help Jasmine, please!" Aladdin whispered, rubbing the lamp.

"One wish left! You're making this really easy, you know." The Genie disappeared from behind Aladdin and reappeared behind Jafar, then scooped up Jasmine in his arms.

"So sorry, boy," Jafar sneered. "I'm afraid your second wish has been denied."

They heard wings flapping. Iago, the parrot, held the lamp in his claws.

"Huh?!" Aladdin looked at his empty hands.

"I'm sorry, Al...," the Genie murmured sadly.

The lamp dropped from Iago's claws into Jafar's hand, and in the same instant, the Genie vanished.

Jasmine screamed. Without the Genie holding her up, she fell straight down and landed right in a big clay pot.

"Jasmine!" Aladdin ran toward her, but the pot sprouted legs—it had transformed into a Heartless. And it scuttled away through the city streets at a tremendous speed.

"Help!"

As Jasmine's cries echoed back at them, Jafar smirked. "And now, I bid you street rats farewell!"

"Stop!" The four of them tried to follow him, but more Heartless already blocked their path.

"Out of the way!" Sora slashed down at them with the Keyblade.

"They're over here, too!" Goofy took out the Heartless that kept appearing. But now they'd lost sight of Jafar.

"Jasmine! *Jasmiiiine!*" Aladdin called out, swinging his sword at the Heartless, and just then the carpet floated down in front of him. "Are you telling me to get on?"

"Let's go, Aladdin!" Sora shouted. "I bet the carpet can take us to Jasmine!"

He hopped on, and then Aladdin, Donald, and Goofy followed.

"...Jasmine..." Hanging his head, Aladdin pounded the carpet with his fist.

The carpet let them off at an enormous statue of a tiger's head.

"The tiger god's mouth is closed!" Aladdin shouted as he jumped down from the carpet. The others followed him.

Goofy cocked his head. "The tiger god?"

"The Cave of Wonders is inside its mouth," Aladdin replied, staring at the huge stone figure. Its eyes glowed with purple flames, seeming to glare at them.

"What's this Cave of Wonders?" asked Donald.

"It's the cave where I found this carpet and the magic lamp."

They looked around. Jafar was nowhere to be seen.

"So, that means there's lots of treasure inside, right?"

"Well, I guess you could say that."

Aladdin moved closer to the tiger's head. Its eyes glowed with dull, menacing light.

"Whoa!" Aladdin fell to the ground, raising a cloud of dust. "I don't get it—the tiger god let me into the Cave of Wonders before, when I found the lamp..."

"Aladdin! Get down!"

He was about to get up, but at Sora's warning, he ducked, and bright bolts of light nearly grazed the top of his head. The tiger god opened its mouth as if it was waking up, and something came rushing out.

"Heartless!" Goofy lifted his shield and rushed at them.

"Why is the tiger god doing this?!" said Aladdin.

"Something's controlling it!" Sora ran to Aladdin and helped him up. "Does anything about it look different from before?"

"...Its eyes are a different color. And the attacking part is new, too."

With sword and Keyblade out, Aladdin and Sora ran up to the tiger god's mouth.

"Can you guys take care of these Heartless?" Sora called back.

"Leave it to us!" Donald jumped, waving his wand.

"Aladdin, go for its eyes!" yelled Sora. He leaped up onto the tiger god's nose and brought the Keyblade down on its right eye. The impact clanged and the tiger god roared. And more Heartless poured out of its mouth.

"*Wa-waaak!*" Donald's magic exploded on the new Heartless, and Goofy rushed at them with his shield.

"All right, one more!" Sora and Aladdin both jumped up again onto the tiger god's nose and attacked. It let out a terrible roar and then, with its mouth wide open, stopped moving.

"We did it!" They jumped back down and hugged in celebration. Having defeated the Heartless, Donald and Goofy joined them.

The purple light went out from the tiger god's eyes, and it loomed silently.

"Let's go!" The four ran on into the tiger's great mouth.

Inside the cave it was completely still. Jafar walked through it with the lamp in his hand. On his shoulder, Iago perched, shifting his feathers.

"With this, I'll be able to find it..." Jafar rubbed the lamp and called out, "My first wish, Genie! Show me the Keyhole!"

The Genie flew out from the lamp, looking dejected. He reluctantly snapped his fingers and the back wall crumbled to reveal the Keyhole.

Still hanging his head, he floated behind Jafar.

"The Keyhole, and the princess... Maleficent will have nothing to complain about now," Jafar murmured, and Iago flapped his wings, agreeing.

And then the very same black-cloaked witch appeared behind him.

"Why, you're here early, Maleficent…"

She made no reaction to Jafar's greeting, but glanced at the princess sprawled on the floor and then quietly strode to the Keyhole. It was as if Maleficent didn't even see him. Jafar's lips curled in annoyance, but he took a deep breath and told her, "The boy who holds the 'key' is on his way."

At that, Maleficent's eyebrows went up ever so slightly. "…That child, again?"

"He's more perceptive than I would have guessed. Why not explain the situation to that other boy—Riku, was it? Doing so may actually prove useful to our—"

Sensing another presence behind him, Jafar turned midsentence. Four sets of footsteps were coming closer. "The street rat…"

When Maleficent turned to look, Sora and the others were standing there.

"Who are you?!" Sora demanded.

Maleficent vanished without a word.

"Jafar! Let Jasmine go!" Aladdin shouted.

"Not a chance," Jafar said glibly. "You see, she's a *princess*—one of seven who somehow hold the key to opening the door."

"Open…"

"…The door?"

Goofy and Donald repeated in turn.

They had heard about the Keyholes, but not about a door. What could it possibly mean…?

"But you fools won't live to see what lies beyond it. Genie! My second wish. Crush them!"

The Genie still floated in the air, limp with misery, and then he looked straight at Aladdin.

"Genie! No!"

"Sorry, Al. The one with the lamp calls the shots. I don't have a choice." Hunching his shoulders helplessly, the Genie began to attack Aladdin and the trio.

"Genie!" Aladdin dodged and kept staring at him in disbelief.

"Why don't I join the fun, as well…?" Jafar swung his snake-headed staff and a great jet of flame shot out toward Sora.

Donald didn't waste any time with his wand. "Blizzard!" Shards of ice flew and doused the flames.

"Putting up a fight, are you?" Jafar smirked and sprang high into the air.

"Hey!" Sora and Aladdin followed him. When he landed again, Jafar stuck his staff into the cavern floor, leaving it standing on its own.

"Look out!"

Goofy jumped up as a lightning bolt from Jafar's staff bounced off his shield.

"You're not gonna beat a royal magician with magic!" With an enormous flourish of his wand, Donald let loose another barrage of ice. As Jafar dodged it, Sora moved in with a flying leap and struck him. Aladdin likewise caught Jafar in his distraction, but the Genie sent him sprawling back.

"Genie…?"

"I'm sorry…Al…" The Genie flailed around, his eyes tightly shut.

"Genie!" Sora called. "What if we got rid of Jafar somehow?"

"Well…sure, without the guy who calls the shots, I wouldn't have to take any…"

"So we just have to beat Jafar! Aladdin, keep away from the Genie! All we have to do is take out Jafar!" Sora raised the Keyblade again and hurtled straight for Jafar.

Aladdin followed him with a ferocious bellow and they closed in. "Yaaaaaahhh!"

"Cover us, Goofy!"

"Got it!"

Donald shot a huge cluster of ice crystals at Jafar, while Goofy jumped in with his shield and kept Jafar's magic from hitting Sora or Aladdin.

Sora grunted and jumped up high to bring the Keyblade down on Jafar. When he moved to dodge it, Aladdin's sword was there waiting.

The boy's sword and the vizier's staff met with a tremendous clash. "Let Jasmine go…!"

"You'll never have her!" Jafar had the upper hand, just barely.

"Aladdin!" Sora yelled, and in the same instant, Aladdin leaped back. Sora hurled the Keyblade at Jafar.

"…Sora!" Donald attacked with his magic, too.

"Here goes!" Goofy ran in and dealt Jafar a heavy blow with his shield.

"Ngh— Aaaaaaargh!" Jafar crumpled with a terrible cry, and then his body was enveloped in darkness.

"We did it!"

The four of them ran to Jasmine, who was still unconscious on the floor, but then—

They thought Jafar had disappeared. They were wrong—now he was floating in the air. "Genie! My final wish!" he cried, holding the lamp high. "I want you to make me an all-powerful genie!"

"…Your wish is my command, master…" Genie covered his face, cowering as he pointed at Jafar without looking and gingerly let loose his magic from his index finger.

The beam of magic grew to engulf Jafar, glowing—and the floor of the cavern cracked open. Jafar fell in.

"C'mon!" Sora and the others jumped into the crack.

In the cavern below, the lowest reaches of the Cave of Wonders, the air rippled with terrible heat. Huge square boulders were lined up in the center like stairs. And to all sides, fiery red lava bubbled and swirled.

"Jafar! Where are you?!" Aladdin shouted.

Then Jafar, now a genie himself, rose up, his body all red as if it had taken its color from the lava. Unlike the friendly blue Genie, Jafar's crimson form had a terribly frightful cast.

With a terrific rumble like an earthquake, Jafar threw balls of lava at them.

"Whoa!" The four jumped out of the way, and Donald's tail caught fire.

"*Quaaaack!*"

"Ha-ha! Idiots!" Iago flapped around behind Jafar, carrying the lamp in his claws.

"The lamp!" Aladdin called. "Get Jafar's lamp!"

There was no way they could win fighting Jafar in his new form as a genie. They had to take the lamp and trap him with its power.

"Hah! Like I'm gonna let you jerks have it!" Iago flew out of their reach.

"Aladdin! You handle Jafar!"

"Right!"

Sora went after Iago, clambering up the square boulders. Aladdin lured Jafar away, dodging the balls of lava that Jafar tossed on him. The brightly plumed parrot perched far off on the highest spot in the cavern, rustling his wings. Sora snuck up as close as he could and swung out with the Keyblade and felt it hit Iago.

"Yeeowch!" Iago squawked and flew closer to Jafar again.

"There he goes!" Sora told Donald.

"Gotcha! *Fire!*" Donald jumped up toward Iago and let the flames fly.

"Ack! Water, where's some water?!" Iago's feathered head was on fire, but then with a huge sweep of his arm, Jafar raised a waterspout to douse it.

"It's no good—we can't get it!" Sora yelled. Iago was diligently keeping away from them now. There was no way they could take the lamp from him.

"Then what do we do?" asked Goofy.

"Well…" Sora got Goofy and Donald, and then Aladdin, together in a huddle and whispered to them.

"Will that really work?" Donald worried.

"It'll work!" Sora thumped him on the back and ran to the very edge of the boulders.

"Hey, Jafar! Over here!" At the same time, Aladdin went to the opposite end. A huge fireball of lava fell toward him, but he dodged it effortlessly. "Is that all you've got?! C'mon!"

Jafar took the challenge and turned his back on the other three. He tried to bring a fist down on Aladdin, as Iago hovered up by the ceiling.

"Goofy, Donald! Now!" Sora called from the corner. Standing at the highest point he could reach, Goofy flung Donald up in the air.

"Here we go!"

"Quack!"

At the same time Sora ran to them. "One, two, *three!*" he yelled and launched himself up first with Goofy's help, and then with Donald's tail end as a foothold, so he flew up high.

Iago squawked as the Keyblade hit his feet, and the lamp tumbled from his grasp. Sora had aimed for the lamp itself, not the parrot.

"Got it!" Sora landed as Iago was scrambling to reclaim the lamp. But Sora got there first. He held the black lamp aloft. "Back to your lamp, Jafar!"

Jafar howled like a storm, and with a swirl of red light, the lamp sucked him in.

"We did it!"

As the four of them stood back, basking in victory, a single piece of paper came fluttering down from above.

"What's this…?" Sora picked it up. The paper was covered in mysterious words, difficult to read.

"Maybe Jiminy will be able to read it," said Donald, peering at it over Sora's shoulder.

Just then the cavern rumbled, and pieces of rock began to fall from the ceiling.

"Gawrsh! It looks like we better get out of here…" Goofy held his shield over his head and looked around desperately.

"But we have to close the Keyhole and get Jasmine, too!" said Sora, looking at Aladdin. They nodded. The magic carpet was there waiting for them.

A terrible roar startled Jasmine awake.

"Where am I...?"

She looked around and saw the great crack in the cavern floor next to her.

What in the world was that...? She tried to look over the edge.

"Princess," said a low voice from behind her.

She turned, and the one who had spoken touched her shoulder...

Just before she lost consciousness again, she caught sight of a handsome boy with silver hair.

The carpet flew out of the crack in the floor, which sounded like it would collapse any minute.

"Jasmine!" Aladdin called. But she was gone. "Jasmine?! Jasmine!"

They all searched the cavern for her, to no avail. Then the Keyhole began to sparkle.

"Jasmine, where are you?!" Aladdin was still looking for her in a panic.

"Sora, we'll find her!" said Goofy. "Take care of the Keyhole!"

"Right!" Sora pointed the Keyblade, and a beam of light shot from the end of it to the Keyhole. He could hear the locking *click*, and then the Keyhole turned into shards of light and vanished.

The entire Cave of Wonders began to shake even more.

"...We'd better go, Aladdin!"

"But we haven't found her— Jasmine!"

"She might have made it back to Agrabah!"

"But—"

With the biggest tremor yet, the walls and ceiling started to crumble.

"We gotta get out of here, Sora!" said Goofy. They had to drag

Aladdin by force onto the magic carpet, and it took off like a rocket toward the entrance.

"Jaaaasmine!" Aladdin's shout was lost in the roar of the collapsing caverns.

In the house where they'd found the magic carpet, Aladdin was hunched down on the floor, unmoving. The lamp sat beside him.

"I'm sorry, Aladdin…"

"So Jasmine isn't anywhere in Agrabah?"

"I don't know, but…"

One of the seven princesses, Jafar had said. He needed Jasmine for something. And so far, Sora knew of two other girls who had disappeared from their worlds.

Alice from Wonderland… And Kairi.

So maybe that meant…

"Aladdin, we'll find Jasmine and make sure she comes home to Agrabah. I promise. We'll save her no matter what."

Someone important to him disappeared…, Sora thought. *I want to find Kairi, too. Aladdin feels the same way…*

"I can't go with you?" said Aladdin.

Sora, Donald, and Goofy looked at one another. "Sorry. We can't take you," Sora replied sadly.

The lamp rattled beside Aladdin, and the Genie flew out. "Hey, Earth to Al, hello! You still have one wish left. Look, just say the word. Ask me to find Jasmine for you!"

Aladdin slowly looked up to stare thoughtfully at the Genie and took a deep breath. "I…I wish…"

The Genie folded his arms and puffed his chest out, beaming as he waited for Aladdin's wish.

"…For your freedom, Genie."

"Al!" the Genie cried in surprise. Dazzling swirls of light engulfed him.

Sora and the others shut their eyes against the brightness, and when they looked again, the golden cuffs on his wrists disappeared. Instead of a ghostlike trail of smoke, the Genie had legs.

"A deal's a deal, Genie," said Aladdin, looking up at him. "Now you can go anywhere you want. You're your own master. I promised I'd set you free with my last wish."

The Genie stared back, looking a little troubled.

"But if you can… I'd be really glad if you could go with them and help Sora find Jasmine. And then, when you find her, bring her back here…"

The Genie turned away from him. "Sorry, Al. I'm done taking orders from people."

Aladdin didn't look away, but kept his gaze on the Genie's back.

"A favor for a friend, though… Now, that's a totally different thing!" The Genie turned to Aladdin again and put an arm around his shoulders. "After all, we're pals, right, Al?"

"Genie…"

"Just leave it to me!" The Genie winked.

"But…won't this be meddling?" Goofy whispered to Donald.

"Meddling? Why, nothing's impossible for the one, the only, the Genie formerly of the lamp! Watch this." The Genie shrank into a puff of blue smoke and swirled under Donald's hat.

"*Waaak!*" Donald lifted up his hat and the miniature Genie's top half poked out.

"With me along, your magic'll get a turbo boost! Limited time offer—you don't wanna miss out on this deal!"

"Is that okay?" Donald rubbed his hat uncertainly.

"Isn't it?" said Sora and held out his hand to Aladdin. "We'll find Jasmine. I promise—just like you promised Genie!"

"Find her, Sora. I'm counting on you!"

Aladdin and Sora firmly shook hands.

CHAPTER 7

MONSTRO
crossroad

"THAT SNAKE OF A VIZIER NEARLY HAD THEM... IF ONLY *someone* hadn't left him to handle it all alone."

In the dark room, Hook glared at the silver-haired boy—Riku.

"Hey, I did my part," Riku said almost indifferently. "I brought the princess, didn't I?"

He was looking at Maleficent as he spoke. Her back was turned to them.

Would she really keep the promise she'd made to him?

Riku understood what he was doing. But he couldn't resist the lure of that promise. And if she really did mean to keep it, he'd do anything. That was what he had decided. If it meant he would have what he longed for... If it was for Kairi.

"Jafar was beyond help, consumed by his own hatred. One must beware of letting it burn too fiercely," Maleficent murmured, slowly turning to face the others. "By the way, Riku, have you not noticed...?"

She gestured toward the dais in the center of the room.

"What?"

"We had a deal, yes? You help us, and we grant you your wish..."

In a wash of dim light, the image of a girl appeared on the dais. She almost seemed to be sleeping there...

"Kairi!" Riku knew it wasn't real, but he ran over to the dais.

"Go to her. Your vessel is waiting."

"Why are you doing all this for me?" Riku said, his voice low with mistrust as he glared at Maleficent. "What's the catch?"

"Catch? Why, there's no catch." She bent down to look into Riku's eyes and said sweetly, "Silly boy. You're like a son to me. I only want you to be happy." Her hand softly stroked his cheek.

"I seriously doubt that."

"Believe what you wish. But lest we forget, I have kept my end of the bargain."

Riku turned away. "Where's the ship?"

"*My* ship it is, lad. But this is no pleasure cruise!" said Captain

Hook, brandishing the namesake hook in place of his left hand. "It won't be a pleasant voyage."

Without another word, Riku walked out of the room.

The Gummi Ship took off from Agrabah and drifted easily through the Other Sky. For whatever reason it seemed to be a quieter route, without many obstructions.

"So, we picked this up back there…" Goofy had the paper they'd found after trapping Jafar in his lamp. He handed it to Jiminy Cricket. "Any idea what it is?"

"It looks like there's a lot written on it…" Looking troubled, Sora peered at the paper now in Jiminy's hands.

"It looks to me like you've found yourselves a piece of Ansem's report," Jiminy replied.

"That's what this is?!"

"Yep, I'm pretty certain." Jiminy looked up at Sora, who was leaning right over him, and then began to read it.

Much of my life has been dedicated to the pursuit of knowledge. And that knowledge has guarded this world well. Not a soul doubts that.

But although I am called a sage, there are things I do not understand.

I believe darkness sleeps in every heart, no matter how pure. Given the chance, the smallest drop can spread and swallow the heart. I have witnessed it many times.

Darkness… Darkness of the heart. How is it born? How does it come to affect us so?

As the ruler of this world, I must find the answers. I must find them before the world is lost to those taken by the darkness…

It is my duty to expose what this darkness really is.

I have conducted the following experiments:

—*Extract the darkness from a person's heart.*

—*Cultivate darkness in a pure heart.*

The experiments caused the test subjects' hearts to collapse, even the most stalwart. How fragile our hearts are. My treatment yielded no signs of recovery. It wouldn't do to let the people of this world see such a terrible sight, so I confined those who had completely lost their hearts beneath the castle.

Some time later, I went below and was greeted by the strangest sight. Creatures that seemed born of darkness... What are they? Are they truly sentient beings? Could they be the shadows of those whose hearts were lost?

One thing I am certain of is that they are entirely devoid of emotion. I must conduct further research.

They still need a name. Those who lack hearts... I will call them the Heartless.

"Heartless... Those who lack hearts...," Sora murmured. "The darkness in people's hearts..."

"Wasn't Leon saying something like that?" said Goofy. "The Heartless seek out the darkness in people's hearts."

Donald gripped the control stick tighter. "Yeah. And he said to be careful."

Sora was thinking hard. Just like anyone else, he got scared sometimes, and he hated things sometimes. There was darkness in every heart, Leon had said.

So then...

"It looks like there must be more to the report somewhere," said Jiminy.

"That part doesn't make any sense," Donald remarked. "We've gotta find the rest of it."

Goofy tilted his head. "Gawrsh, I wonder if the king's read it..."

"What's *that*?!" Donald shouted.

Sora stumbled into the cockpit and saw…

"A whale! It's a great big monster whale!" Goofy ran in circles around the Gummi Ship. The whale rolled its colossal body around in space, and the ship shook as it passed by.

"Monstro!" cried Jiminy Cricket.

"You know the whale?"

"I certainly ought to! He's a whale of a whale, and vicious besides!"

Monstro turned about and came up in front of the Gummi Ship again.

"Whoa!" Donald pulled on the control stick with all his might, trying to reverse course, but Monstro opened his colossal mouth and came straight for them.

"It's too late! He's gonna swallow us!" Sora yelled, and the Gummi Ship was already inside the whale's mouth.

The waves broke softly on the shore. The sea and sky went on forever. The fronds of the cocoyum trees swayed in the sea breeze, and the sunlight was warm on their faces. It was Destiny Island. Sora's island.

"It's true! I saw it myself!" Sora shouted after Riku.

"Are you sure you didn't just hear it this time?"

"What's the difference? I'm telling you, there's a huge monster in there!"

The two boys stood in front of the waterfall. The cool water pouring down sparkled in the sun.

"All right, suppose there really is a monster… You think we can catch it by ourselves, Sora?"

Kairi wasn't there. They were both still little. This was years in the past.

"Yeah! You and me can do anything! …Listen there, can't you hear it growling?"

Sora tapped Riku on the shoulder and looked toward the bushes beside the waterfall. There was a dark passageway behind the bushes. Back then, Sora hadn't known what would begin in that cave.

"*Ssh.* Quiet," said Riku, staring into the passageway. "We've gotta be careful…"

They tiptoed inside.

There was a little cave with tree roots twining around the rocks. The ceiling had a great big hole in it, and they could see out to the bright blue sky.

Stepping into a new place they'd never seen before—just that much was a daring adventure for them.

"See? It was just the wind making that noise," said Riku, looking up at the sky.

"Aw, that's all? I wish it was a monster!" Sora folded his hands behind his head and let out a sigh. "Huh? Wait, what's that over there?"

There was something in the back of the cave. Sora ran over to it.

Riku followed him, less hurried. "A window…or a door?"

It was a big wooden door, taller than Riku and Sora combined, with golden decorations, like something in a castle out of a fairy tale.

"A door…?"

"But there's no way to open it." Riku looked closely, but there was no doorknob or keyhole to be found.

"Geez…is that really all that's here?" Sora kicked at a pebble.

Riku turned back to him. "Hey, Sora."

"Huh?"

"When we grow up, let's get off this island. We'll go on real adventures, not this kid stuff!"

Just then, the wind blew over the hole in the ceiling and howled— the sound Sora had thought was a monster.

But it was somewhere new. A cave they had never been into before. And there could have been a monster. It was enough adventure to make their little hearts pound. A *real* adventure, though—what could be waiting for them out there? What would they find? Riku just couldn't stand to be stuck on this island.

"Sure…but isn't there anything fun to do now?" said Sora, not minding it much.

He couldn't quite understand what Riku had just been saying. He hadn't given much thought to having a real adventure together someday. That was far off, and he wanted to find something to do now. Something fun, right now, at this very moment.

"Oh, I know! Did you hear about the new girl at the mayor's house?"

At that, Riku looked up.

"I heard she……"

The wind went on howling.

That was back before Sora and Riku had met Kairi…

Back when they knew nothing outside of their islands.

"Knock it off!"

Sora startled awake at Donald's shout and sat up.

He must have been dreaming. When had all that happened? It felt like such a long time ago…

"Hey, Sora, are you okay?"

Goofy was looking upward with his shield ready. Beside him, Donald was stamping his feet.

"What are you guys doing?" asked Sora. "Where are we anyway…?"

"Well, we can't be anywhere but inside Monstro," said Jiminy Cricket.

"What about the Gummi Ship?"

"It must be somewhere in here, too." Jiminy looked worried.

Suddenly a treasure chest came flying at them from somewhere up above.

"Whoa!" Sora jumped back.

"I think that big ol' whale just swallowed everyone. And for today's weather…expect showers!" Another treasure chest fell and clanged against Goofy's shield. "*A-hyuck!* Heavy showers!"

"Hey! Who's up there?!" Donald shouted angrily into the air.

"It's me." They could see someone moving up in front of them.

"Hm?" Donald frowned, staring hard.

"Pinocchio! Well, as I live and breathe! If it isn't Pinocchio!" Jiminy scurried toward the figure—it was a boy.

"Pinocchio?" Sora, Donald, and Goofy looked at one another and followed Jiminy. The boy wore a yellow hat and a fine white shirt over shorts, and he was frantically rooting through a treasure chest.

"Pinocchio!"

"Huh? Oh, it's you, Jiminy!"

The cricket hopped up and down in front of Pinocchio's nose. When the others got a closer look, they could see that it wasn't actually a human nose.

Donald and Goofy whispered to each other.

"Hey, is he...?"

"...A wooden puppet, isn't he?"

The boy was not a boy at all, but a puppet.

"What in the world are you doing in here?" asked Jiminy, hopping up onto Pinocchio's shoulder.

"Um... Playing hide-and-seek!"

"I just don't believe it. Here I've been up at night, worried sick about you. Why, of all the— Pinocchio!" Then Jiminy's voice rose in surprise.

"His nose grew!" shouted Donald, jumping up.

"Pinocchio, you're fibbing again!" Jiminy scolded. "You know you're not supposed to tell lies. A lie only grows and grows till you get caught! Plain as the nose on your face!"

"...I'm sorry, Jiminy... I'll never tell lies as long as you're around." As Pinocchio said that, his nose glimmered and shrank back to its normal size.

"You need to be good so you can become a real boy. You promised Geppetto now, didn't you?"

"Oh, that's right! Father!" Pinocchio whirled around and ran.

"Where are you going, Pinocch? Wait!"

But Pinocchio kept on running as if he didn't hear Jiminy at all.

"Come on, everybody!" Jiminy jumped up onto Sora's head.

"Okay… But who is Pinocchio anyway?" Sora asked as they ran.

"He's from the same world as I am. We lived together. Never imagined I'd find him in a place like this…"

"Gawrsh, it can't be good to be inside of a whale!" said Goofy.

"Oh, what a handful that Pinocchio is…" Jiminy took a tiny white handkerchief from his pocket and wiped his face.

The murky interior of the whale's mouth was full of piles of wreckage from other swallowed ships. There was no exit—Monstro's teeth were tightly shut. Far in the back, there was one ship that had managed to keep its shape, with a lantern shining unsteadily from the mast, and the Gummi Ship was nearby. It seemed to be stuck there.

"Father!" Pinocchio ran to the old man who sat on the deck.

"Why, Pinocchio, wherever have you been?" the old man said.

"Umm…"

"Pinocchio, wait!"

Just as he was about to answer, Sora and the others clambered up, their faces just showing at the deck.

"Oh, dear me! So the whale swallowed all of you, too?" The old man helped them aboard.

"Oof! Thanks, mister!" Donald nodded to him.

"Pinocchio sure does like to run off," Sora remarked.

"He must've been worried about Geppetto, too," Jiminy said more charitably. "He's a good boy, after all."

"So who are you…?" the old man asked.

"I'm Sora, and this is Donald…and that's Goofy."

"My name is Geppetto. I'm Pinocchio's father. Say, Pinocchio… Pinocchio?" He looked all around, but the little puppet had disappeared again.

"Jiminy's gone, too!" cried Goofy.

"Let's go find them!" Sora jumped down from the deck and ran after Pinocchio.

They went down the whale's throat, and the walls changed from dim to grotesquely colorful. At the end of that narrow passageway, they came into a more open space, all curved and winding, with random differences in height.

"Pinocchio!" Donald called.

Pinocchio paused at the entrance to another chamber, looking back at the trio tentatively. Jiminy Cricket was riding on his hat.

"Sora!" Jiminy jumped onto Sora instead as they came closer. "I just didn't know what to do when Pinocchio ran off like that…"

He took out his tiny handkerchief again and wiped the sweat from his face.

"What are you doing? C'mon, let's go back," Sora said, but Pinocchio didn't move.

"Y'know, Geppetto's awfully worried about you," Goofy added.

"Stop fooling around! This is no time for games!" Sora told him.

It wasn't Pinocchio who answered. "But, Sora, you used to like games."

"Riku!"

He was standing above them up on a rise. His stunning blue eyes regarded Sora coolly. "Or are you too good for games now that you have the Keyblade?"

"What are you doing here?!" Sora demanded.

Riku jumped down and put a hand on Pinocchio's shoulder. "Just playing with Pinocchio."

"You know what I mean! What about Kairi? Did you find her?"

Riku smiled thinly. "Maybe. If you can catch us, I might tell you what I know."

"Come on!" Sora stepped toward him, but Riku grabbed Pinocchio by the arm and fled. "Hey, wait!"

He broke into a full run after Riku.

"Sora! Wait up!" Donald yelled after him.

"What, Donald?!" Sora stopped and turned. Donald and Goofy were looking at him uncertainly, and Jiminy seemed concerned, too, from his perch on Donald's hat.

"Why *is* Riku here?"

"How should I know?!" Sora snapped, stamping his foot.

"But…isn't that kinda fishy? I've got a bad feeling about this."

"We have to follow them. Or we might never see Pinocchio or Riku again!" With that Sora kept running.

Donald and Goofy exchanged glances, thinking for a moment, then nodded and followed Sora.

The long, narrow passageway was brightly colored but gloomy. Riku paused and hunched over to catch his breath. Pinocchio wasn't with him—he'd run off somewhere else again.

"Why do you still care about that boy?"

Hearing the uncanny voice, Riku turned to find Maleficent standing there behind him. He frowned and looked up at her silently.

"He has all but deserted you for the Keyblade and his new companions." Maleficent touched his cheek and Riku brushed her away.

"I don't care about him. I was just messing with him a little." Riku's eyes gleamed with a fierce, cold light.

"Oh, really? Of course you were. But beware the darkness in your heart. The Heartless prey upon it."

"Mind your own business!" Riku shouted, but Maleficent quietly vanished.

Sora, Donald, and Goofy ran down a long passageway.

"Gawrsh, I don't see Pinocchio or Riku," said Goofy.

"They have to be in here somewhere…," Sora said grimly.

He had no idea what Riku was thinking.

Why is he doing this? Sora thought. *We're supposed to be friends. But now...*

"Sora! There's Pinocchio!" Donald ran toward where Pinocchio was standing, peering at them curiously. And Riku was beside him.

"Riku!" Sora cried.

Riku only stared back without a word.

"What's the matter with you? What are you thinking? Don't you realize what you're doing?!"

"I was about to ask you the same thing, Sora," he replied, shaking his head. "You only seem interested in running around and showing off that Keyblade these days. Do you even want to save Kairi?"

"I do..." Sora stared down at the Keyblade glinting in his hand.

Finding Riku...and finding Kairi. That was what he'd first set out to do. But now, that wasn't all.

He didn't want any more worlds to be destroyed like Destiny Island. He didn't want anyone else to go through something like that. So he was trying to lock all the Keyholes.

That didn't mean he'd forgotten about Kairi.

Even now, he was thinking how much he wanted to see her and how he had to help her.

But...if he only tried to save Kairi, that wouldn't solve anything in the end.

"Please, give me back my son!" Geppetto called from behind them. He must have been unable to stand just waiting for Pinocchio to come back.

"Father!" Pinocchio tried to reach Geppetto, but Riku caught him from behind.

"Pinocchio!"

"Father, help!"

"Sorry, old man," said Riku. "I have some unfinished business with this puppet."

"He's no puppet! Pinocchio is my little boy!" cried Geppetto.

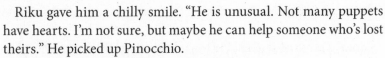

Riku gave him a chilly smile. "He is unusual. Not many puppets have hearts. I'm not sure, but maybe he can help someone who's lost theirs." He picked up Pinocchio.

"Wait—are you talking about Kairi?" said Sora.

"A puppet that lost its heart to the Heartless... It might hold the key to helping Kairi." Riku smiled for real. "How about it, Sora? Let's join forces to save her. You and I can do anything."

Sora held the Keyblade, ready to fight.

"What, you'd rather fight me? Over a little puppet?" Riku stared at him unblinkingly.

"Pinocchio's not just a puppet. He has a heart. Or at least a conscience!" Sora retorted, his voice full of strength and determination. "It's a tiny little voice, but I can hear it loud and clear. And it's telling me that letting you have Pinocchio is wrong!"

"Then you leave me no choice, Sora." Riku let go of Pinocchio with a shove and looked down, balling his fists.

"Pinocchio! Pinocchio!" Jiminy hopped over from Donald's hat to Pinocchio, who just barely opened his eyes.

"Jiminy... I'm not gonna make it...," he said weakly, but then his nose grew a little. "Oh! I guess I'm okay!"

Pinocchio got to his feet, and Jiminy happily hopped up and down.

Just then a huge Heartless dropped down from above them—the Parasite Cage.

"*Wak!* Incoming!" Donald held out his wand. The Heartless was a big ball, with a wide mouth like a crack, and long arms waving like seaweed in a current.

"Riku..." With the Keyblade ready, Sora stared at him, but Riku seemed to look right through him. A black haze surrounded Riku's body...the same as the dark energy that had engulfed him back on Destiny Island.

"Where are you going?! Riku!"

But Riku disappeared into that black glow, as if to drown out Sora's shouting.

"Waaaak!" The Parasite Cage spat bubbles at them, knocking Donald back.

"Jiminy, Pinocchio! Geppetto! Get back, guys!" Goofy held up his shield in front of them.

Sora was staring after Riku, where the black glow had dissipated. Donald yelled his name, and he rushed at the Parasite Cage.

"Graaaah!" Sora brought his Keyblade down on its head. The impact was almost like striking metal, and the thing opened its mouth.

"Sora!"

"Aim into its mouth, Donald!"

"Blizzard!" Donald waved his wand and a great cluster of ice flew into the Parasite Cage's mouth. At the same time, its rubbery arm smacked Sora and sent him flying.

Goofy ran to him. "Are you okay?"

"I'm fine! Let's get rid of this thing!" Sora rubbed his mouth and got up again with the Keyblade ready.

"Wak!" When Donald's magic struck the Parasite Cage, it opened its mouth again. And then Sora rushed in, swinging the Keyblade with all his might.

Riku...!

It sounded like Riku knew where Kairi was.

And Riku...was turning to the darkness, trying to save her. Maybe.

Sora didn't know what to do about it. Those feelings flowed into the Keyblade, and it seemed as if he hit the Parasite Cage with them.

He'd jumped into the thing's mouth, and the others were getting nervous for him. Just as Donald called Sora's name, light shot out of the Parasite Cage's mouth.

"...There!" It spat out Sora and its body turned into light. Then the glowing heart slowly floated up, and the Parasite Cage dissolved with the light.

That was when Monstro's body itself began to shake.

With all the fighting, the whale must have decided that it wanted the rabble-rousers out of its belly.

"Sora, let's get out of here!"

"Right… But where are Geppetto and Pinocchio?"

The trio ran back toward the Gummi Ship.

"I told them to go ahead and get aboard," said Jiminy Cricket, who at some point had taken up his perch on Donald's hat.

"Gawrsh, I hope they're okay…"

"Anyway, we'd better hurry!"

And just as they flung themselves aboard the Gummi Ship, there was an enormous tremor, and a blast of wind attacked the ship.

"*Qua-waaaak!*"

"*Wahoo-hooey!*"

Monstro sneezed and the Gummi Ship shot back out into the Other Sky.

"Whew…," Donald sighed, holding on to the control stick. Behind them Monstro, looking a little ill, swam away to find somewhere more peaceful.

"I hope Geppetto and Pinocchio are all right…," Goofy worried.

"Yeah. Hopefully they landed safely somewhere… *Quack!*"

"I just know they're all right," said Jiminy. "So long as they're together, Pinocchio will be a good boy, no matter where they go."

Sora sat huddled on the floor with the Keyblade across his lap, almost inaudibly murmuring his friend's name. "Riku…"

CHAPTER 8

NEVERLAND
believe

THE GUMMI SHIP SPED QUIETLY ACROSS THE OTHER SKY.

Sora looked up at Goofy. "Maybe I've been wrong…," he said, frowning.

Unsure what to say, Goofy turned to Donald in the pilot seat.

"What're you wrong about? You're looking for Kairi, aren't you?" Donald shouted back.

"But…"

"Don't worry about it, Sora."

"But I do want to see her…and Riku…" Sora hugged his knees to his chest.

"We want to see the king, too!" said Goofy.

"And I've wanted to see Pinocchio and Geppetto," Jiminy Cricket added.

But Sora's gloomy expression didn't change.

"Aw, Sora, that face doesn't suit you!"

"Hmm…" Sora was lost in thought.

"If you keep makin' that face…," Goofy started.

"I know, the Gummi Ship won't run…"

"*A-hyuck*. Right! C'mon, Sora, smile!"

At Goofy's insisting, Sora got himself to smile.

"There, just like that! That'll keep the ship going!" Goofy grinned, giving him a thumbs-up.

"Yeah, you're right… Being sad won't help me find Kairi." Sora finally got up and looked out at the Other Sky from the cockpit.

"You got it, Sora!" Donald cheered.

"Sorry I had you guys worried." A little embarrassed, Sora scratched his head and moved next to the pilot seat. "Can you see the next world yet?"

"Not really. It oughta be around here, but…" Donald shot a beam to break up a space rock blocking their way. And then— "Oh no! This is real bad!"

Goofy ran flailing into the cockpit.

"What, Goofy?"

"Back there! Behind us!" Goofy pointed toward the stern and ran in circles around the cockpit.

"Well, I can't exactly look behind me when I'm—" Donald turned for a second to look at Goofy. *"Quaaack?!"*

"What's going on?" Sora turned, too, and saw another huge ship heading straight for them. "It—it—it's a pirate ship!"

"First a whale and now pirates?!" Donald pushed the control stick all the way forward, trying to get the Gummi Ship into a speed that would let them escape. But the pirate ship was still gaining on them.

"It's gonna ram us!" cried Donald. "Everybody hold tight!"

A huge impact rocked the Gummi Ship.

Aboard the pirate ship, in Captain Hook's cabin, Kairi was stretched out on the sofa. Riku stared at her hard. "So Kairi's no more than a lifeless puppet now?"

"Precisely," Maleficent replied, standing behind him.

"And her heart…"

"Taken by the Heartless, no doubt."

Riku turned to her, his fists clenched. "Tell me! What can I do?"

There was desperation in his voice. Maleficent spoke gently as if answering a child's urgent questions. "There are seven maidens of the purest heart. We call them the Princesses of Heart. Gather them together, and a door will open to the heart of all worlds. Within lies untold wisdom… There, you will surely find a way to recover Kairi's heart."

She leaned in toward Riku's downturned face. "Now, I'll grant you a marvelous gift… The power to control the Heartless."

A sickly greenish light spread out from Maleficent like a miasma and moved to envelop him.

"Soon, Kairi… Soon." Riku turned to look at her once more. She didn't even twitch, sleeping as still as a doll.

*   *   *

"Ow, ow, ow…" Sora got up, poking at the bruises he'd gotten here and there. "Donald…? Goofy?"

They must have been thrown from the Gummi Ship in different directions again.

"I can hear the ocean…"

Actually, he could hear waves all around, murmuring from every direction. He'd landed on the deck of the pirate ship. A big round moon hung in the sky, and the sea surrounding the ship was a completely different color from the brilliant turquoise waters of Destiny Island—here it was a deep blue. But the sound of the waves was the same, making Sora feel a little bit at home.

This was Neverland—the fantasyland where the dreams of children are born.

Sora walked up the deck toward the bow, and then he felt a presence behind him.

"I didn't think you'd come, Sora."

He turned to the familiar voice.

It was Riku, looking down at Sora from the bridge, the sea breeze riffling his silver hair. He smiled. "Good to see you again."

"I've missed you, too."

Riku snorted. "Really? While you were off goofing around, I finally found Kairi."

There beside him, Kairi sat—or rather, she'd been placed sitting up, like a doll. There was no strength in her posture at all, and her half-open eyes were dark and lifeless.

"Kairi!" Sora tried to run to her, but a hook thrust out to block his path.

"Not so fast. No shenanigans aboard my vessel, lad!"

Hook, the pirate captain, stood there with his shipmates.

"Riku, why are you siding with these guys?!" Sora shouted.

This isn't like Riku at all. Not the Riku I know…

"The Heartless obey me now, Sora," Riku said with a faint smile. "I have nothing to fear."

Sora gritted his teeth and glared at Riku. He had no idea what to do.

"And I've picked up a few other tricks as well. Like this, for instance…" Riku raised one hand, and Sora's shadow lifted up from the deck.

Horrified, Sora jumped back with the Keyblade ready.

"But I don't really have time to play with you. Sorry, Sora."

Then the floor opened up beneath Sora's feet, and he fell down into the hold.

"Riku…!"

Hearing Sora's shout trail off into the darkness belowdecks, Riku brushed his bangs back. "Let's get under way already. And keep Sora away from Kairi until we're ready to land," he told Captain Hook, then picked up Kairi and went back into the cabin.

"Hmph. That scurvy brat thinks he can order me around?!" the captain spat, flourishing his hook.

Smee, the first mate, sniffed with his big red nose under his glasses and said, "What shall we do, Cap'n?"

"Nothing! The hold is crawling with Heartless. Let *them* keep an eye on the brats."

"But, Cap'n, you-know-who is also down—" Smee began.

Hook held up a finger to his lips. "Shh! Did you hear that, Smee? Oh, that dreadful sound…!" He looked around with his shoulders hunched in terror.

"No, Cap'n."

"Are you quite sure? Did I imagine it?" His bold demeanor had deserted him entirely, and he grabbed Smee by the shoulders as if for support. There was one thing that he just couldn't bear. "Ohh, my poor nerves…," he moaned, shaking his head.

"Whoa!"
"*Yipe!*"
"*Quack!*"

He landed on something soft.

"Get up already, Sora!"

It was Donald's voice from under his behind. Apparently, Donald and Goofy had broken his fall once again.

"Where are we…?" Sora stood up and looked around. It seemed to be belowdecks, but there was hardly enough light to tell. They poked around impatiently, looking for a way out. Sora had to find Kairi again.

"Here's a window!" They went to the tiny window, and Sora peeked out.

"See anything?" asked Donald.

"Not really…" Sora shook his head. It was just too dark.

"This way's no good, either… The door won't open." Goofy pushed and pulled on the wooden door, but it didn't budge.

"*A-hem!*" There was a tiny cough from behind Sora. Startled, he turned, but no one was there.

"Huh…?"

"How ya doin' there? Looking for a way out?" A boy jumped out from the shadows behind some barrels. He was dressed all in green, including his cap, which had a red feather in it.

"Who are you?" Goofy said warily.

The boy puffed out his chest. "I'm the answer to your prayers!"

Donald frowned and tapped his foot, trying to decide whether the boy was friend or foe.

"But you're stuck in here, too, aren't you?" said Sora.

The boy in green burst out laughing. "I'm just waiting for someone!"

"Who?" Sora asked, and a tiny little light flew in circles around him.

"Tinker Bell, what took you so long?"

The trio stared in surprise. The little light stopped in front of the boy and took on shape—a fairy. She wore a dress, green like the boy's outfit, and her glow twinkled as she hovered closer to the boy's face.

"Great job. So you found Wendy?"

The fairy didn't seem to be speaking. But with every twinkle, she made a tiny chiming sound, and somehow the boy understood what she meant to say, as if that was her language.

"Hold on—there was another girl there, too?"

"That has to be Kairi!" Sora moved closer. "Where are they?"

The fairy fluttered her glowing wings, looking less than pleased at Sora's approach.

"Aw, Tink, don't be mad... Huh? Are you crazy? There's no way I'm leaving Wendy behind!"

Tinker Bell fluttered even more violently.

"Aha, she's a girl, too! She must be pretty jealous!" Donald whispered to Goofy.

Tinker Bell glared at him and flew right over to kick him in the bill.

"*Wak!*" Donald held his bill in both hands.

Tinker Bell glanced from the corner of her eye and covered a giggle before she flew back out of the little window.

"Hey, c'mon, Tink! Open the door!" the boy called after her, flustered, but she didn't come back.

"Aww, gee..." Sora looked at the glittering trail Tinker Bell had left in her path. "Umm..."

At a loss, the boy scratched his head, then stood up straighter and held out his hand. "I'm Peter Pan."

"I'm Sora. This is Donald, and this is Goofy. Nice to meet you!" Sora tried to shake his hand, but Peter Pan pulled back instead.

"I'm going to find Wendy. ...So we're in this together, but only until we find her, got it?" he told them a little self-importantly.

Then they heard a click.

"The door's open!"

Tinker Bell must have opened it after all. They hurried out, but a swarm of Heartless appeared practically from beneath their feet.

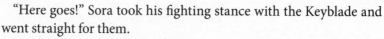

"Here goes!" Sora took his fighting stance with the Keyblade and went straight for them.

"Me, too!" Goofy followed him.

"*Fira! Thundara! Blizzara!*" Donald shot off spells as he jumped. But the shadow beneath him seemed to be crawling. "Hm? ...S-S-Sora!"

Sora looked back and saw his own shadow, which Riku had conjured before. It had a shadow Keyblade, too, with which it was attacking Donald. "*Quack! Wak!*"

The shadow's attacks were no less fast and fierce than Sora himself. It was all Donald could do to run away.

"I guess this is where I come in..." Peter Pan, who had been lingering by the door with his arms folded, launched into the air. He swooped down on Sora's shadow and dealt it a single perfect blow.

"Ha! Take that!" Again and again, he swooped at the shadow, wearing it down.

"Hey, don't take all the credit!" Seeing Peter Pan fight like that sparked Sora's competitive spirit. He made a huge leap and brought the Keyblade down on the Heartless.

"Whew..."

After defeating the Heartless, they took refuge in another room to catch their breath. Peter Pan was somehow floating above the trio's heads. Sora's shadow had apparently disappeared to escape him.

"So, uh, how come you can fly?" Goofy asked, as if he couldn't stand not knowing.

"Anyone can fly. You wanna try it?" Peter Pan alighted on the floor and held his fingers to his lips to whistle. The little sparkling light of Tinker Bell flew around them and then took shape in front of him.

"Just a little bit of pixie dust..." He held Tinker Bell by the wings and flew over the others. "There, now you can fly!"

Glittering dust fell from Tinker Bell and Peter Pan onto the trio.

"Really? For real?" Donald jumped up, flapping his arms like a bird, but belly flopped back on the floor. Sora and Goofy did the same, but one after the other, both fell again.

"See, *we* can't fly!" Donald complained. Tinker Bell hovered in front of him, twinkling with laughter.

"So how *do* you fly?" Sora and Goofy folded their arms, concentrating. Tinker Bell flew around, scattering her sparkling dust as if to tease them.

In the captain's quarters, Hook and Riku were deep in discussion.

"What?" Hook fumed. "So Wendy isn't one of the chosen ones?"

"There are seven supposedly, and Maleficent says she's not one of them," Riku replied flatly and turned away. "Hoist anchor as soon as possible. And leave all the dead weight behind, including her."

"After the trouble of capturing her?!" Hook stamped his foot. "And why those seven? What is Maleficent planning anyway?"

"Who knows?" Riku looked apathetically out the porthole at the dark sea. It was nothing like the ocean at Destiny Island. *It's not our ocean.* "As long as it means getting Kairi's heart back, I couldn't care less."

"*Hah!* You're wasting your time! The Heartless have devoured that girl's heart. I'll stake me other hand, it's lost forever."

"No. They haven't gotten her heart." He spoke quietly, unruffled.

I'll find her heart…no matter what it takes.

"Cap'n Hook…" A voice interrupted them via the speaking tube that piped into the cabin.

Hook grimaced and went to answer. "What?"

"The prisoners have escaped… And, er, Peter Pan is with them."

"Blast that Peter Pan!" Hook spat.

The boy was a particular rival of his. In fact, Hook had convinced himself, it was thanks to no other than Peter Pan that he had a hook in place of his hand.

"All right, then! Bring the hostage to me cabin, Smee. Hop to it!"

Sora and the others fought their way through the Heartless across the belly of the ship.

"So...how do we get back up above deck?" Goofy wondered. They'd searched every nook and cranny, but hadn't found a staircase or a ladder.

"This is the last room down here," said Donald. When he opened the door, Peter Pan and Tinker Bell darted through first. "Hey, wait up!"

The trio followed them into yet another dim room. Tinker Bell, glittering, stuck close to Peter Pan. "What is it, Tink?"

She flew up and paused at a grate in the ceiling.

They heard a girl's voice. "Peter? Peter Pan?"

Peter Pan flew close, putting his face right up to the grate. "Wendy!"

Now they could see a girl in a blue dress through it.

"Please hurry, Peter! The pirates are coming!"

"I'll be right up there. Just hold on!" Peter Pan looked for a way to get up to the room above.

"Wendy?" Sora called, unable to keep quiet as he stared up from the floor.

"Yes?"

"Is there another girl in there with you?"

"Oh, why, yes—but she seems to be asleep. She hasn't budged an inch..." Wendy looked back.

Trying to follow her line of sight, Sora climbed up onto a box, and then he could see Kairi's leg. "Kairi? Wake up! Kairi!"

Kairi's finger twitched. But then he couldn't see her anymore—and Wendy screamed.

"Sora! C'mon, let's get up there!"

At Peter Pan's urging, Sora scrambled atop another box and made it up through a gap in the grate on the other side of the ceiling.

"Wendy! Are you in there?" Peter Pan called, knocking on the door to the room where Wendy just was. But there was no reply.

"Is the door locked?" Sora and Goofy tried ramming it, to no avail.

"Let's find another way!" Donald ran in the opposite direction. At the same time, Peter Pan kept trying to ram the door along with Sora and Goofy.

"Hey, there's a ladder over here!" Donald shouted, and the others exchanged glances, then climbed up the ladder.

They came up into a small cabin. And there…

"Riku…" Sora stared.

Riku was holding Kairi, who was still motionless as if in a deep sleep. He stepped back without a word. The other three only watched.

"What's happened to you, Riku?!" cried Sora. "Even if you can use the Heartless to get Kairi's heart back—if you have to hurt someone else to do it, that's just going to make her sad!"

Riku only narrowed his eyes.

"Riku!" Sora called again, and then a shadow at Riku's feet slowly rose from the floor.

It took on Sora's shape. And it was coming at them.

"Augh!" His shadow knocked him back.

Riku simply walked into the pitch-black darkness that came up from beneath him and disappeared.

"Riku! Wait!" Leaning on the Keyblade, Sora got to his feet. Riku was already gone.

"Sora, we better get rid of this thing first!" said Goofy.

"But Riku—and Kairi—!"

"Sora, c'mon!"

Finally Sora shook his head forcefully, as if to get something out of it. His shadow knocked Donald into the wall. Sora faced it with the Keyblade ready.

He jumped with a furious roar and swung at the shadow. With a terrible clang, the shadow's own dark Keyblade blocked it. They had all the same strengths—they were too evenly matched. The fight could go either way.

"Don't worry, you've got backup!" Donald began to wave his wand.

"I'm gonna take care of this thing!" said Sora. "You guys go with Peter Pan and find out how to get back down to that other room!"

Sora and the shadow both knocked each other flat. But he got up again and faced it. "I'm fine! Go!"

Riku...

What Riku was doing was wrong. Hurting other people to help Kairi was wrong.

This world was in danger of being consumed by the darkness. Ignoring that to save Kairi was wrong.

I want to help her, too..., Sora thought. *I do.*

But...with our world gone, if we just save Kairi, where can we go back to? Don't we have to go back home, to our island?!

"I'm making it so the three of us will always be together."

He felt as if he'd heard Kairi's voice from somewhere.

I won't lose. This shadow won't beat me.

So Riku and Kairi and I can sit on the beach together again, talking and laughing.

I can't lose...!

Sora struck the shadow, and it collapsed on itself, sinking into the floor.

"You did it!" Goofy cheered from behind him.

Sora took some deep breaths and stared at his shadow. It crept over the floor and settled by his feet.

"Wow, not bad, Sora. You beat it all by yourself!"

"Yeah..." He sighed, a little winded, but looked at Goofy with a grin.

"Sora..." Goofy sounded a little worried.

Then Donald, who was searching on the floor along with Peter Pan, made a discovery. "I found the door!"

Peter Pan made a trapdoor in the floor spring open and flew down to the room below.

"Let's go!" The trio followed him.

"Wendy!" Peter Pan landed close to her. Wendy was on the floor, unconscious. Tinker Bell flew twinkling around him, but he waved her off. "Well, this is as far as I can go, Sora. I gotta help Wendy."

He picked her up and flew out a porthole. Tinker Bell, having been so nastily ignored, sulked and flew off somewhere else.

"Is that…it?" Goofy scratched his head.

"Should we go back to the Gummi Ship?" said Donald.

"Yeah, let's go!"

At Sora's strangely cheerful voice, Donald and Goofy exchanged glances. Just then they could hear a commotion from above.

"C'mon!"

They hurried back up above deck.

When they emerged from the hold, Captain Hook was there to greet them. "Quite a codfish, that Riku—running off with the girl without even saying good-bye."

The maritime winds howled over the deck.

"Run off where? Tell me where he went!" Sora brandished the Keyblade at Hook.

"To the ruins of Hollow Bastion, where Maleficent resides. But you won't be going there." Hook held up a glass lantern that was handed to him by Smee. Inside it was not a flame, but Tinker Bell, sparkling helplessly. "Unless you intend to leave your little pixie friend behind?"

Sora barely shook his head. Of course they couldn't abandon Tinker Bell.

"Hand over the Keyblade, and I'll spare your lives. Be glad I'm merciful, unlike the Heartless! So, which will it be? The Keyblade or the plank?" With a sweep of his hook, the pirate captain indicated the plank jutting out over the water.

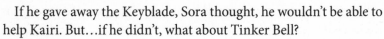

If he gave away the Keyblade, Sora thought, he wouldn't be able to help Kairi. But…if he didn't, what about Tinker Bell?

"Sora!"

He moved toward the plank as if driven that way by the Heartless. Donald and Goofy began to help him, but Hook had the point of his namesake in the lantern, at Tinker Bell's throat. "Not so fast!"

Then they heard the ticking of a watch.

"It's him! The crocodile that took me hand!" Hook peered warily into the water and jumped back. The enormous crocodile opened its mouth wide, its beady eyes fixed on the pirate.

"He's after me other hand! I can't stay here! Go away! Ah, I can't stand the sight of him! …S-Smee, you take care of them!" In a panic, Hook fled into his cabin.

The Heartless crept closer to Sora, pushing him farther out onto the plank. The crocodile waited in the water below for dinner to fall into its gaping jaws.

"Fly, Sora!" he heard Peter Pan's voice whisper. "Just believe, and you can do it!"

I can fly. If I believe.

Sora closed his eyes and jumped backward off the plank. The crocodile's jaws closed—but Sora flew up into the air.

"But, but—how could that be?!" Smee stammered. While he stood there flabbergasted, Peter Pan swooped in and snatched away the lantern.

"Peter Pan!" Sora landed beside him on the plank.

"Hey, you stuck around to save Tink. You didn't think I'd leave you all behind, did you?!" Grinning, Peter Pan opened the lantern for Tinker Bell to fly out.

"Oh no, oh no!" Smee ran away from the Heartless. They turned on Sora instead. Donald lifted his wand, and Goofy held out his shield.

"You're all going down!" With the hostage set free, Sora charged into the swarm of Heartless, and the others followed.

Now he'd defeated his own shadow—normal Heartless were no challenge to him at all. And with Tinker Bell and Wendy safe from Hook, Peter Pan had nothing to hold him back, either.

They called to one another as they fought. "Not too bad, Sora!"

"Not too bad yourself!"

"We're not so bad, either! *A-hyuck!*" Goofy took a huge leap and struck at a flying Heartless. Donald shouted, piercing the air with spell after spell.

Soon there wasn't a single Heartless left on deck.

"Now all that's left is Hook!"

Peter Pan stopped Sora from barging into the captain's quarters and instead lightly rapped at the door.

"Is that you, Smee?" they heard Hook say. "Did you finish them off?"

Peter Pan stifled laughter and held his nose to reply. "Aye, Cap'n. They walked the plank, every last one of them."

It sounded just like Smee. Sora exchanged glances with Donald and Goofy.

"Is that so now?!" Hook bellowed and burst out of the cabin past them. As he looked this way and that for Smee, who wasn't there, Peter Pan snuck up from behind with his dagger and jabbed the captain's stern.

"Yeowch!" Hook jumped around. "Pe-Peter Pan—*blast* you!"

"Ready to make a splash, you old codfish? It's your turn to walk the plank!" Peter Pan threw his dagger at Hook.

"I'll have vengeance for me left hand, you dirty brat!" He drew the sword at his hip and lunged at Peter Pan with alarming speed.

Peter Pan jumped out of the way and flew in loops above Hook's head. "Ha! Only if you can reach me!"

"And he's not fighting alone!" Sora rushed in with the Keyblade while Hook glared at Peter Pan.

Evading them, Hook was moving ever closer to the edge.

"Hah! Got you!" Sora taunted, driving Hook toward the railing until he leaned backward over the water—where he could hear the ticking sound again.

Hook shrieked in alarm. "It—it—it's him! He's here!" He shoved Sora aside with sheer force and went scurrying around the deck. Sora and the others could only stare.

"Say, Peter Pan...," Goofy called out, and the boy flew closer. Goofy lowered his voice. "Who's this fella that's got Captain Hook so scared?"

Peter Pan laughed. "Oh, it's just the crocodile—the one that's been waiting for someone to walk the plank! Hook really can't stand him."

Having run clear around the deck in panic, Hook stood wheezing. He glanced out at the water and shuddered.

"But why is he ticking?" Goofy wondered.

"When the crocodile ate Hook's hand, it was holding his precious pocket watch. So now that's in his belly, too, and when he comes close, you can hear it ticking." Peter Pan looped in the air, snickering.

"Gee, I feel kinda sorry for him," said Sora, scratching his head.

"Feel *sorry* for him?" Donald retorted. "He took Wendy and Kairi and Tinker Bell all prisoner! That's the kind of guy he is! *Fire!*" He waved his wand and set Hook's sleeve aflame.

Hook yelped, and then his rear was on fire, too, but he began to chase after Donald, swinging his sword frantically.

"*Quack! Wawawaaaak!*" It was Donald's turn to run in a panic.

"So, how tough is Captain Hook?" Goofy asked, startled.

"Hmm. I wonder..." Peter Pan shrugged. Then, with a smirk, he went after Hook again with his dagger.

"Neverland's not yours for the taking, you know!"

Hook removed his jacket to beat out the fires on it and glared furiously at Peter Pan. "Blast you, you insolent brat!"

"Why don't we finish this, Hook?" Peter Pan landed on the deck with his knife out toward the pirate.

"Perfect—except I'll be finishing *you*!" With his jacket back on, Hook made a thrust at Peter Pan. But the boy cleanly evaded and kept doing so, as he cleverly led Hook toward the plank where Sora had been driven not long before.

"Ha-ha! Over here, Hook!" he taunted, flying again.

"Why you—!" Hook leaped at Peter Pan, dramatically lunged and missed. And below him was nothing but water. "*Yaaaaargh!*"

He fell into the ocean with a tremendous splash. A single sheet of paper, having fallen from his pocket, drifted slowly after him.

"That's gotta be part of Ansem's report!" Donald managed to snatch it out of the air.

The ticking crocodile homed in on Hook, who noisily swam for his life. "Heeeeeeelp!" His howls echoed over the Neverland sea.

The waves quietly washed against the pirate ship. That sound was so familiar to Sora…

The Neverland sea was calm now, like the ocean at Destiny Island. Leaning on the balustrade, Sora stared out over the water.

"Huh," said Goofy. "Kairi couldn't wake up, so maybe she's really lost her—"

"*Sssh!*" Donald cut him off, shaking his head.

"Sora…," Peter Pan started saying from behind him.

"I still can't believe it…," Sora murmured and looked up at the starry night sky. "I really flew! Wait till I tell Kairi. I wonder if she'll believe me? Probably not."

"You can bring her to Neverland sometime! Then she can try it herself," said Peter Pan.

Sora turned to him. "If I believe, I can do anything, even fly. So I'll find Kairi. I know I will. There's so much I want to tell her…about flying, and the pirates, and everything that's happened." His eyes shone, free from doubt.

I'll believe. I won't give up.

Then Tinker Bell fluttered down, twinkling at them.

"Sora, let's go see the clock tower," said Peter Pan.

"The clock tower?"

"Tink says there's something there."

The trio took off into the air, following Peter Pan to the clock tower.

"Wendy!" Peter Pan called. She was sitting on the edge of the clock tower, gazing over the city. The enormous clock tower looked as tall as a skyscraper, with all the lights from countless buildings and houses spread out below. Each of the four walls had a great clock-face, telling the time for miles around.

Sora, Donald, and Goofy had met Wendy only briefly aboard the pirate ship. Uncertain how to talk to her, they looked at one another, until Wendy spoke first.

"Are you Sora?"

"Yeah… Er, nice to meet you, Wendy."

"And…you two must be Donald and Goofy. Peter Pan told me all about you." Wendy smiled sweetly, but then she looked a little bit worried. "What about Kairi?"

Sora shook his head.

"Oh, I see… Well, don't give up, Sora!" she said brightly, as if to dispel the bit of gloom that had come over Sora, and stood up. "Look! Isn't it such a lovely view? And thanks to this clock tower, you can tell the time from anywhere in town."

Sora stood beside her and looked down. He'd never seen a view like this before—the lights of the city seeming to cover the whole world.

Now he had another thing to tell Kairi.

He sprang back into the air and flew around the clock tower. "Huh…? The clock on this side is broken."

"Yes, it looks like only one of them is," Wendy said a little anxiously.

"I wonder if we can fix it?" Donald flew over to look at the clock-face that showed the wrong time. "Maybe it just needs a little nudge!"

He whacked the minute hand as hard as he could with his wand and managed to move it a tiny bit.

"C'mon, now!" Donald kept whaling away at it, and when he'd finally pushed the minute hand to the number twelve, the clockface began to glow. And...

"The Keyhole!" Donald flew up higher. The Keyhole had appeared on the clockface. Sora drifted closer and pointed the Keyblade at it.

A beam of light shot from the tip of the Keyblade into the Keyhole and sealed it with a click. Then something tumbled out of the Keyhole.

"Whoa!" Goofy fumbled to catch it. "It's a navigation Gummi!"

Donald soared into the sky, and just then, the clock struck twelve.

"...Peter, it's time," Wendy said and began to walk down the corridor along the tower's edge. Peter Pan flew slowly beside her. "Are you really going back to Neverland?"

"But we can see each other anytime!" He held tight to Wendy's hands. "As long as you don't forget Neverland, that is."

Sora watched them together. After a moment, he went and said, "Wendy..."

She looked up at him and smiled shyly. "As long as I don't forget... It's true. Peter will always be with me. So don't forget Kairi, either! If she remains in your heart, Sora, you're sure to find her again."

"...Yeah. You're right."

Tinker Bell flew around Donald, twinkling brightly.

"Donald, Goofy... Is it time to go?" said Sora. They soared into the sky after him.

"Okay, Peter Pan, we're off!"

"See you later, Sora!" Floating by the tower, Peter Pan waved to them. Beside him, Tinker Bell seemed a little sad.

The trio returned to the Gummi Ship.

HOLLOW BASTION
last princess

RIKU WAS IN THE LITTLE CAVE ON DESTINY ISLAND.
Sora was with him.

A memory from when they were still small…

But even though he remembered it clearly, Riku wasn't sure just how long ago this had happened.

Why had they gone into that cave?

"Hey, Sora."

"Huh?"

"When we grow up, let's get off this island. We'll go on real adventures, not this kid stuff!"

Just then, the wind blew over the hole in the ceiling and howled—the sound Sora had thought was a monster.

"Sure…but isn't there anything fun to do now?" said Sora, not minding it much. "Oh, I know! Did you hear about the new girl at the mayor's house? I heard she arrived on the night of the meteor shower…"

Riku turned to look at the door behind them. A great big keyhole had appeared on it…

A little groan escaped Riku. He couldn't even remember when that had happened. It hurt to try.

When? Right before they met Kairi—their secret adventure—when was it?

It was hard to breathe. He broke out in a cold sweat.

"That was reckless to bring her here without at least using a vessel," said Maleficent. Riku was still hunched over.

This was Hollow Bastion, Maleficent's abode—so called for its aura of vast emptiness. It was a gloomy place, as if the castle itself might be swallowed up by the darkness at any moment.

"Remember, relying too heavily on the dark powers could cost you your heart," she went on.

Just as a drop of sweat fell from Riku's forehead to splash on the floor, a low roar from somewhere echoed in the castle chapel. He shivered and stood up, but Maleficent never moved.

"A castaway... Although his world perished, his heart did not. When we took the princess from his castle, he apparently followed her here through sheer force of will." Her eyes went narrow as she smiled at Riku. "But fear not. No harm will come to you—he is no match for your power."

Riku looked up at her then. "My power...?"

"Yes—the untapped power that lies within you. Now, child, it's time you awakened that power and realized your true potential..."

Riku was enveloped in a pale greenish glow...

The Gummi Ship sped smoothly through the Other Sky. Donald sat in the pilot seat with Goofy and Sora beside him, showing the new page from Ansem's report to Jiminy Cricket.

"Let's see now..." Jiminy began to read.

> When I tracked the movements of the Heartless, I suddenly happened upon a strange door in the deepest recesses beneath the castle. It had a large keyhole, but seemed to be unlocked. So I opened the door.
>
> And behind it...was an enormously powerful core of energy. It may be the ultimate goal of the Heartless. But what could that energy be?
>
> The Heartless feed on the hearts of living beings, and they yearn for that energy core. So what is beyond the door must be a heart as well...the heart of this world itself.
>
> But what do the Heartless mean to do with the heart of the world?
>
> That night, I observed a great meteor shower in the sky. I am studying the material from the meteorites that fell. What a find! The stuff is foreign to our world—elastic to the touch, and when two pieces are brought together, they bond easily.

"He's talking about Gummis!" Donald exclaimed.

The Gummi they'd just picked up had a bouncy elasticity to it, and it would indeed easily stick to another Gummi.

"There's more," said Jiminy, who read on.

> *None of the records make any mention of such a substance. Was it introduced to this world when I opened that door?*
>
> *Our world is so small, and the space surrounding it so vast—I wonder what other strange materials are drifting out there. Could there be uncharted worlds in the skies above?*
>
> *I should stop musing on such unrealistic dreams.*
> *For now, there is no way to venture outside this world.*
> *My people and I are all but prisoners in this tiny place.*

"And that's all we have so far." Jiminy placed the new paper in his file with the piece of the report they'd picked up in Agrabah.

Sora folded his arms and cocked his head. "A door…"

"You ever seen anything like that, Sora?" asked Goofy.

"Yeah… On Destiny Island."

He thought the door in that cave was probably the same as the door that Ansem's report mentioned. When it opened, he'd been knocked back so that he couldn't really tell what was happening, but somehow, it had felt like there was something terrible on the other side.

Goofy tilted his head, too. "And the keyhole is the same as the Keyholes that we've been lockin' up."

But that still didn't tell them very much.

"It looks like there's still more somewhere," said Jiminy Cricket.

"I guess we'll have to find it…" Sora folded his hands behind his head and looked at the pilot. "Are we at Hollow Bastion yet, Donald?"

That was the place Hook had been talking about.

"Well, about that… Er, I can't find it."

"Huh?"

"There's a whole lotta nothing where it ought to be…"

"Shouldn't we ask Cid to install the new navigation Gummi?" said Goofy, holding out the one he'd caught at the clock tower.

"Sounds like that's what we have to do... But then, how'd Riku get to Hollow Bastion?" Donald frowned. It shouldn't have been possible to travel between worlds without a vessel, like the Gummi Ship or Captain Hook's pirate ship.

"...Anyway, we'd better stop back at Traverse Town," said Sora.

"Right. Off we go." Donald pulled back on the control stick and the Gummi Ship gained speed.

Riku...

Sora stared out at the Other Sky with troubled eyes.

Traverse Town was peaceful and welcoming.

When they opened the door of the Accessory Shop, Cid was puffing on a cigarette as usual. He waved. "Hey there! Sora!"

"We found another navigation Gummi!" Goofy handed him the gleaming Gummi block.

"Mm-hmm. So you'll be able to open up even more routes with this. Okay, leave it to me." Cid headed out to the Gummi Ship, leaving the trio behind in the shop.

"Gawrsh, I think we could use a break," said Goofy, yawning. "It looks like we have some time, so why don't we go over to see Aerith and those fellas?"

Beside him, Sora was lost in thought, staring at the floor.

"Sora!" Donald said urgently.

He finally looked up.

"Now just remember what Donald said to ya," said Goofy. "No frowning, no sad faces."

Sora smiled a little anxiously. "How can you be so cheerful? There's still no sign of your king... Aren't you worried?"

"Aw, phooey, we're not worried about the king," said Donald, stubborn with determination.

"He told us to go out and find the Key Bearer, and we found you,"

Goofy went on. "So as long as we stick together, it'll all work out okay! Ya just gotta believe in yourself, that's all!"

Sora closed his eyes. "Just believe…"

"*I believe in you.*"

Out of nowhere, he heard Kairi's voice. In the same moment, a strange feeling came over him.

It was a deluge of light—it led somewhere.

When was that…? It was like a dream he'd had on Destiny Island…but different.

In the midst of the dazzling light…a scene appeared.

"Where am I…?"

A little girl ran up to an old woman who was sitting in a chair. The old woman gazed fondly on the girl and slowly began to tell a story.

"*Long ago, people lived in peace, bathed in the warmth of light.*

"*Everyone loved the light. But then people began to fight over it. They wanted to keep it for themselves. And darkness was born in their hearts.*

"*The darkness spread, swallowing the light, and the hearts of many people. It covered everything…and the world disappeared.*

"*But small fragments of light survived…in the hearts of children.*

"*With these fragments of light, children rebuilt the lost world. That is the world we live in now.*

"*But the true light sleeps, deep within the darkness. That's why the worlds are still scattered, small and divided from each other. Someday, a door to the innermost darkness will open, and the true light will return.*

"*Even in the deepest darkness, there will always be a light shining within to guide you. So you mustn't give in to darkness. Believe in the light, and the darkness will never defeat you. Your heart will shine with its power and push the darkness away—the power to bring happiness.*

"*Do you understand, Kairi…?*"

"Kairi?!" Sora called out, and the old woman vanished. The much younger Kairi was looking around anxiously. There was nothing else but bookshelves full of books. Sora floated in the air behind her.

"Kairi…" He reached out to her, but she disappeared, too, as if she was only a mirage. "Huh?"

Sora came to, and he was in Cid's shop.

"What's the matter?" asked Goofy, worried.

What just happened to me? Sora thought.

"Um, nothing," he said, looking up to the sky.

Kairi, did you call to me…?

"Hey, all done!" Cid walked back into the shop. "I installed that navigation Gummi. But…are you kids actually planning on going there?" He frowned.

"You mean, to Hollow Bastion?" said Donald.

"Yeah, there. It's basically Heartless central by now." Cid folded his arms, looking grim.

"D'you know a lot about Hollow Bastion, Cid?" Goofy asked.

Cid closed his eyes for a moment and then spoke. "Well, I'm not gonna tell you not to go, but be careful. Don't say I didn't warn ya."

That was all he had to say on the matter.

"We're going," said Sora. "Riku's there…and probably Kairi, too."

"Well, all right, then…"

The trio left the shop.

"They're going, aren't they…?" Aerith stepped out from the back of the shop.

"Yeah… Never thought I'd hear the name of that place again…" Cid stared into space with his brow furrowed.

Hollow Bastion. It had once been the world where Cid and Aerith and their friends lived.

The enormous castle towered before them, surrounded by cliffs of water. Great bubbles and boulders were suspended in the air, and the place felt altogether mystical—or rather, uncanny.

This was Maleficent's abode…Hollow Bastion.

"I know this place...," Sora murmured, gazing up at the castle.

"Gee, that's funny." Goofy cocked his head. "You haven't been here before, have you?"

A castle that he couldn't have seen before, or even heard of—but somehow, he felt like he'd been here before...

"I don't know why... I feel this warmth inside, right here." Sora touched his chest. It was a warm feeling, not painful, and yet it seemed to squeeze him there tightly.

It was familiar somehow...

"Aw, you're just hungry," Donald said blithely.

"Hey, I'm serious!" Just as Sora was about to spring at Donald, a tremendous sound echoed from the watery cliffs. It almost sounded like a ferocious animal roaring.

"*Quack?!*" Donald jumped and looked around. At the moment, there didn't seem to be any Heartless here, or any people.

"Let's go!" said Sora. They climbed up to the castle by the floating boulders, heading toward the strange roar.

"No vessel, no help from the Heartless... So tell me, how'd you get here?" Riku said to the huge animal from a floating boulder.

The Beast had sharp teeth and claws, and he was looking straight back up at Riku.

"I simply believed. Nothing more to it." The purple cape over his furry body fluttered in the wind. "When our world fell into darkness, Belle was taken from me. I vowed I would find her again no matter the cost. I believed I would find her." The Beast's low, rumbling voice rose. "I will have her back!"

"Take her, if you can!"

With a vicious roar, the Beast leaped at Riku, but he nimbly dodged and countered with his sword.

Growling, the Beast fell.

"Riku! Stop!" Sora's cry rang out. Riku turned, the wind tossing his silver hair.

"So you finally made it. About time. I've been waiting for you, Sora." Riku calmly went on. "We've always been rivals, haven't we? You've always pushed me, and I've always pushed you."

"Riku…?"

"But it all ends here. There can't be two chosen ones." Riku smiled faintly.

"What are you talking about?"

"Let the Keyblade choose its true master!"

Riku reached out, and the Keyblade began to shake in Sora's grasp, as if a powerful force was pulling it away from him—then it flashed into light and vanished.

"Wha—?!"

"*Wak?!*"

"*Hyuck?!*"

The trio all shouted in shock. The Keyblade rematerialized in Riku's waiting hand.

"Maleficent was right…" Riku's fingers closed tightly around the Keyblade. "You don't have what it takes to save Kairi. It's up to me. Only the Keyblade master can open the secret door…and change the world." He lifted it high.

"But that's impossible. How can it be you…? *I'm* the one who fought my way here with the Keyblade!" Sora shouted.

Riku smiled broadly at him. "You were just the delivery boy." He lowered the Keyblade. "Sorry, your part's over now. Here, go play hero with this."

Riku tossed a wooden sword to Sora. It clattered on the ground, and then Riku walked away.

"No…" Sora fell miserably to his hands and knees.

"Come on, Goofy." Donald turned to follow Riku.

"Huh? But…" Goofy looked from Sora to Donald, the one broken-hearted on the ground and the other about to walk away. "I know the king told us to follow the key and all…but…"

Donald started walking, as if he meant to leave Goofy behind, too, in his hesitation. Goofy kept glancing at one and then the other.

"Sora…" Then Goofy helplessly followed Donald, too.

Donald's steps paused. "Sora, sorry."

And the pair left like they were running away from something.

What do I do…? What am I supposed to do now? Sora's thoughts ran. *I don't have the Keyblade anymore. I don't know what to do. Donald and Goofy went with Riku… I thought they were my friends.*

He felt like crying.

Just then the wind picked up. He heard a low growl. The Beast was trying to walk.

"Hey, don't move. You're hurt!" Sora rushed over and held out his hand, as if there were any way he could support the Beast's weight.

"Why…did you come here?" the Beast rumbled, his breathing labored. "I came to fight for Belle." He staggered to his feet again. "And though I am on my own, I will fight. I won't leave without her."

Sora looked at the wooden sword on the ground by his feet. It was just like the ones they had played with on Destiny Island.

Why did I come here…? What was I going to do?

Sora picked up the wooden sword and followed the Beast. "Me, too. I'm not gonna give up now. I came here to find someone very important to me…"

As if in response, the Beast looked up at the castle.

Pipes ran twisting all along the walls of the gloomy grand hall, wrapped in eerie silence. In the wide corridor leading to the grand hall there were six capsules, three on each side, and each capsule contained a beautiful girl. Alice…Jasmine…and the other Princesses of Heart, all gathered there by Maleficent's machinations, all seeming to be deep asleep.

And in the center floated Kairi, as if suspended there by some mysterious power.

Without even a glance at the princesses in the capsules, Maleficent stood at the entrance to the grand hall and looked back. Her black cloak billowed.

"Oh purest of hearts! Reveal to me the Keyhole!"

Beams of red light rose from each princess and met where Kairi lay. The unified beam of light shone past Maleficent, across the grand hall, to the so-called Portal to Darkness. Where the light struck the portal, a great red Keyhole appeared—and in the center floated the crystallized power of the princesses' hearts.

Sora and the Beast climbed up the steep path to the castle. It had seemed so far away before, but now they were seeing it up close. Sora stood before the gigantic gate, staring up at its towers. As if it had been waiting for them, the gate opened with a huge groan.

"Be on your guard," said the Beast. "They're close—I can feel it. Are you ready for them?"

Sora nodded and stepped inside. And then—

"Belle?!" the Beast exclaimed. In the middle of the dark corridor stood a woman in a yellow dress. The moment the Beast ran toward her, Belle's form dissolved into darkness, and only a small Heartless was left.

The Beast let out a roar of fury and launched himself at the Heartless. Then the door to the passage in front of them opened, and Sora saw Riku, Donald, and Goofy there.

"Just quit while you can," Riku said, unruffled.

"Not without Kairi!"

Riku frowned—and black fog surrounded his body. Now he was dressed in black, brandishing the Keyblade. "The darkness will destroy you."

"You're wrong, Riku. The darkness may destroy my body, but it can't touch my heart." Sora held up the wooden sword, determination in his voice. "My heart will stay with my friends. It'll never die!"

"Really? We'll just see about that!" Riku stretched out his hand and a blue-white light shot from it. Knowing it was too late to dodge, Sora closed his eyes and braced himself.

"Sora ain't gonna go anywhere!"

It was Goofy standing in front of him with his shield out. The blue-white light struck the shield and fizzled out.

"You'd betray your king?" Riku snapped at Goofy.

"Not on your life!" Goofy looked back at Sora. "But I'm not gonna betray Sora, either. He's become one of my best buddies, after all!" He gave Sora a wink and a thumbs-up, and then turned to Donald. "See ya later, Donald! Could ya tell the king I'm really sorry?"

Goofy held his shield ready toward Riku.

"Wait, Goofy!" Donald shouted. "We'll tell him together!"

He ran over to Sora, too, and aimed his wand at Riku.

"Donald…"

"Well, you know… All for one and one for all," Donald said without looking at Sora, as if he was still ashamed.

"I guess you're stuck with us, Sora," Goofy said, giving Sora an apologetic look.

"Thanks a lot…Donald, Goofy." Then Sora stared hard at Riku.

"How will you fight without a weapon?" Riku spat.

"I know now—I don't need the Keyblade. I've got a better weapon. My heart."

Sora stood up straight and earnest, and Riku snorted.

"Your heart? What good will that weak, little thing do for you?!"

"My heart may be weak. But it's not alone. It's connected to all the friends I've made!"

Tidus, Wakka, Selphie. And Leon, Aerith, Yuffie, Cid, Merlin and the Fairy Godmother. Alice, and the nameless flowers in the lotus forest. Tarzan and Jane, and Kerchak. Aladdin and Jasmine and the Genie. Pinocchio and Geppetto. Peter Pan and Wendy, and Tinker Bell, and the Beast. Everyone he'd met on this journey so far.

And…there were Donald and Goofy, and Jiminy Cricket, and the king whom he had yet to meet.

And Kairi.

All of those hearts were connected to his.

"I've become a part of their heart, just as they've become a part of mine. And if they think of me now and then, if they don't forget me… then my heart can't disappear." Sora stood ready to fight with the wooden sword. "I don't need a weapon. My friends are my power!"

The Keyblade began to shine in Riku's hand. And then the wooden sword Sora held glowed as well—and it became the Keyblade.

"No! How—?!" Riku stammered.

In Sora's hand once again, the Keyblade sparkled and shone.

"This can't be happening!"

Riku rushed at Sora with the dark sword. Sora blocked the heavy blow.

"Riku—!"

"Sora!"

That day on Destiny Island, when they'd fought with wooden swords—it seemed so, so long ago now. Riku and Sora had both become much stronger since then. Riku had the powers of darkness...and Sora held the Keyblade.

"We're gonna fight, too!" Donald ran into the fray.

"Here we come!" Goofy ran at Riku with his shield up, and Sora jumped back. Then Goofy's shield struck Riku, and Donald let loose some magic. With all the battles the trio had been through together, they had come to fight as one, completely in tandem.

And Riku was knocked back hard.

"Maybe I can't win against you alone, Riku, when you have the darkness giving you power!" said Sora. "But..."

"But he's got us, too!" Donald declared with a jump.

Riku, on his knees, grimaced and pounded the floor.

"Riku..." Sora offered a hand to help him up. But Riku only swatted it away and ran.

What happened...? Why?

Gasping for breath as he ran, Riku had only questions.

Is Sora really stronger than me...? Or is it something else?

We were always rivals. And I always won. Even if I lost, it would only be dumb luck.

Except when it was about that... About Kairi.

Maybe I'm really no match for him, after all...

"Know this." The voice came from close behind him. "The heart that is strong and true shall win the Keyblade."

"Who's there?!" Riku whirled to see a man in a dark hooded cloak, shimmering with eerie bluish light.

"The Keyblade chooses. And it will not choose one without a strong heart."

"Are you saying my heart's weaker than his?!"

"For that instant, it was."

Riku looked down in frustration. The hooded man stepped closer.

"However, you can become stronger. You showed no fear in stepping through the Door to Darkness. It held no terror for you. Plunge deeper into the darkness...and your heart will grow even stronger."

Riku shook his head. "What should I do...?"

"It's really quite simple. Open yourself to the darkness—that is all." The man slowly raised a hand toward him, and Riku's body glowed with pale green light. "Let your heart itself become all-encompassing darkness..."

Maleficent stood before the apparatus in the grand hall, gazing into the portal.

"So, the path has emerged at last." Beside her, Riku looked at it as well. His voice was somehow lower than usual. In the portal, the crystal of power shone red, illuminating them with a dismal glow.

"It will become the Keyhole to the darkness."

A multitude of pipes ran toward the portal, and in its center, darkness swirled balefully.

"Unlock it, and the Heartless will overrun this world," said Riku.

"What do I care? The darkness holds no power over me. Rather, I will use its power to rule all worlds." A hint of a smile played over Maleficent's face.

"Such confidence," Riku remarked a bit mockingly. A Keyblade as black as night appeared in his hand.

"Oh?" Maleficent marveled at the dark Keyblade. But then her voice turned angry. "Impossible!"

Nothing at all was happening to the portal.

"The Princesses of Heart are all here!" she fumed.

Riku went on staring impassively up at the portal. "A princess who's lost her heart will never be able to release her power."

Then he turned to look at Kairi, where she floated in midair. His eyes were cold and cruel.

Then a shout rang from outside the grand hall, and they could hear the clashing of weapons.

"The king's fools are here. I'll deal with them myself. You stay here and guard the princesses." Maleficent walked unhurriedly down the stairs.

As he watched her go, Riku's body glowed with blue light.

Sora and his companions stood in front of the door, catching their breath.

"This must be the deepest part of the castle..." Sora stared up at the door, gripping the Keyblade tightly. He had defeated so many Heartless to get this far. He had met so many people and seen so many strange new things.

But maybe that would all come to an end soon...

Beyond this door would be Kairi. And Riku.

Riku...

We'll get to run together across the beach on Destiny Island again. I just know it.

I don't believe that you're completely taken over by the darkness.

"Gawrsh, maybe the king'll be there, too?" said Goofy.

"I dunno...," Donald fretted. "But I bet we'll find some clues!"

Behind them, the Beast growled. "Let's go. ...Hold on, Belle..."

Sora opened the door.

A wide corridor led to a soaring chamber, the floor decorated with a rose emblem. It seemed to be the castle chapel. They walked warily inside.

And then...there was the witch.

"I'm afraid you're too late," said Maleficent, looking down at Sora. "Any moment now, the final Keyhole will be unsealed, and this world will be plunged into darkness. It is unstoppable."

"We'll stop it!" cried Sora. "After coming this far, there's no way we're gonna let that happen!"

The Keyblade in his hand shone brightly, as if all the strength of his heart poured into it with a light that would keep the world from darkness.

"You pitiful fools. You think you can defeat me? Me—the mistress of all evil!"

The floor with the rose emblem lifted up with Maleficent upon it.

"Come, my minions!" She waved her staff and Heartless emerged from the floor.

"Sora!" Donald called.

"Let's get her!" Sora rushed toward Maleficent and leaped up high, but a dragon-shaped Heartless knocked him back. "Donald, Goofy! Beast!"

"Got it!"

The other three trounced the Heartless that tried to attack Sora, and he leaped into the air again. "Now it's one-on-one!"

"Is that what you think?" Maleficent waved her staff again and cried, "Meteors of heaven, unleash thy fury!"

Balls of light rained down on Sora. With a shout of alarm, he fell from the piece of floor that held Maleficent aloft.

"Sora!" Goofy ran to him and gave him a potion.

"Well? Do you still think you can be any match for me?!" Maleficent taunted.

"We'll beat you, don't worry!" Once Goofy helped him to his feet, Sora jumped at her again.

Donald blasted away a Heartless that swooped for him. "We've made it all this way fighting together!"

"And we're not gonna lose to any darkness!" Goofy added.

The Beast roared, too, and lunged at a Heartless.

Sora swung the Keyblade at Maleficent with all his might, but she blocked his strike.

Even if she has more magic, she's not stronger. Because real power comes from caring about other people!

"I'm...not gonna lose!"

Maleficent was thrown back by Sora's power. He jumped down from the rose-crested floor and brought the Keyblade down on her.

With a terrible scream, she sank to the floor, clutching her chest.

"Did we win?!"

"No—how—could I lose!"

Darkness enveloped Maleficent, and without hesitation, Sora and the others leaped into it after her.

"...That little boy with just a Keyblade... How could he...defeat me...?" Maleficent groaned, clutching at herself in pain. Someone appeared behind her.

"Do you need any help?"

"Riku?!"

Maleficent looked up. It was the boy to whom she herself had granted the power of darkness.

"Wait, Maleficent!"

"...So, here we are all together." Riku smirked at Sora, who had followed Maleficent.

"Huh? ...Is that...?" Donald looked at the black Keyblade in Riku's hand.

"Yes. A Keyblade." Riku held it aloft. "But unlike yours, this Keyblade holds the power to unlock people's hearts. Allow me to demonstrate... Behold!"

He turned and thrust the Keyblade into Maleficent's chest.

"What— Riku?!"

Darkness surged from Maleficent where the Keyblade pierced her.

"Now—open your heart, surrender it to the darkness! Become darkness itself!" Riku called out as the darkness surrounded him.

"Riku!"

He glanced at Sora and then vanished into the dark.

Maleficent let out a high, fierce cackle as she began to glow with wicked green light. "This is it! This power! Darkness—the true darkness!"

Black energy blazed like fire, and in the midst of it, Maleficent transformed into a pitch-black dragon.

"What happened?!" cried Sora.

"...The darkness in Maleficent's heart changed her form," said the Beast. "She's become a dragon."

"C'mon, guys!" Sora rushed at the dragon, but she stomped her enormous foot on the floor. "Whoa!"

Sora lost his balance from the impact and fell, but he immediately jumped up again and struck out with the Keyblade from beneath the dragon's chin down her throat.

The dragon roared and breathed green fire. Sora barely managed to dodge.

"Hey! *Fira! Blizzara! Thundara!*" Donald pelted out spells at the dragon's head, and Goofy handed him potions to recover his magic power. The Beast made a running leap...

"Beast!"

The Beast slammed his weight against the dragon's face. While she was stunned, Sora jumped again and struck.

"Got her!"

Their glances met as they landed.

"One more time!"

Sora and the Beast both leaped into the air again and attacked. The dragon roared as if to shake the castle at its foundations and melted into a ball of darkness, which sank into the floor and vanished.

Riku reappeared, murmuring, "How ironic... She was just another puppet after all."

"A puppet...? What do you mean?" Sora demanded.

Riku turned to him. "The Heartless were using Maleficent from the beginning. She failed to notice the darkness in her heart eating away at her. A fitting end for such a fool."

Maleficent's black cloak lay tattered on the floor. Riku ground his foot into it with contempt. Darkness rose up and he vanished into it.

"Riku…" Sora stared at the dark energy that faded out after him. And there in its wake…a sheet of paper was left behind.

"It's more of Ansem's report!" Goofy hurried over but picked it up very carefully.

"…Now what do we do?" Sora said glumly.

"Well, first of all let's find Kairi!" Donald told him.

They returned to the chapel where the first battle with Maleficent had taken place and looked around.

"Hmm… It doesn't look like we can go any farther in…" Tilting his head, Goofy knocked on the walls.

If this was a dead end, there had to be other paths. They would have to backtrack and search the middle of the castle again.

But the Beast was staring at a corner of the chapel. "Belle's heart… It's here."

"Here, where?" Donald waddled closer—and the Beast rammed his fist into the wall. *"Wak!"*

The wall crumbled to reveal a passageway.

"Belle!" The Beast hurtled in, and the others followed.

The passageway led to a mezzanine overlooking the grand hall. And there were the six princesses, asleep in their capsules illuminated by white flames.

"Belle…" The Beast fell to his knees before her capsule.

"Sora! Here's Alice!"

"And Jasmine!"

Sora heard Donald and Goofy, but his glance went elsewhere, toward the enormous apparatus. Atop the stairs where all the pipes ran, there was something like an altar, where a heart-shaped gate stood.

And there—

"Kairi!" Sora ran up the steps to Kairi who was sprawled on the floor and knelt beside her to pick her up. "Kairi! Kairi, open your eyes!"

But she was totally limp in his arms, unmoving.

"It's no use." That was Riku's voice.

And yet—there was something harsh and strange in the sound of it. What had happened to him…?

"That girl has lost her heart." Riku looked down at him from atop the gate. "She cannot wake up."

"What? You…" Sora gently set Kairi back down and stood up, glaring at whatever thing had taken Riku's form. "You're not Riku."

The real Riku would never call Kairi "that girl"! he thought.

"The Keyhole cannot be completed so long as the last Princess of Heart still sleeps." Riku jumped lightly down, almost as if he floated.

"Princess…? Kairi's a princess?"

"Yes. And without her power, the Keyhole will remain incomplete." Riku brandished his dark Keyblade. "It is time she awakened."

"Whoever you are, let Riku go! Give him back his heart!" Sora readied his Keyblade, too.

"First, you must give the princess back her heart." Riku pointed his Keyblade at Sora.

"Ngh!" Sora's chest hurt… It was so heavy. He grabbed at his chest and fell hunched over.

"Sora?!" Donald called, running toward him.

"Don't you see yet?" said Riku.

"Wh…what's…" Sora groaned.

What's happening to me? Is it…something in my heart?

"The princess's heart is responding. It has been there all along. Kairi's heart rests within you!" As he said that, Riku's voice became something else entirely.

"Kairi… Kairi's inside me?"

"I know all that there is to know."

Sora lifted his face to stare at Riku. "Who…*are* you?"

"It is I, Ansem, the seeker of darkness!" Riku slowly stepped toward him.

"*Quaaack!*"

"Hey, you stay away from Sora!"

Trying to protect Sora, Donald and Goofy leaped at Riku—at Ansem—but he knocked them back and sent them tumbling back down the stairs.

"So, I shall release you now, princess. Complete the Keyhole with your power. Open the door and lead me into everlasting darkness!" He brought the dark Keyblade down upon Sora's head—

"*Sora!*"

It was Kairi's voice. He knew he had heard it.

He raised his Keyblade and blocked the stroke of the dark Keyblade.

"Forget it! There's no way you're taking Kairi's heart!"

The two Keyblades clashed.

"No matter where I go or what I see, I know I can always come back here."

Kairi's heart... Yeah. Kairi was always with me. She's been right here with me all this time.

"I'm making them so the three of us will always be together."

Riku and I lost each other. But Kairi's always been here. In my heart, along with Donald and Goofy, and all the other people I've met on the way. We aren't just connected. We're together.

That's why I won't lose!

With a huge impact, Sora sent the dark Keyblade flying from Riku's hand.

"Riku!"

For just a moment, he thought he'd seen the real Riku there—but then Riku disappeared. Sora kept calling his name, frantically looking around, but he was simply gone.

"Sora! Sora, look!" shouted Donald.

"The—the Keyhole...!" Goofy pointed. The depths of the

heart-shaped gate roiled, crackling with energy like lightning bolts. Sora raised his Keyblade at it. But nothing happened.

"It won't work! The Keyhole's not finished yet!" Goofy yelped.

"What can we do?!" Sora demanded.

Goofy looked at Kairi. "Maybe we've gotta wake Kairi up... Kairi's power...er, the last princess... Wait. If we can free her heart..."

Kairi's heart. *How can I free her heart when it's stuck in me?* Sora thought, touching his chest.

The dark Keyblade was there on the floor.

"A Keyblade that unlocks people's hearts...," Sora murmured. "I wonder..."

"Sora...?" Donald stared at him uneasily.

"You don't mean—!" Goofy started.

Sora picked up the dark Keyblade and walked over to the sleeping Kairi.

"Sora, wait!" cried Goofy, but Sora only looked at the other two and smiled.

Right... I have to open my heart.

Sora turned the dark Keyblade so he was holding it backward and unwaveringly plunged it into his own chest.

This'll set free Kairi's heart.

He let go of the dark Keyblade, and it floated up, shining blackly, and dissolved into six glowing lights. The lights scattered and disappeared into the princesses.

"Sora?! Sora!" Goofy went to him, and before his eyes, a single light emerged from Sora's chest. It drifted away and glowed above Kairi's chest before it vanished.

"Sora, where are you?"

Kairi slowly opened her eyes. In the same instant the Keyhole took its complete form.

"Soraaaa!" Donald shouted, running toward him.

Kairi caught Sora in her arms as he fell—but there was no weight, and he turned to light that sparkled and vanished.

"Sora…?"

The last glints of light in Kairi's hands floated up and faded. Donald jumped up, trying to gather them back together. "Sora! Come back, Sora!"

What's happening to me…?
Falling…falling…into darkness……

"No! He can't be— I won't let him go!" Kairi leaped to her feet.

A man's voice echoed in the grand hall. "So, you have awakened at last, princess."

Ansem.

His long silver hair fluttering, the man strode to Kairi's side.

"The Keyhole is complete—you have served your purpose. But now it's over."

"Don't make another move!" Donald glared hard at Ansem.

Ansem stopped short. "Impossible…"

Another figure appeared in front of him. Engulfed in light, Riku spread his arms as if to block Ansem from going any farther.

"Riku?!" cried Kairi.

"You've got to run!" said Riku. "The Heartless are coming!"

Kairi nodded to him and turned to flee.

"What about the Keyhole?" Goofy wondered.

"*Wak!* Let's just get out of here!" Donald followed her and so did Goofy.

A single little Heartless jumped down from the stairs, trying to follow them.

"Kairi, hurry!" Goofy called.

She stopped to look back. "But I can't leave them behind!"

Riku, who was holding back Ansem, and Sora who had disappeared…

"We can't stay here!" Donald yelled to her.

"…I know." Kairi ran down the steps that led from the grand hall to the chapel. The little Heartless trailed her.

Goofy saw it and jumped, startled. "There's a Heartless after us!"

"I'll take care of 'im!" Donald rushed at the Heartless, and shouting, he whacked it on the head with his wand a few times. But it just stayed there in a tiny huddle. "Confounded Heartless! Get lost, will ya?!"

The Heartless raised what seemed to be its face and looked straight at Kairi.

"Sora?" She had no idea why she would think that—and yet... "Sora, is that you?!"

She gazed at the little Heartless.

"Uh-oh!" said Goofy. "The rest are after us!"

Before they knew it, more Heartless had surrounded them. Donald and Goofy exchanged glances and jumped into the thick of the swarm.

"This time, I'll protect you." Kairi spread her arms to shield the little Heartless. All at once, the other Heartless pounced. She took the little one in her arms and fell, covering him, and the Heartless swarmed over her. "Sora!"

"Kairi?!" Donald and Goofy turned. They couldn't see her through the throng of Heartless.

But suddenly a brilliant light shone out and blasted the Heartless away from Kairi. They glowed and vanished.

"What's goin' on?!" Goofy yelped.

In the center of the light, Kairi stood in Sora's arms.

"Kairi... Thank you."

She opened her eyes. "Sora!"

Donald and Goofy echoed her and ran to his side. More Heartless were already closing in on them again.

"Go! Now!" It was the Beast. They thought he had stayed with Belle, but he was there roaring and scattering the Heartless.

"Beast! Come with us!" cried Sora.

"I told you before—I'm not leaving without Belle," he replied, still ready to spring at the next enemy. "Now, go! The Heartless are coming!"

"All right. Let's get out of here!" They ran, Sora holding tight to Kairi's hand.

FRAGMENTS

THE PATH WENT ON THROUGH THE UNENDING DARKNESS.

He couldn't see what lay ahead. There was no light anywhere.

"Sora, Kairi... I'm sorry..."

A lone boy walked the winding path—Riku. To either side, everything disappeared into darkness, but maybe, if he kept going, there would be a way out.

"Is this the afterworld?" he wondered. Behind him, there was no path, only an expanse of darkness. He stumbled in his exhaustion. "I'm not ready. Not yet. Not until I see Sora and Kairi one last time..."

Pale bluish light surrounded him.

"Riku, can you hear me? I'll be there soon."

"Who's that?" Riku turned, but no one was there. Nothing but more darkness.

"I have the other Keyblade—the Keyblade from this side."

He kept looking around. There was nobody else here—and yet he was hearing someone's voice.

"I've been trying to get through to you. But the darkness in your heart kept me away."

"Who are you?" Riku said into the darkness. "What's happened to me?"

"Your heart overcame the darkness. But it was too late for your body. That's why your heart is here—in the place of darkness where hearts are gathered."

"So what do I do?" he asked, gazing down the dim path.

"The Door of Darkness will open soon...but it's a door we can't enter. It has to be closed from both sides. To do that, we need two keys and two hearts. Maybe we were both destined to come here, to close the door."

"Destined, huh? You seem to know everything." Riku went on talking to the invisible voice in the dark. "So tell me—are Sora and Kairi okay?"

"Don't you feel the echoes of their hearts? But how you perceive them...that depends on what's in your heart."

Riku closed his eyes. Behind his eyelids he saw Sora...and Kairi.

I'm not wrong... Now I know I wasn't.

"Thank you...," Riku murmured, almost a whisper.

HOLLOW BASTION
toward light

THE GUMMI SHIP WAS GLIDING ALONG AGAIN THROUGH the Other Sky.

"I wonder if Riku's okay…," said Kairi, gazing fixedly out the window.

"I bet he's fine," Sora replied. "He's pretty tough."

"…Yeah, you're right." Kairi nodded.

Sora stood behind her, looking out the same way. "Hey, Kairi… Have you ever seen anything like this before? The first time I was on this ship, I was thinking how I wanted you and Riku to see it."

Kairi put her hand up to the window. Whether they were stars or just pieces of drifting space rock, all the things out there sparkled. A view they'd never seen before—that was what she and Sora and Riku had wanted to see back on Destiny Island. "It's so beautiful…"

Suddenly the Gummi Ship rocked.

"Quack!"

"What happened, Donald?" Goofy went up by the pilot seat.

Jiminy Cricket looked uneasy, too. "Heartless, all the way out here!"

The Gummi Ship fired its lasers and shot down the Heartless floating out in space. In the places where there had been asteroids or mysterious blocks in the way, now there were new kinds of Heartless. They came at the Gummi Ship with their big mouths gaping open.

"Wak! Hold on, everyone!" shouted Donald. "It's full speed ahead, Traverse Town or bust!"

The Gummi Ship accelerated and zoomed away.

They landed once more in Traverse Town.

"Hi, Aerith, we're back!"

As if she had known Sora and his companions would be returning, Aerith was there to greet them in the First District town square. "Welcome back…Sora. And you must be Kairi?"

Kairi nodded.

"So you found her." Aerith smiled.

"Yeah. But Riku…" Sora looked down and bit his lip.

"He'll be all right. I'm sure he will."

"I guess so…" Sora fell quiet.

Goofy jumped up behind him. "Oh yeah! Aerith, that Ansem feller's report you were talkin' about—we found it!"

"Really? That is good news!"

"Jiminy's got all the pages!" Donald crowed, like he was making himself sound more excited for Sora's sake.

"Jiminy?" said Aerith.

"Oh—I guess we haven't introduced him. He's our friend!"

In reply, Jiminy jumped up out of Donald's pocket. "How do you do, Aerith!"

"Nice to meet you…Jiminy."

From his perch on Goofy's shoulder, Jiminy politely doffed his hat.

"What a wonderful friend!" Aerith crooned. Goofy and Donald nodded brightly. Beside them, Kairi quietly looked at Sora.

They went with Aerith to the Second District hotel. Leon and Yuffie were already in a room, waiting for Sora.

"Welcome back, Sora!" Yuffie grinned.

"Hi, Yuffie. It's good to be back…"

"So you found Kairi, huh?!"

"Yeah." Sora looked at Leon, who was leaning back against the wall with his arms folded and his eyes closed. "Hi, Leon."

"Tell me what happened."

"Okay…" Sora and the others began to recount all that had taken place at Hollow Bastion.

Leon sighed. "So the darkness is flowing out of that Keyhole…"

"And there are more and more Heartless everywhere," said Goofy. "It sure looks like that's why."

"And the only way to stop them…," Aerith began, gloomily looking at Sora.

He held up the Keyblade. "Seal the Keyhole, right?"

"Maybe," said Leon. "But no one knows what will happen once it's sealed."

"Well, we can't just stay here," Sora protested. "We have to do something. I've got a friend back there!"

Riku was still there. He had to be.

"That's right…," Leon agreed. "And Riku's Keyblade must have been born of the captive princesses' hearts—just like that Keyhole you saw."

"But my heart…was missing." Kairi clasped her hands over her chest.

"Then it must have remained incomplete," Leon went on. "And once that Keyblade was destroyed, the other princesses' hearts should have been freed."

"Then the Beast and Belle must be together again!" Donald said with a bit of cheer.

"Maybe Jasmine and Alice are awake, too," Goofy wondered.

"But I thought…that the Keyhole would make the darkness stronger," Aerith added. "I mean, it is strong, but still…it ought to be stronger now."

"The other princesses are probably staying in the castle, holding the darkness back," said Leon.

Sora and Kairi looked at each other. The princesses staying in the castle…?

"We've gotta help them!" said Donald.

"If anyone can, it's you." Leon nodded to them firmly.

"Oh, that's right…," Aerith remembered. "We haven't read Ansem's report yet!"

Jiminy Cricket hopped up and handed her the pages.

"We just found that page in Hollow Bastion," said Donald, peering over Aerith's shoulder.

"I'll read it." Aerith began.

> *Simply astonishing! Today, I had a guest from another world. He is a king, and his vessel is built from the material that composed the meteors.*

"That's *our* king!" Donald leaped up.
"There's much more," Aerith said.

> *He had much to tell, and we talked for many hours, but one story in particular caught my interest—that of a key called the "Keyblade."*
> *It is said to hold phenomenal power. One legend says its wielder saved the world, while another says that he wrought chaos and ruin upon it. I must know what this Keyblade is.*
> *A key opens doors.*
> *It must be connected to the door that I have opened.*

"So the king's met Ansem!" The news about King Mickey had Donald and Goofy in higher spirits.
"And he knew about the Keyblade!"
"We heard about it from the king, too," said Aerith.
"...Gawrsh, I wonder where he went." Goofy cocked his head.
They'd been to more than a few worlds by now, but they still hadn't found the king. Could there be other worlds that they simply couldn't reach?
"There are only more and more questions," said Aerith.
"But there are some things we know," Sora replied. "We know what we have to do."
He looked at Kairi and nodded.
Yuffie took a step closer to him. "You have to go back to Hollow Bastion, Sora."
"We will!" Sora said emphatically.

"But the route was jammed with Heartless—they'll wreck our ship before we ever make it!" Donald kicked at the floor.

"And we didn't find any new Gummi blocks, either…," Goofy sighed.

"Talk to Cid," said Leon. They nodded to one another and left the hotel for Cid's shop.

"Hollow Bastion, huh…?" Yuffie murmured, watching Sora go, and then she looked to Leon. "You know, I can hardly remember it."

After a moment, Leon pointed out, "Well, it's already been nine years."

"I wonder how they're all doing…," Aerith said softly, turning her gaze out the window to the night sky.

"There you are, Sora," said Cid with his elbows on the counter.

Sora stood at the counter and looked up at him. "We need to go back to Hollow Bastion."

"But the route's like a traffic jam of Heartless! Can't you do anything, Cid?!" Donald demanded, jumping up and down.

"Pretty sure doing something about a Heartless traffic jam would be a job for you guys," Cid retorted.

"*Wak!* Well, what *are* we supposed to do?!" Donald stamped his webbed foot.

"It's a chicken-or-egg problem, huh?" Cid rubbed his chin. "Let's see now…"

"There must be some way," said Sora.

"Simple. You gotta go around instead of through." Cid leaned his elbows on the counter again, as always, and looked straight at Sora. "Install a new navigation Gummi and take a new route."

"But we don't have any new navigation Gummis!" said Donald.

"I know, I know…" Cid shrugged to Donald and turned back to Sora. "Go to the secret waterway, Sora. There's a nav Gummi down there."

Goofy perked up. "Really?!"

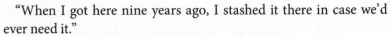

"When I got here nine years ago, I stashed it there in case we'd ever need it."

"Nine years ago…?" Kairi spoke for the first time.

"That was when we escaped from Hollow Bastion and ended up here."

"So that means Hollow Bastion is…" Goofy exchanged glances with Donald.

"It's our home world." With his eyes half-closed, Cid went on with gravity in his voice. "Never thought a kid like you would be the one to need that nav Gummi."

"I'm not a kid!" Sora pouted.

"You mean, you're not *just* a kid?" Cid grinned and winked at him. "You go and get that Gummi. I'll do a little maintenance on the Gummi Ship for ya, and the king's men here can be my assistants."

"Aye-aye, sir!" Donald jumped up and saluted.

"Go on now. And take Kairi."

"Okay! Let's go, Kairi." Sora took her hand, and they went to the underground waterway.

Shielding Kairi, Sora fought through the Heartless in the Second District, and they ran into the secret waterway.

It was deserted and dim, but the murals on the walls gave off a soft glow.

"Places like this are always kind of exciting, huh?" said Kairi, looking up at the murals.

"It's like that cave back on our island!"

"Yeah… Look at this mural. It's almost hypnotizing, isn't it?"

The painting of the sun seemed to gaze down on them with a mysterious warmth. As Sora walked closer, the sun began to shine.

"Wow…it's so pretty!" Kairi gazed at it, wide-eyed. A beam of light fell into Sora's hand, and the sun changed into a crescent moon.

The light that fell into his hand was a Gummi block.

"Is that a Gummi?" asked Kairi.

"Yeah. We'd better hurry up and take it back to Cid."

Kairi looked up again at the moon. "A light deep within the darkness…"

"Oh, your grandma's story, right?"

"Sora, how…? Oh, that's right. We were together all along."

He smiled at her. "You know what's funny? I looked everywhere for you, but you were with me the whole time. But finally we're together again, Kairi." Then his smile faded a little. "Now it's time to get Riku back."

"You think it'll ever be the same again between us?" She looked down, too, and her voice was small. "Riku's lost his…"

"He'll be okay! I turned into a Heartless, and you saved me, right?"

Lost in the darkness…I couldn't find my way. I was stumbling along, and I started forgetting things…my friends, who I was. Even inside my head, it was dark. The darkness almost swallowed me. But then I heard Kairi's voice…and it brought me back.

Sora gazed straight at her. "So here we are, thanks to you."

"I didn't want to just forget about you, Sora. I couldn't!"

"…I guess that's what it means, that our hearts are connected. The light from our hearts broke through the darkness… I saw that light, and that's what saved me."

Kairi nodded. *Whatever happens, wherever we go, our hearts are connected, Sora.*

She recited a line from her grandmother's story. "No matter how deep the darkness, there will always be a light shining within."

"I guess it's more than just a fairy tale."

"Well, let's go and save Riku!" she said, determined. But Sora shook his head.

"You can't go."

"Why not?"

"Because it's way too dangerous."

"C'mon, Sora. We made it this far by sticking together. You can't go alone!" Kairi shot back.

I just want to go with you, she thought.

"Kairi, even if we're apart, we're not alone anymore. Right?"

At Sora's earnest look, she smiled brightly and put her shoulders back. "I can't help?"

"Well, you'd kind of be in the way."

"Okay. You win," she relented and took something out of her pocket. "Take this."

It was a charm made of thalassa shells, five of them tied together in the shape of a star.

"I'm making them so even if one of us gets lost, we'll make it back here safe and sound. ...So the three of us will always be together."

"It's my lucky charm. So you *have* to bring it back to me!" she said, teasing a little, leaning over the charm in his hand.

"Don't worry. I will." Sora closed his fingers over it.

"Promise?"

"Promise," he said solemnly, looking into her eyes.

"Don't ever forget, Sora. Wherever you go, I'm always with you."

"I know."

The moon in the mural gleamed down on them.

The Gummi Ship launched into the Other Sky.

"Sora, did you get to say bye to Kairi?" Goofy asked quietly.

Sora was looking out the rear windows at Traverse Town receding behind them. "Yeah. I told everyone good-bye."

"But Cid just said, 'See ya!'...didn't he?" Donald remarked in the pilot seat. "Doesn't that mean he thinks we'll be back there?"

"I guess so..."

Then one of the instrument lights in the cockpit began to blink.

"There's a new warp hole near Traverse Town!"

The engineer from Disney Castle was contacting them. "Chip! Are you guys all right?"

"Sure we are! Queen Minnie and Daisy are just fine, too!"

Chip's cheerful voice squeaked through the cockpit.

"But…why the sudden radio, then?" Donald said into the communicator.

"You know there are more Heartless suddenly appearing in all the worlds, right? So Dale and I thought maybe something funny was going on in the Other Sky, and we looked into it. We were hoping we might find out something to help you!"

"Gee, thanks!" Goofy called toward the communicator. Then they could hear a lady's voice over the speakers.

"Donald, Goofy? Do you copy?"

"Your Majesty!" It was the queen. Donald and Goofy both stood up ramrod straight.

"More and more stars are disappearing from the sky. The king must be terribly worried, too. Please, help the king and the Key Bearer save the worlds…"

"You can count on us!" said Goofy, and then the communicator lost the signal.

"Aw, nuts," Donald grumbled. "We got cut off…"

"What was that…?" asked Sora.

"A top-priority message from our castle!" Goofy replied. "And we promised after we find Kairi and Riku and the king, we'd have everyone over to the castle, right?"

"Yeah! You've gotta meet Queen Minnie and Daisy, too!" Donald added.

"We can do it, Sora!"

"We'll be able to go back and see everyone in no time!"

"Yeah…!" Sora agreed, and the Gummi Ship plummeted into the warp hole.

Hollow Bastion loomed against the bleak sky. The trio looked up at the castle and then at one another.

"Let's go!" said Sora.

"Right!" Donald and Goofy nodded, and as they did, Heartless sprang out of the ground.

"*Quack!*" Donald jumped.

"Gawrsh, there really are a lot…"

"Well, we have to go!" With his Keyblade up, Sora ran.

"Hey, Sora…," Goofy said, even as he slammed into Heartless with his shield. "What if these Heartless are like you were, and they're all somebody from somewhere, people who just lost their hearts and got changed into Heartless?"

"Maybe…but we can't let anything stop us right now."

"That's right! We're not gonna lose!" Donald shot off spells at them, and then they heard a roar.

"Beast!" He had chosen to remain behind at Hollow Bastion, and now he appeared above them at a higher foothold.

"You may need my strength," he growled and rushed at the Heartless.

Still swinging the Keyblade, Sora asked, "Where's Belle?"

"Still in the castle." The Beast glanced up at the castle from the corner of his eye and knocked aside a Heartless.

"Not because the Heartless got her?!" said Goofy, giving Donald a magic-recovering potion.

"No. She stayed for a reason. The other princesses are with her as well." The Beast crouched at the castle gate, catching his breath.

"I wonder why?" said Donald.

"Well, let's go ask them." Sora stared up at the gate.

When he'd entered this castle before, Donald and Goofy hadn't been with him. But now they were all together with the Beast, too.

They'd be okay. There was no way they could fail.

They opened the gate to Hollow Bastion—the castle of emptiness.

No matter how many Heartless they defeated, more rose up to take their place. Sora and the others fought with all their might to get through the castle. But at least they wouldn't get lost—they'd been here before.

"Sora, this way!" called Donald, waving his wand.

"Wait, just a second, Donald!"

"But the Beast already went on ahead!"

"By himself?!"

Scattering Heartless as they went, the trio hurried to the door through which the Beast had vanished. *It should lead to the library,* Sora thought.

"Beast!" They ran through—and there, the Beast and Belle were together in a warm embrace.

"*Wak!*" Donald covered his eyes but peeped out at them through his fingers.

"Beast..." Belle gazed up at him, smiling, then turned to the others. "You've come to seal the Keyhole, right?"

She gently let go of the Beast and moved closer to them.

"Belle... It's really dangerous here," said Sora, looking up at her. "Why are you staying?"

"We've been holding back the Keyhole with our own power. But... we can't hold out much longer."

"We'll take care of it!" Sora said resolutely.

"...We should go to the grand hall, then. Quickly. The other princesses are watching over the Keyhole." Belle touched Sora's shoulder.

"Sora, let's go," said Goofy.

"Right!" Sora nodded, and they headed back into the depths of Hollow Bastion to the grand hall.

The six princesses gathered in the grand hall, standing around the Keyhole.

"You're here at last! We've been waiting for you, Keyblade master." A woman in a beautiful white gown greeted them. "I'm Cinderella. My world has already disappeared."

Cinderella looked down sadly.

"Where's Ansem?"

At Sora's question, the princesses all exchanged a glance, and a woman in a low-cut blue dress stepped forward. "My name is

Aurora. Ansem is no longer here. When the Keyhole appeared, darkness poured out… It swallowed Ansem, and he disappeared."

"Disappeared…?"

Aurora looked grim.

A black-haired girl in a yellow skirt picked up the explanation. "Ansem may be gone, but the flood of darkness hasn't stopped. We're working together to hold it back." She looked up at the Keyhole.

"What's your name…?"

"Oh, how silly of me. I'm Snow White. My world is gone, too…"

"I cannot forget the look on his face…" Aurora's brows knit tighter. "As the darkness engulfed him, he was smiling."

"Sora! Please hurry!" That was Jasmine, the princess of Agrabah. "The darkness is going to escape the Keyhole."

"It's all we can do, just to hold it back," Alice added fearfully.

"And we can't manage for much longer…" Snow White shook her head.

"All right." Sora nodded. "We're on our way."

"In the meantime, we'll do what we can, too." Snow White smiled at him.

"That Keyhole manifested through our power, they say, but in fact, I still find it hard to believe," Cinderella remarked. "I never knew I had any power like that. I think the other princesses feel the same way, too."

"I never thought I'd be wielding a Keyblade, either."

"I suppose it's like that…" Cinderella nodded.

"I'm so glad that we have one another here," said Aurora. "If the Keyhole had only needed one princess, how terribly lonely it would be for her."

The princesses looked at one another then, each smiling in her own way.

"You helped me during that silly trial, Sora," Alice said brightly, stepping closer to him. "So now, it's my turn to help everyone else!"

"Yeah! What an awful trial that was!" Donald added, and Alice laughed.

Then Snow White spoke. "Sora… There's someone very dear to me, but I just don't know what happened to him. So I want to protect this place. I don't want to see any more worlds disappear."

"Me, too," Sora replied. "I can't stand the thought of any more worlds disappearing or any more people getting swallowed up."

Snow White smiled, but her eyes shone with tears.

"I have the Beast here with me, but we want to go home to our world…" Belle looked at him, too. "Please, Sora."

"I'm worried about Agrabah… But I'm sure Aladdin will be all right, whatever happens." Jasmine closed her eyes as if remembering the desert city.

"*A-hyuck!* It'll all be okay!"

"*Wak!*"

Goofy and Donald tried to cheer up Jasmine, then looked at Sora. "We'd better get going."

"Right!"

Sora climbed the stairs and stood in front of the heart-shaped gate. The Princesses of Heart were facing it and praying. He stepped through the gate…

"There's the Keyhole!" Donald pointed to a heart in a strange emblem at the back of the room.

"Yeah…" Just as Sora lifted the Keyblade, something made the Keyhole vibrate uncannily.

"*Yipe!* Something's here!" Goofy jumped and clung to Sora. Darkness flowed out from the Keyhole and from it came an enormous Heartless—the Behemoth. It was like a huge, ferocious bull, with two long horns, and when it roared, they were surrounded with purple flames.

"Here we go!"

"Right!" Sora gripped the Keyblade. He wouldn't let anyone stop him—or anything.

Until he saw Kairi again…and brought Riku back.

Until everyone was home in their own worlds… Until they were home on Destiny Island.

"Donald! Goofy!" he called. He was fighting for these friends, too. And he wouldn't lose.

Light flashed out from the Keyblade and struck the Behemoth. Donald fired magic into its mouth, and behind him, Goofy helped them with potions—it was their surefire strategy.

"Got 'im!"

The Behemoth let out a final roar, slowly turned into light, and faded away.

"Now let's lock up that Keyhole!" said Goofy.

Sora pointed the Keyblade at the Keyhole in the heart emblem. A beam of light shot into it from the tip of the Keyblade, and they heard a resounding click.

"We did it!"

The heart emblem began to shine, and the Keyhole disappeared. The trio went back out to tell the princesses that the portal was closed.

"Huh…?" Donald cocked his head. They had emerged, not into the grand hall, but some mysterious chamber they'd never seen before. Clinging mist obscured their sight.

"Where are we?" Sora murmured. And a strange sensation came over him—it was almost as if someone else had passed through his body.

"Ah, it seems you are special, as well."

The voice came from behind him. Sora whirled around. "Who's there?!"

A man stood there in a deep black cloak with a hood that hid his face. Sora couldn't even tell whether it was a person in that cloak or a Heartless.

"Ansem…?" Goofy raised his shield.

"That name rings familiar…"

On their guard, the trio glared at the strange figure.

"You remind me of him," he said.

"What's that supposed to mean?!" Sora demanded.

The man looked calmly down at him from beneath his hood. "It means you are not whole. You are incomplete. Allow me...to test your strength."

He seemed to glide over the ground instead of walk as he moved closer to Sora, and light erupted from his raised hand.

"Whoa—!" Sora was knocked back hard.

"Sora!" Goofy tried to run to him, but two swords flew at him and sent him sprawling.

"*Firaga! Thundaga! Blizzaga!*" Donald pelted out his spells, but each barrage of magic disappeared when it neared the mysterious figure's cloak.

"Impressive. This will be enjoyable..."

"What're you talking about...?!" Sora shouted, jumping up.

"It is beyond your comprehension for now. We will meet again."

"Who *are* you?!"

"I am but an empty shell." As if he were made of smoke, the man vanished without a trace.

Then, as Sora still stood ready to fight, a familiar voice spoke from behind him. "Good work, Sora."

They turned to see Leon standing in front of the heart-shaped gate, resting the Gunblade on his shoulder.

"We're back...?" Sora said, confused.

"What happened?" Leon asked.

"Never mind, it's nothing... What are you guys doing here?"

"We came in Cid's ship!" Yuffie replied from her perch on the banister.

"This was our childhood home," said Aerith. "We wanted to see it again."

Leon glanced around dismally. "It's in worse shape than I feared. It used to be such a peaceful place..." His gaze fell.

"Don't worry. If we defeat Ansem, everything should be restored." Aerith tried to comfort Leon, then looked at Sora. "Your island, too…"

"Really?"

Aerith nodded, smiling.

Yuffie jumped down from the banister and said sadly, "But…it also means good-bye."

"Once the worlds are restored, they'll all be separate again…" Aerith looked down.

"Then I'll just visit you guys with the Gummi Ship!" Trying to be cheerful, Sora ran to Yuffie's side.

"It's not that simple," said Leon.

Sora turned to him. "Why not?"

"Before all this, no one knew about the other worlds, right? Every world was isolated, divided by unseen walls." Aerith looked expectantly at Leon.

"The Heartless destroyed those walls," Leon went on. "But if the worlds return, so will the walls."

"Does that mean we won't be able to fly in the Gummi Ship?!" Donald exclaimed, running up to Leon as if he might argue the point.

"It'll be useless."

Hearing Leon's curt words, Sora bit his lip. "So you're saying we'll never…" He couldn't finish the sentence. His shoulders drooped.

Donald and Goofy looked at Sora miserably.

"You won't be able to come visit Disney Castle…"

"And we won't get to go to the beach at Destiny Island…"

"We may never meet again," Leon told them, "but we'll never forget each other."

"No matter where we are, our hearts will bring us together again." Aerith smiled sweetly.

"Besides," said Yuffie with a grin, "I couldn't forget you even if I wanted to."

"Hey, what's that supposed to mean?!"

She laughed and ran to the other side of the hall, as if she had to flee from Sora.

"Thank you, Sora. I think the darkness is getting weaker now," said Alice, spreading her hands.

"But be careful..." Jasmine looked around nervously. "I can feel something huge and sinister... Ansem..."

"It's the heart of the darkness," said Aurora. "It must be where he went."

"Then we'll take the Gummi Ship there and deal with Ansem and the Heartless," Sora said resolutely.

"An answer worthy of the Keyblade master." Cinderella smiled.

"Sora... There's one more thing I want to tell you." Aerith looked terribly serious.

"...Aerith?" he said anxiously.

"The last page of Ansem's report. I found it in the library."

"So you found the whole thing?" Sora took the stack of pages she handed him, still looking straight at her.

"Ansem disappeared when this world fell to the darkness. We all thought that he died defending people from the Heartless, but..."

Goofy finished for her. "But Ansem was the one who brought 'em here, wasn't he?!"

"That's right. Even though he was known as a sage..." Aerith looked down, troubled.

"Say, Aerith, could you read the rest of the report for us?"

"All right..." She took the pages and began.

Opening the door to a world's heart causes its walls to crumble. The fragments are seen as shooting stars. The material known as Gummi blocks are in fact pieces of those walls, which surround the worlds.

Supposing that the appearance of the Heartless is the cause of the walls collapsing…then I cannot allow that key, called the Keyblade, to close the doors.

I will be unable to see the hearts of the worlds.

If the princesses and the Keyblade are connected, they should resonate. I have chosen a particular girl to send off into the Other Sky and observe.

"Is this…about Kairi?" Sora murmured.

"The hearts of the worlds…? Gawrsh, what could that be?" Goofy wondered.

"It's probably the world's core, which Ansem was trying to reach," Aerith replied.

"But what's there?"

"Wait. I'll keep reading."

Just as people have hearts, so do worlds. Each one of the stars scattered in the night sky is a world, and deep within each world lies a door to its heart.

The Heartless come from people's hearts, as does the darkness. And the Heartless seek to return to a greater heart.

The core of a world's heart—even I cannot know what might be found in such a place. I must find out. There I will pursue the answers to these mysteries, the mysteries of the heart. And when I encounter the world's heart, I will become all-knowing.

My path is set. My body is too frail for such a journey, but I must do this. I will cast it off and ascend…I will plunge into the depths of darkness.

"Ansem abandoned his own body for the sake of his research…," Aerith murmured.

"That's *weird*!" Sora blurted. "He was only doing all that for himself anyway!"

"That's true... And then he opened the door." Aerith mournfully lowered her gaze.

"We'll close it, Aerith!"

"I hope so...," she said with her hands clasped, like she was praying.

"Please, Sora. Your courage can bring back our worlds." Snow White bowed her head.

"Once the darkness is gone...everything should go back to the way it was before," Cinderella added.

Leon looked down at Sora. "Just like we were able to come back to Hollow Bastion... You'll all have your worlds to go back to."

"Then our island... Will Kairi be back there?"

The blue sea...the blue sky. He missed Destiny Island so much.

"Of course!" Cinderella said sweetly.

"But... We can't go home until we've found Riku and the king. Right, guys?" Sora turned to Donald and Goofy.

"Right! 'Cos we're gonna bring them back!"

"We sure will!"

The three nodded to one another and then set off for the core of the world.

CHAPTER
11

END OF THE WORLD
another key

THERE WAS THE CORE OF THE WORLD. THE PLACE where darkness gathered, the deep darkness that sought to consume everything.

"...So Ansem must be there somewhere." Sora stared out at the darkness floating in the distance.

"The king's probably there, too," said Donald, gripping the control stick tighter.

"And Riku," Goofy added.

The journey they'd set out on in search of people had become a journey to save them—and to save the worlds. And of course they hadn't given up on finding the ones they searched for, but now the trio were of one mind—one heart.

"Don't forget about me now!" said Jiminy Cricket, perched on Donald's hat.

"'Course not!" Sora replied. "We've come all this way together!"

"But from here on out, it's only gonna get more dangerous," said Donald, trying to look up at Jiminy. "So you better stay hidden!"

"Right. I won't come out, unless you need me." Jiminy slid back into Donald's pocket.

"Let's go, Donald!" said Sora, and Donald pulled on the control stick. The Gummi Ship plunged into the darkness.

They emerged from a small cave into a mysterious boundless space. The lavender sky seemed to go on forever, an eerie color hinting at twilight, as if the sun had just set.

"Can we walk here...?" Donald tiptoed out, and the surface beneath him rippled like water, but it wasn't. It was like they had to walk atop nothingness.

"There's something off in the distance," said Sora, staring at the far-off shape. Something out there floated like a cloud, and stone pillars stood in a line.

"Gawrsh, is this all that's left of the worlds the Heartless destroyed?" Goofy squinted a little at where Sora looked.

"Those worlds will be restored if we beat Ansem, right?" said Sora.

"You betcha!" Donald replied, unquestioning.

We have to believe if we're going to beat Ansem, Sora thought. *But...*

"If we do beat him and the restored worlds are all disconnected, what's gonna happen to this place? And to us?"

"Well, uh..." Donald folded his arms, thinking.

This was the world of the Heartless, made of the fragments of shattered worlds. So what would happen if this world itself disappeared?

"...Maybe we'll just disappear," Goofy said reluctantly.

Sora looked at him uneasily.

"But no worries," Goofy went on, trying to bolster his spirits. "Even if this place goes poof, our hearts ain't goin' nowhere. I'm sure we'll find our pals again. Yup, I just know that we will!"

"Yeah. You're right." Sora nodded and opened his hand. There on his palm was Kairi's thalassa shell charm.

I know it. Because we believe.

Peter Pan showed me that if I believe, I can fly.

Aladdin showed me that I've got to keep my promises, no matter how hard it is.

And Tarzan showed me that I'm with friends I can really believe in. Everyone's taught me so much. Our hearts are connected.

So I'm going to give it back, no matter what. I'll come back, no matter what, Kairi.

Sora put the charm in his pocket and started to walk. Donald and Goofy followed him.

"I guess we should just head for that cloud, huh?"

"Sounds about right..."

Then the Heartless appeared.

"This'll be the last of 'em! C'mon!" Goofy raised his shield.

Sora nodded and flung himself at the Heartless.

*   *   *

In that lavender space that looked like it would never end, finally they came to the stone pillars they'd seen before.

"Is this where we're supposed to go…?" Donald worried. Then an uncanny dark sphere appeared in front of them, glowing with black energy.

"That's…," Sora began.

Goofy looked back at him. "Sora, have you seen one of these before?"

"Yeah—look out!"

"*Waawawaaaak!*"

In front of Donald there was a Heartless like a huge bull.

"Didn't we beat this fella back in Hollow Bastion?!" cried Goofy.

It was the same as the Heartless that had appeared when they went to close the Keyhole in Hollow Bastion—the Behemoth.

"So, we can do it again! C'mon!" Sora rushed in and leaped up to strike it under the chin with the Keyblade.

"*Wah-hoooey!*" Goofy jumped at it.

"*Fira!*" Magic shot from Donald's wand. They were definitely hurting it.

"Here goes!" Sora ran up behind it and climbed up onto its back and dealt a heavy blow on top of its head. It let out a terrible roar.

"Piece of cake!" Donald puffed out his chest. The Behemoth turned to light that floated up into the sky. A crack appeared in the enormous stone in front of them.

"Gawrsh… Where could Ansem be?" Goofy wondered.

"Maybe if we jump into this crack we'll find him." Donald looked down into it. He could see a hole at the bottom where light poured out.

"Let's go!" Sora went ahead and jumped into the fissure. It was a dark cave with strange rock formations here and there—and all sorts of colorful Gummi blocks were embedded in them.

"Looks like there's something down at the bottom..." Goofy peered down from his foothold.

"*Waaak!* Heartless!" Trying to do the same, Donald was taken by surprise when Heartless appeared behind him and lost his footing.

"Donald!" Sora grabbed ahold of his shirt. A Heartless like a large ball attacked them. "Whoa!"

Still holding on, Sora fell, too.

"Donald! Sora!" Goofy lunged to catch him and plummeted down headfirst.

"Hey, Donald, you okay?"

Sora stood up, warily looking around. It looked like they'd fallen all the way to the bottom.

"I think so... Ow, ow, ow..." Donald got up, too, just in time for Goofy to fall onto him headfirst. *"Quack!"*

"Oh, hey, Donald... Sora! I sure am glad you guys are okay."

"Get off me and *then* I'll be okay!" Donald tried to push Goofy's behind off him.

It seemed to be a rule that whenever the three of them fell from somewhere higher up, someone had to land on someone else.

"Where are we...?"

Nearby it was pitch-dark. A little ways off, they could see a blue light.

"...What's that?" Sora went closer and touched it. The moment he did, they were flung somewhere else.

"Wawawaaak!" Donald squawked.

Sora had closed his eyes against a dazzling brightness, and when he opened them again, he saw the familiar streets of Traverse Town.

"How'd that happen?" said Goofy, looking around. And then more Heartless appeared. "Shucks, they just won't let us be!"

He sent them flying with his shield.

"Look, there's another blue light over there!" Sora ran to it and touched it.

"Now we're in Alice's world!" shouted Donald. At least, it looked just like the green courtyard where that trial had taken place.

"Another blue light!" Goofy went closer and touched it, and then they were in Tarzan's Deep Jungle.

They touched the blue lights and traveled through one world after the next. Agrabah, then Neverland—each one a world where they had locked the Keyhole. All the worlds they had been to were scattered here as if to greet them.

"Gawrsh, what's happening?" In Neverland, Goofy cocked his head.

"I think these are all pieces of the worlds that the Heartless invaded," said Sora. He touched the blue light, and they were whisked off to the next world.

"We haven't been to this place before..." Donald peered at the strange surroundings, now a corridor in a building somewhere.

"Look, there's some kinda funny emblem over there." Goofy ran closer to the red-and-black emblem at the end of the hall. "It looks like that thing where the Keyhole was in Hollow Bastion..."

Sora looked up at it from beside him. It was like a big heart shape, but there was something eerie about it.

"Here's a door!" Donald exclaimed. They went to the door he spied in the middle of the hall and opened it.

In the middle of the room inside, there was a big hemisphere of glass or crystal. Pipes ran into it, infusing it with something.

"What...is that?" Sora stood in front of the machinery supporting the hemisphere. It had something that appeared to be an instrument panel.

Donald looked closely at Sora. "Are you gonna touch it...?"

"Maybe we better not... What if a buncha Heartless come flying out?" Goofy worried.

"C'mon, let's see what it is!" Sora flipped what looked like a switch.

"Oh, those born of the darkness, devoid of hearts…"

"It's talking!" Donald jumped. The voice that came from the machine chanted as if reciting a poem.

"Shh!" Sora held a finger to his lips, shushing Donald.

"Ravage all worlds and bring desolation. Seize all hearts and consummate the one great heart. All hearts to be one and one heart to encompass all. This is the realm of 'Kingdom Hearts.' The great darkness, sealed within the great heart. Progeny of darkness, return to the eternal dark. For the hearts of light shall unseal the path. Seven hearts, one keyhole, one key to the door. The Door of Darkness bound by two keys. The Door to Darkness, which seals the light. None shall pass but shadows, returning to the darkness. Oh, those born of the heart, those with no hearts, fallen children of the dark, devour every heart until the Door of Darkness opens!"

"What the heck is 'Kingdom Hearts'?" Sora muttered.

"Well, he said it's 'all hearts.'" Goofy cocked his head.

"Progeny of darkness… That must mean the Heartless, right?" Donald looked up at Sora.

"But didn't we close all the doors?" said Sora.

"There's gotta be another door we have to close to seal away the darkness…," Goofy replied. "The Heartless are still around, after all."

"Aw, man, none of this makes any sense…," Sora sighed. They went back out to the corridor.

Goofy looked back at the strange emblem. "Huh?"

"What, Goofy?"

He ran to the emblem and picked up a piece of paper. "Sora… It's more of Ansem's report!"

"I thought the part we found in Hollow Bastion was the end of it?" Sora peered at the page in Goofy's hand.

"Jiminy!" Donald called, and the little cricket hopped out of his pocket.

"Hmm… Well, it certainly looks like *this* is the last page of Ansem's report." Jiminy took the page from Goofy and began to read.

Existing only as a heart, I have returned to the Heartless, and yet there is no hint of a transformation.

The body is certainly gone. But its memories remain, and I have yet to take the form of a Heartless. Much is still unknown.

To reach the realm of darkness, one must go through the doors of Kingdom Hearts, the place where the worlds' hearts connect.

There are many worlds, some of which we know nothing about.

The world in which we live, the realm of darkness, the realm of light. And the world between. Whither lies the true paradise?

Where does the body go when it separates from the heart?

I know that when the heart returns to the Heartless, the physical form disappears. But that is merely true in this *world. In another world, might it not still exist?*

If this is the case, then another version of oneself can exist elsewhere.

A being that is neither darkness nor light, belonging nowhere, abandoned by its heart, a mere shell of its former self, spurned by light and darkness alike.

However, I am certain that if one's self exists here, then by definition the other cannot truly "exist." Call it then a nonbeing, a "Nobody."

"It's just more stuff that doesn't make any sense…" Goofy frowned.

"There've been an awful lot of things we don't understand in Ansem's report, but I've been able to figure it out here and there. This part, though…" Jiminy Cricket shook his head. "It's really above my head, too."

"The true paradise…"? "The world between…"?

"Nobody"…?

"There's that 'Kingdom Hearts' stuff again," said Sora.

"I wonder just what he's trying to say." Jiminy cocked his head and retreated back into the pocket.

"Whatever! It just means we gotta beat Ansem!" Donald said ferociously.

"Yeah…I guess you're right." Sora nodded and gripped the Keyblade. "Let's go."

"Right!"

The three jumped into the black glow at the corner of the hall.

They came out into another cave. Purple sandy stuff covered the floor, and there were strange markings on the walls like the ghosts of dead trees. Fragments of buildings and pieces of wood were strewn about, wreckage from an otherworldly storm.

The trio passed slowly through the cave.

"Gawrsh, this place gives me the willies…," said Goofy, shivering.

"Yeah, but we've got to keep going," Sora replied. Donald and Goofy both nodded.

The branch-like markings on the walls grew more twisted. It was impossible to tell what they were supposed to be.

"So this is the end of it…maybe?" Donald looked up at the exit. "I guess there's only one way to find out."

The moment they moved on to the next floor, the Heartless attacked.

"*Wha-hooey!*" A vicious blow knocked Goofy back.

"Hey! What's the big idea?!" Donald waved his wand and hit the Heartless square in their (probably) faces.

"They're over here, too!" yelled Sora. He defeated one after another, but more kept appearing.

"Hey, Sora! Look at that!" Goofy pointed to a heart-shaped emblem in the back of the cave.

"That…looks like the one we just saw in that room…doesn't it?" said Donald as he fired off spells.

"Yeah, but not just that! See?" Goofy gave the Heartless in front of him a good whack with his shield, and then a crack appeared in the heart emblem.

"So it's a door that'll open if we beat the Heartless?!" said Sora.

"I think so!" Goofy replied and rushed another Heartless.

"Okay, let's get rid of them!"

One by one, the trio took out the Heartless that came at them.

"…This has to be the last of 'em, right? *Firaga!*" Donald blasted away the last Heartless and the heart emblem crumbled to reveal a hole that led onward.

"We did it!"

They ran to the hole in the wall. Through there, it was calm and silent.

Fine sparkling sands flowed out of the walls, making little dunes. Unlike in the places they'd been through so far, a few plants grew here.

"Looks like there aren't any Heartless in here…" Donald stepped forward, glancing around warily. In the quiet, the sand gritted beneath his feet.

"There's a door."

They walked closer to it.

"…Huh?" Sora's head tilted.

Donald looked up at him. "What's wrong?"

"Don't you hear something? There!" Sora cocked an ear toward the voice he heard.

"Careful… This is the last haven you'll find here. Beyond, there is no light to protect you. But don't be afraid. Your heart is the mightiest weapon of all. Remember—you are the one who will open the door to the light…"

"I don't hear anything," said Donald.

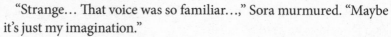

"Strange… That voice was so familiar…," Sora murmured. "Maybe it's just my imagination."

But he knew he heard it.

The voice he had heard on Destiny Island… That voice from his dreams.

"Maybe you need a break!"

"Let's take it easy for a bit… I'm tired, too!" Goofy sat down on a pile of sand.

"Hmm… I guess so." Sora sat beside him and flopped out on his back.

"Oh yeah… Aerith gave me some goodies." Beside him, Donald took a little bundle from his pocket.

"Hey, when did she give you that?" Sora sat up and stared at the bundle, wrapped up in white paper and tied with ribbon.

"When we said good-bye in Hollow Bastion!" Donald unwrapped it. There were cookies inside.

"Oh, boy!" Goofy took one and tossed it into his mouth. "Mm, it's yummy!"

"I want one!" Sora grabbed another and chomped.

"Nice and sweet!" said Donald with his mouth full.

"Those cookies at the tea party in Alice's world were tasty, too," said Goofy.

"They sure were!"

Donald and Goofy nodded.

"Oh, and the bananas in Deep Jungle—those were really good!"

"When did you find bananas?!"

They sat there cheerfully remembering things from their journey. There, before the final door…

Refreshed after their break, they opened the door, and what lay beyond was…a brilliant blue sky and sea and a white sandy beach.

"Is…is this my island?!" Sora ran out to the beach. It was definitely the same beach. He wasn't seeing things.

Except…there were no cocoyum trees. And…the waterfall was dried up, too.

The bridge to the little islet was gone.

"How…" Sora jumped to the islet, where he'd always talked with Riku. Donald and Goofy followed him.

"Riku!"

The other boy was there, dressed in black.

"This world…has been connected."

It was Ansem's voice.

Riku slowly turned, and at the same time, the islet vanished. He and the trio were left floating in the air.

"Tied to the darkness… Soon to be completely eclipsed." As he spoke, the other islands were disappearing.

"Wa-wa-whoooa!" Goofy jumped, startled to see the ground gone.

"There is much to learn." With Ansem's words, the sea turned to darkness. "You know so little. One who knows nothing can understand nothing."

Cracks split the sandy shore. Rocks and trees melted into darkness and congealed again into something mineral and purple black. Sora was riveted, watching the twisted changes taking over his home.

"Take a look at this tiny place." Riku, speaking with Ansem's voice, spread his arms, his face turned upward to the sky. "To the heart seeking freedom, this island is a prison surrounded by water. And so this boy sought to escape from his prison. He sought a way to cross over to other worlds. And he opened his heart to darkness."

Before Sora's eyes, Riku transformed into Ansem.

"Riku!"

"Don't bother. Your voice can no longer reach him where he is. His heart belongs again to darkness. All worlds begin in darkness, and all so end. The heart is no different. Darkness sprouts within it, it grows, consumes it. Such is its nature. In the end, every heart returns to the darkness whence it came."

Ansem's shadow stretched long over them.

"You see…darkness is the heart's true essence."

"That's not true!" cried Sora. "The heart may be weak. And sometimes it may even give in. But I've learned…that deep down, there's a light that never goes out!"

"Believe in the light, and the darkness will never defeat you. Your heart will shine with its power and push the darkness away—the power to bring happiness."

"So you have come this far, and still you understand nothing. Every light must fade, every heart return to darkness."

With a sweep of Ansem's hand, the island began to rumble and shake.

"Wa-waaak!" The ground split open beneath Donald's feet, and he fell, as if the chasm sucked him in. The crack split further and Goofy tried to run from it, but he fell in, too.

"Donald! Goofy!" Sora reached down, desperately trying to help his friends, but before his eyes, the whole island broke in two and a dark cloud boiled up.

"Behold, the endless abyss! Within it lies the heart of all worlds—Kingdom Hearts!"

Darkness burst out of the crack and ate away at the earth, devouring the world, and then Sora.

"Look as hard as you are able. You'll not find a single speck of light. From those dark depths are all hearts born—even yours! Darkness conquers all worlds!"

Ansem's voice echoed through the dark. In front of Sora an enormous mass of darkness materialized—an even deeper darkness within the darkness.

"You're that thing…!"

It was the huge shadow that Sora had fought back on Destiny Island.

With a terrible roar the shadow brought its fist down to crush him. But Sora raised the Keyblade and blocked it.

"I'm not giving in to the darkness…!"

In the swirling dark his Keyblade shone brightly, cutting through the great black shadow. The shadow screamed.

"I won't—I won't give in!"

Darkness clutched at his feet, swallowing him up.

And the shadow was consumed in the greater darkness, which then took some dire form, something like an enormous ship… Atop it, the upper half of a horrible dark monster writhed. Tubes sprouted from the monster's belly and connected to Ansem's back.

Floating there, Sora stared him down. And then he heard a shout.

"Soraaaaa!" Waving his wand wildly, Donald was sinking toward the monster as if through quicksand.

"Donald!" Sora swam down through the darkness, calling to him.

"Sooooooraaaaa! Hey, Sora!" From another side came Goofy's voice.

Both his friends were about to be swallowed up by the darkness. What could he possibly do?

Just as he was nearly taken over himself by the thick darkness of despair—someone spoke to him.

"*Giving up already? Come on, Sora. I thought you were stronger than that.*"

It was Riku's voice, ringing inside him.

"Giving up? No way, not me!"

Sora flew out of the black cloud.

Ansem's laughter echoed in the abyss. In a ball of dark red haze atop the enormous ship-like thing, something shone.

"Heeeeeelp!" It was faint, but Sora definitely heard it—Goofy's voice.

"Goofy?!" He plunged into the haze.

"Sora!"

"Goofy!" He was there in a cavernous hole, fighting Heartless alone. Sora flew in to knock them down. "Where's Donald?!"

"I can't find 'im…!"

"He must be around here somewhere!" Sora and Goofy flew out of the hole.

"Maybe he's in another clump of this red mist?" said Goofy.

Sora ran up the creature's back and jumped off from the front— where a huge, hideous face was waiting for him.

"Sooooooraaaaa!"

There he could just barely hear Donald calling him from inside its mouth.

"C'mon, Goofy!"

"Right! Here we go!" Goofy rushed at it and Sora followed him.

The thing's eyes narrowed and suddenly shot out lightning. Sora winced.

Goofy spun like a tornado, hitting the face with his shield. "Hold on, Sora!"

"I'm okay!" Sora flew up and struck its eyes with the Keyblade.

The creature opened its mouth and let out a terrible shriek. Sora and Goofy flew into its mouth.

"Sora!"

"Donald!"

Sora hugged him. "You're okay?!"

"Aww, phooey, this is nothin'!"

"Gawrsh, you kinda sounded like you were about to cry," Goofy remarked.

"Well, now we're all together." Sora looked at the other two.

"And that means nobody can beat us!" Goofy struck a brave pose.

"Right!" Donald nodded.

They flew out of the creature's mouth.

"Ansem!" Sora called out.

Ansem slowly rose, taking up a weapon like a double-ended sword, with a long blade at either end. He roared.

"We won't give in to darkness!"

Ansem seemed to be laughing at Sora's declaration. He whirled the double sword.

"Wa-waaak!" Donald jumped to avoid it and let his magic fly. "Hey—what's that?!"

Where the magic struck, deep black darkness gushed out and gathered into an enormous sphere above their heads.

"Aaah-hooey!" The sphere was about to drag Goofy into it. Sora caught his arm and held him back.

"Gawrsh, that scared me…" Goofy wiped cold sweat from his face.

"Donald, Goofy! It's time for our formation!"

"Right!"

Sora barreled at Ansem. Behind him, the sphere shot out beams, but they were deflected by Goofy's shield. And from behind the shield, Donald waved his wand.

With a ferocious yell, Sora struck at Ansem with the Keyblade. Ansem thrashed about and screamed in agony.

"Firaga! Thundaga! Blizzaga!" Donald waved his wand, pelting out magic with all his might. Where the spells hit, there were huge explosions.

"All right! One more time!" Sora flew at Ansem again and brought the Keyblade down on his head.

They couldn't hear anything but Ansem's scream. Ichor erupted from the enormous monster. And then—light shone from Ansem's chest and engulfed the entire creature with a colossal explosion.

"Did we beat him?!" Sora landed and looked back at the monster. But it was gone—only Ansem stood there, leaning forward on his knees and groaning.

"Ansem…!"

Sora ran at him with the Keyblade ready.

"It is futile. The Keyblade alone cannot seal the Door to Darkness."

"The Door to Darkness…?"

Ansem stretched his hand out behind him, where there was a white door. "Kingdom Hearts! Fill me with the power of darkness…"

The white door barely began to open. Darkness spilled forth from it. Was *this* the Door to Darkness?

"You're wrong!" cried Sora.

All hearts are born in darkness? I don't believe that.

Hearts are born in light.

Even if there is darkness in our hearts, there's light to drive it away.

With every person we meet, our hearts are connected, and the connections turn to light.

"I know now without a doubt—Kingdom Hearts is *light!*"

The darkness twining around them became beams of light that struck Ansem. "What—?!"

Amid the dazzling brightness, Ansem's gaze was fixed on the door. The seeker of darkness was enveloped in a burst of light.

"Light… But…why…"

And then, with the light, Ansem faded away…

"We've gotta shut the door!"

At Donald's cue, they ran to the white door. On the other side, darkness was pulsing there about to rush out.

Sora pushed at the door. "*Ngh… It's so heavy…*"

The huge door didn't move. Goofy peeked inside and jumped. "Whoa!"

"Stop staring and keep pushing!" Donald snapped, but then he looked inside, too. "The Heartless?!"

In the gloomy space inside, innumerable black shadows writhed.

"*Qua-waaak!* Hurry!" yelled Donald. But the door simply wouldn't budge.

"Don't give up!" The voice came from the dark inside, and another hand appeared on the door.

"Riku!" It was him—he was on the other side, trying to pull the door shut.

"C'mon, Sora! Together, we can do it!"

"Okay!" Sora pushed with every ounce of strength he had. Donald and Goofy were trying with all their might, too.

"There…just a little more!" Riku murmured, but behind him the shadows twisted. They gathered and grew and began to take form.

"It's hopeless!" But the moment Donald shouted that, a light cut through the clustering shadows.

"Huh…?" Donald and Goofy peeked inside again, and silhouetted against the light was a very familiar figure.

"Your Majesty?!" Donald cried.

Their king, Mickey Mouse, was standing right there, holding a golden Keyblade aloft. "Now, Sora! Let's close this door for good!"

"But…" With the door still open just a tiny crack, Sora hesitated.

If they closed it now—what would happen to the king? …And Riku?

"Don't worry," said Mickey, as if he could hear Sora's thoughts. "There will always be a door to the light!"

"Sora, you can trust King Mickey!" Goofy told him. Sora nodded.

Riku glanced back for a moment. "Now! They're coming!"

Mickey looked at his two retainers—and his very dear friends. "Donald, Goofy… Thank you."

There was hardly any time left…

"Take care of her, Sora," Riku said softly.

Whatever reply he might have made stuck in his throat, but Sora nodded firmly and sniffled a little bit.

And then with everything he had, Sora pushed.

Inch by inch, the door closed. He couldn't see Riku anymore.

"Sora! The Keyblade!" Donald shouted.

Sora raised his Keyblade. On the other side of the door, in the darkness, King Mickey raised his Keyblade, too.

The two Keyblades locked the Door to Darkness.

They could hear that sound, the click of a lock—then the door glowed with brilliant light and vanished.

"Sora…"

He heard a small voice from behind him and turned. "Kairi!"

She was standing there alone. "Sora!"

He ran to her and clasped her hand in his. Just then, with a terrible rumble, the realm of darkness began to collapse beneath their feet.

"Kairi! Remember what you said before? I'm always with you, too! I'll come back to you. I promise!"

"I know you will!"

The drifting ground pulled them apart. They held on to each other as long as they could—and they had to let go. They called each other's names, one more time...

And then a rain of light poured down, obscuring everything in its glow. The rain was shards of light and darkness, too. Shooting stars streaked up into the sky, and with a warm, gentle rushing, the worlds returned to how they were meant to be.

Separate. The worlds flew apart, and Kairi stood alone on the shore of the blue sea.

It was Destiny Island. Kairi walked over their beautiful island. It hadn't changed a bit from when Sora and Riku were here. The sunlight sparkled on the water and stung her eyes.

But Sora wasn't here, and neither was Riku. As if to make sure all of the island was still there, she headed to the cave.

There was the doodle on the wall, where Kairi and Sora had drawn each other.

Light poured into the cave and illuminated the drawings.

And she saw Sora, adding something to the doodle. He was sketching his own hand, holding up a paopu fruit to the drawing of Kairi.

If two people share one, their destinies will become intertwined... There was a legend like that about the paopu fruit.

Kairi said his name, and he turned to look at her with a grin— then he flashed into light and vanished.

It was only a dream...or some kind of mirage. A tear slid down her cheek.

Kairi picked up a stone and added more to their doodle—her hand holding a paopu fruit up to Sora's mouth.

Sunlight streamed down into the cave. She could just barely hear the soft whisper of the waves.

You'll come back, Sora. I know you will.

EPILOGUE
everlasting tales

A SINGLE PATH STRETCHED ON THROUGH THE GRASSY field as far as they could see.

"Gawrsh, I wonder where we are…" Goofy looked around but saw nothing besides the rolling plains. The Gummi Ship was gone, and there was no sign of any other people.

"Well, now what do we do?" said Donald, looking back at Sora.

"We've gotta find Riku and King Mickey," Sora replied.

Goofy sighed. "But, uh… Where do we start lookin' for that door to the light?"

"I dunno, but…"

The three looked at one another and each heaved a sigh.

A brown dog crossed the path in front of them, wagging his tail.

"Pluto?!" Donald exclaimed.

It was the king's dog, Pluto, who had run off back in Traverse Town.

"Hey, Pluto, where've you been?" Goofy ran up to him.

Pluto stood there, tail wagging, and they saw there was a letter in his mouth.

"Is that…?"

"It's the king's seal!" Donald rushed to Pluto, too.

"Hey, have you seen King Mickey?" Sora asked him.

And then Pluto sprang into a run.

"Hey, wait!" Sora ran after him. So did Donald and Goofy.

As they chased Pluto, their laughter rang out over the plains.

"Sora..."

He thought he heard a voice from somewhere. He turned, but no one was there.

"Remember, Sora. You are the one...who will open the door to the light."

—THE END—